P9-BYJ-614

Driftwood Dreams

T. I. LOWE

Tyndale House Publishers, Inc.
Carol Stream, Illinois

Visit Tyndale online at www.tyndale.com.

Visit T. I. Lowe at www.tilowe.com.

TYNDALE and Tyndale's quill logo are registered trademarks of Tyndale House Publishers, Inc.

Driftwood Dreams

Copyright © 2019 by T. I. Lowe. All rights reserved.

Cover photograph of chairs illuminated copyright © Pernilla Hed/Masterfile. All rights reserved.

Cover photograph of birds copyright © schankz/Shutterstock. All rights reserved.

Cover photograph of sand copyright © stockphoto mania/Shutterstock. All rights reserved.

Cover photograph of clouds copyright © Burben/Shutterstock. All rights reserved.

Author photograph by Jordyn Strickland, copyright © 2019. All rights reserved.

Designed by Faceout Studio, Jeff Miller

Edited by Kathryn S. Olson

Published in association with the literary agency of Browne & Miller Literary Associates, LLC, 52 Village Place, Hinsdale, IL 60521.

Unless otherwise indicated, all Scripture quotations are taken from the *Holy Bible*, New Living Translation, copyright © 1996, 2004, 2015 by Tyndale House Foundation. Used by permission of Tyndale House Publishers, Inc., Carol Stream, Illinois 60188. All rights reserved.

Scripture quotations in chapter 15 are taken from the Holy Bible, *New International Version,*® *NIV.*® Copyright © 1973, 1978, 1984, 2011 by Biblica, Inc.® Used by permission. All rights reserved worldwide.

Driftwood Dreams is a work of fiction. Where real people, events, establishments, organizations, or locales appear, they are used fictitiously. All other elements of the novel are drawn from the author's imagination.

For information about special discounts for bulk purchases, please contact Tyndale House Publishers at csresponse@tyndale.com, or call 1-800-323-9400.

ISBN 978-1-4964-4045-7

Printed in the United States of America

25	24	23	22	21	20	19
7	6	5	4	3	2	1

To my daughter, Lydia Lu.

Dare to dream.

No one lights a lamp and then puts it under a basket. Instead, a lamp is placed on a stand, where it gives light to everyone in the house. In the same way, let your good deeds shine out for all to see, so that everyone will praise your heavenly Father.

MATTHEW 5:15-16

1

Standing in the midst of the ebb and flow of her daily chaos always gave Josie Slater the same feeling as standing in the surf—it was ever-changing, yet she felt trapped in the same spot with her feet slowly sinking in the sand. She absently handed an order slip to a passing waitress while ringing up the couple sitting at the counter in front of her.

"This place is amazing." The middle-aged man handed over a couple of bills.

"Why, thank you." Josie offered a polite smile along with his change. She didn't even have to be present in the moment anymore to serve up generous portions of Southern hospitality to tourists.

"The candied pecan waffles were delicious," the wife added as her husband helped her off the stool.

The couple had been sitting there chatting Josie up for the better part of the last hour about their thirtieth wedding anniversary trip to the Grand Strand. They were both dressed in brand-new swimwear and were pasty white, except for the fresh streaks of sunburn across their noses. Even if they hadn't told her, they were broadcasting their tourist status. Josie often wondered why vacationers couldn't figure out how to properly apply sunblock. Over the years she'd seen various red-and-white stripes, Rudolph noses, hairline sunburns, and handprints.

Even with their neon noses, Josie thought they were

the cutest and wondered if such happiness was ever going to be in the cards for her. Seemed the only card she owned was the one that kept her rooted behind this counter, parroting courteous responses to customer accolades.

The man wrapped his arm around his wife's shoulders. "And just think, we were about to walk on by, but the people piling in and out of this old building made us curious enough to step inside."

"A hidden gem is what Driftwood Diner is." The wife added a generous tip to the old-fashioned milk can that served as the tip jar for counter service. "It's the best meal we've had since arriving."

Josie couldn't agree more. She was right proud of the establishment created at the hands of her parents. The timeworn, rusted shanty sat proudly, even with its arthritic lean to the left, on the sand of coastal South Carolina and had been a prominent fixture in the Sunset Cove community for nearly four decades. Its breakfast fare was legendary, and it usually took just one taste of the biscuits and gravy to have a newbie hooked for life. Josie's father replaced the traditionally used ground sausage with chopped shrimp, taking the already-decadent dish over the top.

"Y'all have a good time at the beach, and be sure to come back for lunch." She waved goodbye to the couple.

"Oh, we will. I have to try the shrimp burgers." The husband waved one last time before guiding his wife out the screen door.

Josie continued on autopilot, gathering dirty dishes and wiping down the counter while her mind wandered toward happier thoughts of the upcoming weekend meeting with the Sand Queens.

Just as the aged shack had held its ground against passing storms over the years, so had Josie and her two closest friends, Opal Gilbert and Sophia Prescott. The Sand Queens of Sunset Cove had affectionately earned their moniker from their mothers, who practically raised them on the very sand in front of the diner. Their bond was as solid as the galvanized screws that secured the tin roof to the graying clapboard structure.

Josie had witnessed a similar bond with the motley crew of geriatric ladies who were making their way into the diner at the moment. Well . . . her dad said *ladies* was too generous a word for the Knitting Club, considering they were a thorn in many a Sunset Cove resident's side. *Busybodies* was the term most folks used for the half-dozen or so old ladies of various shapes, sizes, and races.

"Josephine, this gout is killing me. Get us to our table 'fore I fall out," Ethel grouched, limping into the dining area, carrying her walking cane like a purse strap in the crook of her arm. She was dressed in her blue uniform, so Josie knew the ole grouser would be making customers miserable at the post office later in the morning. How the woman had kept her position as head postmaster for over forty years was an unsolved mystery. She also seemed to make it her mission to call everyone by the wrong name.

Case in point, Josie's name was not Josephine, but she chose to ignore it just as she did anything that could be considered confrontational. Instead, she pointed to Ethel's arm. "The cane would be more helpful if you'd actually use it, Miss Ethel."

"Oh, hush up." Ethel plopped into her chair as several other women followed suit, each one groaning and grunting while settling in at the long wooden table.

Josie gravitated to her favorite of the bunch with her order pad in hand. "Good morning, Miss Dalma. What can I get you?"

Dalma Jean Burgess grinned up at Josie, showing off

the fact that she had forgotten her teeth. Who knew where they would turn up? Josie made a mental note to look for them later when she stopped by Dalma's house.

"I'm fine, dear. I had a bowl of cereal earlier." Dalma plucked a sugar packet out of the small mason jar on the table, tore it open, and dumped the contents into her mouth.

Josie's eyes narrowed and scanned the tiny lady who didn't even make it past five feet in height nor one hundred pounds in weight. Dalma wore a pair of worn brown corduroy overalls with a fine silk blouse in a blush shade. A straw hat sat lopsided on top of a head full of long, wavy white hair. With the eighty-nine-year-old's ever-present smile and quirky wardrobe, she reminded Josie of a friendly scarecrow one would find in the corn patch out at Pickering Farms. Except for the pink bedroom slippers on her feet, that was.

"Miss Dalma, you're out of milk," Josie stated after refocusing on the woman's comment. Milk was on the shopping list she needed to knock out after her shift. "How'd you manage eating cereal?" She reached into the back pocket of her jean shorts to make sure the list was still there.

Dalma waved off Josie's concern, the overhead lights glinting off the giant ruby ring on her index finger. "I had vanilla ice cream. Works just as good as milk." She shrugged her thin shoulder and winked one of her cloudy-blue eyes. "Tastes better than milk, as a matter of fact. Will you add another pint to the shopping list?"

Even though Dalma had retired more than ten years ago, she would always be considered the town's librarian. Josie recalled Saturdays spent sitting on a rug in the children's room while Dalma acted out whatever book she was reading for story time. No one could tell a humorous story like Miss Dalma, and yet her own story seemed quite tragic in Josie's opinion. She'd lived long enough to bury her husband and only child, leaving her alone except for her church family and the Knitting Club. And, well, Josie too. Five years ago, Dalma's mind seemed to start slipping, so Josie stepped in and designated herself as caregiver.

Josie scribbled *two fried eggs, coffee* on the order pad before moving her attention to Bertie, who was unofficially the ringleader of what should have been named the Busybody Gossip Club.

"I heard a certain someone has moved back to town," Bertie drawled while keeping her eyes focused on a menu she probably had memorized. She patted down the side of her freshly teased gray hair with her free hand, going for casual but failing.

A name, followed by an image, skirted through Josie's mind regarding who that certain someone could be, but she quickly shut down those thoughts and chose not to take Bertie's bait. Besides, there was no way he would ever return to the small town of Sunset Cove for good, not when the world was his oyster.

"Would you like the Sea Traveler's Special today, Miss Bertie?" It was her usual and Josie was trying to hurry things along, but when Bertie used the menu as a fan and grinned wide, she knew there would be no hurrying along whatever was going on.

"Ah . . . traveling the world . . ." Bertie sighed. "Such a romantic idea. Don't ya think, Josie?"

Josie's chest began to burn. It was the same reaction produced each time he drifted into town for a quick visit with his family. She always made herself scarce during those times, not wanting a reminder of all the dreams that one man represented that would never be hers. It was no one's fault but life itself, and Josie would willingly lay down those dreams all over again to be there for her father. Some folks declared her too shy, while others outright claimed she was too passive. Maybe she was a little more of both than she should be, but more importantly, Josie was loyal to a fault. And sometimes that loyalty needed her to put herself aside for the betterment of others.

"Did you hear me, honey?" Bertie's question dripped with false sickly sweetness, but Josie saw past it to the pot the old lady was working on stirring.

"Excuse me, ladies." Josie waved over one of her waitresses. "Tracy, please take these ladies' orders." She shoved the pad into Tracy's hands and hurried to the counter to find something, anything, to do to tamp down her emotions. She took a minute to shoot Opal a text, asking if she was planning on stopping by. When an answer didn't come in after a few beats, she slid the phone back into her pocket and rang up a customer with a take-out order.

After a small rush of customers passed through, Josie felt somewhat settled. She scanned the Knitting Club's table and caught Dalma pouring maple syrup into her cup of coffee. She was just a wisp of a woman but had filled a giant void in Josie's life. A smile pulled at her lips as she thought about helping Dalma plant tomato bushes the week before even though the lady adamantly declared they were strawberry plants.

Josie's reverie came to a screeching halt as the screen door squeaked open and ushered in not only a briny breeze, but also a vision from her past.

With a pronounced air of confidence, August Bradford walked over to the counter and halted in front of a dazed Josie. Her heart jolted at the sight of him, something only this man could elicit. He spoke—or at least his lips moved—but she couldn't hear anything over the roar suddenly residing in her eardrums.

The Knitting Club's table kicked up in volume, sounding like a bunch of hens clucking away, but there was no focusing on what they were clucking about either. She knew the answer anyway and had a feeling their timing wasn't coincidental. All Josie could do was just stand there and stare, as if looking into his silvery-blue eyes had turned her to stone. With a hint of purple near the center, those uniquely hued eyes were made to belong to an artist such as August Bradford. The thick fringe of black eyelashes only emphasized their beauty. It was enough to spawn jealousy in Josie, her own fair lashes barely visible, but it didn't. It only tempted her to stand there and stare unabashedly. Mouth agape, that's exactly what she did.

"Are you okay?" A throaty voice penetrated the roar in her ears as a hand waved in front of her face.

Oh, my . . . that voice . . .

The words simply wouldn't come—only pitiful squeaks of breaths escaped—so Josie did the only thing to come to mind. She hightailed it into the kitchen.

As the swinging door flapped a few times before shutting behind her, she knelt behind the workstation and tried working some oxygen into her seized-up lungs. The normal comforting scents of fried seafood and sizzling breakfast meats did very little to calm her as she slowly inhaled and exhaled.

"What in the world's ailing you, Jo-Jo?" Her dad turned his back to the grill, wiped his hands on his apron, and ambled over to check on her.

She shook her head when her tongue remained frozen.

The burly man glanced out the small circular window in the door and grumbled under his breath. "We got two girls out sick today and customers lining up. Whatever this is, you need to get over it."

"I just n-n-need . . . a minute," she managed to stammer out while wiping away the sheen of perspiration that had broken out on her forehead.

With another grumble under his breath, her dad pushed through the door and then let out a guffaw boisterous enough to have Josie scooting over to the door. She cracked it open just enough to catch sight of the dark-haired man at the counter. Seeing him was so exhilarating it was nearly devastating.

"August Bradford! All the way back from New York City! How are ya, boy?" Jasper moved around and grabbed the *boy*, who was close to a foot taller than him, into a bear hug.

"Good to see you, Jasper." August returned the hug with as much exuberance while chuckling in such a deep baritone it seemed to rumble throughout the building.

"Are you just passing through?" Jasper gave August's shoulder a firm clap before moving behind the counter.

"No. I'm home to stay." August settled onto one of the stools.

"Really? I figured those hoity-toity galleries up north wouldn't give you back to us."

"Nah. I have a few of my pieces on display in a couple different galleries there, but my uncle offered me the front space in his music studio here." August shared the impressive information with as much humbleness as if he had merely said his art would be on display at the run-down flea market up the road. It was a charming characteristic Josie had always admired about him.

Dishes clanged from behind her and drowned out whatever August was saying. She glanced over her shoulder and gave the guy on dish duty a stern glare, which he returned with a confused shrug as he dropped another pan into the giant stainless steel sink. She turned back to the cracked door and leaned her head out a little farther.

"Well, ain't that great. Sure is good to have you home." Jasper nodded his head, agreeing with his own statement.

August returned the nod. "It's great to be back. I was right homesick."

"I bet that uncle is gonna have you busy with the camp, too."

August let out another throaty chuckle. "Oh yeah. The list is a mile long, but I'm pretty stoked to be helping."

"What's the name of it again?"

"Palmetto Fine Arts Camp. We're scheduled to open the second week in June."

"You boys only got two months to get it together then."

Josie watched as August's eyes shifted from the chatty man and caught her peeping out the door. He bit the corner of his lip before looking back to her dad. "The camp construction is complete. All we have to do is go in and put our stamp on the place."

The two men talked a few more minutes with Josie catching only snippets of their conversation until a few groups cleared out and were quickly replaced by new customers. She knew her reprieve was about to come to an end.

"I know you ain't in here just to see my purty mug. You want biscuits and gravy and apple-stuffed pancakes."

August grinned. "Yes, sir. I'm hanging out with my kid brothers this morning, so I'll need three orders, please."

"I better make it four, then. Those boys know how to eat. I'll get it going." Jasper turned his head in the direction Josie thought she was hiding. "Jo-Jo, get on out here and serve August a cup of coffee."

Josie nearly jumped out of her skin at the mention of

her own name, making the door bang against the side of her forehead.

"She all right?" Josie heard August ask as she worked on rubbing the sting away.

"Who knows with that girl? Probably just hormonal or something." Jasper waved off August's concern and shuffled into the kitchen.

"Kill me dead now," she mumbled to herself, mortified.

"You ain't got time to be dead." Jasper gave his daughter a stern look, leaving no room for argument as he pointed to the door. "Get out there. Now."

Embarrassed and flustered as she was, Josie somehow managed to make her way out of the kitchen and over to the coffeepot. She poured a cup and placed it on the distressed-wood countertop in front of August without spilling a drop.

"Thanks." August lifted the cup in her direction before taking a sip.

"Thank you," she replied, feeling foolish. *Thank you?* She followed it up by blurting out more idiocy. "I'm welcome." After all these years, how could August Bradford still make her so tongue-tied and rattled? She was a grown woman, for crying out loud.

August was decent enough not to call her out on her jumbled response. The only reaction he offered to her word folly and twitchy behavior was a wry smile, which he covered graciously with the coffee cup.

His free hand smoothed over one of the planks. "I've always loved these countertops."

He seemed to be waiting for her to respond, but her eyes were fastened on the planks with her mouth pressed in a tight line. Some of the boards were naturally grayed, while others had light washes of white or teal. It was one of the last projects she had completed with her mom. Of course, her dad had grumbled at first but relented when they hauled in all of the reclaimed wood and set out to renovate the entire counter space, lengthening it enough to accommodate ten mismatched wooden barstools Opal helped them find.

Josie's eyes unlatched from the counter and flickered around the dining hall, where a collection of rustic pieces of art—mostly fashioned from driftwood, seashells, and anything else that had washed up on shore—hung on the weathered shiplap walls. Several weathered signs hung precariously about as well. One of Josie's favorites stated, *Time near the coast doesn't move by the hour; it moves by the currents, plans by the tides, and follows the sun.*

The diner was a relaxed space, inviting people to come on in whether they had shoes or not, but it no longer held that comfort for Josie. Not one new piece of art had been added since that awful life storm turned her and her dad's life upside down.

Blinking the memory away as best she could before it blinded her, she managed a somber nod before moving to the other end of the counter to refill another patron's cup of coffee.

She kept busy with taking orders, ringing customers up, and checking on Dalma. At one point, from the corner of her eye, she caught August swiping a postcard from the stand beside the register. On the front of the card, intended for tourists, was a picture of the diner with blue skies and ocean waves in the background. After grabbing a stray pen from the counter, he began doodling something. As curious as Josie was, she willed herself not to look over and inspect it.

Thankfully, August's take-out order came up shortly. Before she could key it in the register, her dad interrupted.

"It's on the house."

August shook his head and fished out the wallet from the side pocket of his blue board shorts. "No, no. Let me pay."

"Nonsense. This is my welcome-home gift." Jasper made a show of pushing the bag containing the foam carryout containers into August's reluctant hands. "Don't you dare be rude like that, boy."

Admitting defeat, August put away his wallet and accepted the bag. "Yes, sir. I appreciate it."

"You hitting the surf today?" Jasper asked, wiping his hand along the grease-stained apron.

"That was the plan, but the water is like glass." August stood up from the stool. "You gotta go surfing with me sometime."

Jasper cackled at the idea and slapped the pronounced O of his belly. "It's been too many years and way too many shrimp burgers for that."

"Nah, man. It's never too *anything* to pursue what you love." August fixed Josie with a meaningful look. "It was good seeing y'all."

"You too." Jasper easily sent the polite remark back while Josie stood beside him in her mute state. She had not uttered an intelligible word directly to him the entire time. "And tell your folks I said hey."

"Will do." August spoke to Jasper, but his eyes remained on Josie, like he was waiting for something. When she remained silent, he appeared to give up whatever he'd hoped for and turned to leave. The Knitting Club began calling out to him, but he was smart enough to only give them a gentlemanly nod and brief wave. Before he made it completely out the door, Opal blocked his path. The shimmering halo of blonde-tipped auburn curls floated every which way as she did her little clap-and-hop dance at the sight of August.

Josie tried not to stare as August and Opal exchanged what looked like pleasantries. The friendly pair laughed at one point with Opal patting his arm.

Opal was an artist in her own right, who took what most people considered junk and restored it into newer, more unique pieces that she sold from her downtown store, Bless This Mess. Back in their youth, Josie and Opal had taken art classes with August at school as well as a few at the community center. Opal was social enough to befriend him, and Josie had been too awkward to do anything but admire him from afar.

Evidently time hadn't changed some things.

"I'll be by sometime this week," August's deep voice rang out as he headed outside, much to Josie's relief.

Opal nodded and waved before skipping over to the counter with a sweet smile on her fairylike face. Dressed in a peasant blouse, long skirt, and thick Birkenstocks, she was the epitome of cool and calm in the middle of the stuffy restaurant.

Even with several ceiling fans rotating overhead, sweat dewed along Josie's brow. She brushed away a damp lock of blonde hair that was beginning to stick there and mumbled, "Hey."

"Isn't it wonderful August has finally made his way home?" Opal's green eyes sparkled with enthusiasm.

"Umm . . ." Josie busied herself with wiping down the already-clean counter until Opal snickered. "What?"

"You still don't know how to come to terms with your crush on that man, do you?" Opal snickered again.

"I'm too old to have a crush on anyone. And who says I ever had one on him?" Josie's cheeks lit with knowing she'd just told two fibs. By the smirk on her friend's face, she could tell Opal knew it too.

"You're twenty-five years old. . . . Keep telling yourself

that," Opal said as she scooted behind the counter and helped herself to a glass of sweet tea as she had been doing for as long as Josie could remember. She then moved over and settled on the stool in front of the cash register. Her first sip almost sputtered all over the clean counter as she picked up the postcard and turned it for Josie to see. "Seems you're not the only one!"

Eyes wide in shock, Josie took in the simple yet astonishingly accurate sketch of her silhouette. She was amazed that a plain ink pen was used to create such a rendering and that a fifty-cent postcard served as the canvas.

"Oh, my goodness . . ." The wild beating of her heart started up again, and the oxygen to her lungs was so sparse she grew pure dizzy.

"Are you also too old for love letters?" Opal pointed to the scribbling underneath the drawing. *Untie your tongue and give me a call sometime.* Along with the simple one-line note, August included his number.

"Humph . . ." Josie paced behind the counter while Opal sat on the stool in all her coolness.

Suddenly the Sand Queens' upcoming get-together felt foreboding. Opal and Sophia would have quite a fun time at her expense. They were like sisters, which meant they were loyal but loved to rib one another.

Exasperated, Josie left her friend at the counter, marched straight outside, and plunged herself into the ocean. No, not really, but she sure did consider it.

●   ●   ●

An hour slipped by after August's grand reappearing and departure, followed by the Knitting Club and Opal departing as well. With them gone and the morning rush winding down, Josie could finally take a breath.

"Finally, some peace and quiet," Josie spoke too soon as the screen door swung open to produce another thorn. "Could this day get any worse?"

As the newly arrived thorn made it to the counter, he produced a gun from the pocket of his baggy basketball shorts. A loose tank top and a black ski mask completed his outfit.

Josie held out a hand, palm side up, and wiggled her fingers. "Give me that thing right now!"

"You need me to call the cops?" a customer asked as others began gasping and muttering.

Josie snatched the gun out of the reluctant thief's hand. "No thank you. This young man is just pulling our leg. No harm done." Josie smiled, trying to apply a good serving of Southern charm, but by the befuddled look on the woman's face, she wasn't buying it.

"But he had a gun," another customer pointed out, eyes wide.

Josie tsked. "It's only a water gun. See?" She aimed the gun toward the ceiling and pulled the trigger, producing a stream of water.

The thief's shoulders slumped. He released an exasperated huff and plopped down on a stool. "But I really need to rob you this time. I'm being for real."

"I'm not in the mood for this today, Theo Williams," Josie spoke quietly as she tossed the gun underneath the counter. It certainly looked like a real gun. Thinking better of it, she hid it underneath a stack of bags.

Jasper barreled out of the kitchen. "What in the sam hill is going on out here?"

"Theo's here to rob us again," Josie answered.

Jasper grumbled and shook his head. "Son, you need to stop causing a ruckus."

"He's your son?" a woman asked, edging closer to

witness the little incident at the counter with several others following suit.

Josie exchanged a smirk with her father because Theo looked nothing like them, and not only because his skin tone was several shades darker than theirs. Josie was tall, and her father was built sturdy. Poor Theo was short and scrawny.

"No, ma'am, but we claim him. How 'bout y'all go back to your breakfast and I'll have some sweet glazed biscuits brought out—on the house—for the disturbance." Jasper motioned for them to return to their tables, and after a few more moments of rubbernecking, they left the scene of the crime behind the counter.

Josie moved her attention to Theo. His ski mask was rucked up, making his face look like it was melting. "Why don't you take that thing off? You've got to be burning up in it."

"Someone might be able to ID me if I take it off."

"Really, Theo?" Josie leaned over the counter and snatched it off, revealing a sweaty mess of a young man. "What did I tell you last time about trying to rob us?"

Theo shrugged. "That you'd wring my neck next time."

Josie dismissed the threat with a flick of her wrist. "After that."

Theo sighed. "If I needed money, to ask nicely for it."

"Then why didn't you?"

"It makes me look needy."

Josie scoffed. "I think you just enjoy the theatrics of the robbery." She knew it was more on the lines of pride, and it didn't help matters that Theo was a little on the slow side.

A few years ago, she'd taken Theo to the doctor's office after he fell off the deck outside and was unable to get in touch with his mother, Deandrea. Doc Nelson,

the town's longtime pediatrician—known for his overuse
of unusual expressions—explained that basically Theo's
light bulb was on, but it wasn't screwed all the way into
the socket. After that, Josie began helping out Theo and
Deandrea when she could. He was nineteen now and
thought he was the man of the house, trying to help his
mother make ends meet, but that usually ended up causing more of a problem than anything.

"How much is the electric bill?" Josie asked, knowing
it was due.

"One hundred eight dollars and twelve cents. That's
all I was gonna take." His big brown eyes began to water,
and then his stomach rumbled loudly.

Josie patted his hand, resting on top of the counter.
"I know, Theo. You hungry?"

"I could eat."

"I'll grab you a plate of food. After you finish, I need
the garbage taken out and they could use some help washing the dishes in the kitchen. Once you're done with that,
I'll pay you one hundred and thirty dollars." She fixed a
glass of tea and placed it in front of him. "That sound
like a deal?"

"But I only need one hundred eight dollars and twelve
cents." Theo looked a little confused but relieved.

Josie's heart ached a little, knowing her thief was honest and sincere, even if he went about things in the wrong
manner. She also knew he and his mother had fallen on
hard times, so she would do what she could to make this
difficult season a little easier for them. "You work hard
until closing and you'll earn a bonus."

"I can do that," Theo responded with a good measure
of enthusiasm. He smiled wide enough to show off the
endearing gap between his front teeth.

Josie couldn't help but chuckle while heading into

the kitchen to get Theo some food. "What a day," she mumbled to herself and was actually a little thankful for the bogus robbery. At least it helped to get her mind off a certain other man who made her heart do other peculiar things besides ache.

2

"Hmm . . . Just as good as I remembered it." August savored the velvety bite of biscuit coated in rich gravy as he sat in the dining room of his parents' beach house. Being back home and sharing his favorite breakfast with his brothers, pure contentment easily settled over him.

"Good enough to make you stay this time?" Tucker asked. The teenage boy stuffed an entire rolled pancake into his mouth all at once, nearly losing a chunk of sautéed apple in the process.

Always having to copy the older ones, Zachary tried to pull off the same maneuver with his pancake.

"Whoa, little guy." August placed his hand on the youngest boy's arm.

"But I'm five. I ain't *little*," Zachary protested but controlled himself and only took a giant bite instead, losing a chunk of apple down the front of his shirt.

August leaned over with a napkin and made quick work of cleaning up the mess. He studied both his brothers, one tall and lanky with messy black hair like himself and the other fresh-faced with a headful of chocolate curls. He looked over at Tucker as the teenage kid started devouring the extra plate of food Jasper had included, and was even more baffled by the facial hair on the kid's chin. He moved his attention to Zachary, regretting how much he'd missed already, and vowed to build a relationship with the little guy.

"Yeah, no. I'm not going anywhere else. You two punks are trying to get all grown on me. I can't miss out on any more of this." August reached over and pinched the whiskers on Tucker's chin before giving them a playful yank. His brother batted his hand away while smirking at him.

Zachary stroked his smooth chin and nodded. "Yeah. I'll be getting that soon, too."

The two older guys chuckled at their kid brother.

August thought about another person with whom his absence had caused him to miss out on a lot. Josie Slater had never been known to be articulate. Put the poor girl in front of a podium or just him, and she'd stammer herself into a hot mess. He found it endearing and she had so much spirit, he naturally gravitated toward her. And when she worked on her artwork way back when, he was drawn even more to the passion she poured into it. He knew he'd found a confidante who not only understood his artistic world but resided in it as well.

He often daydreamed about them painting a life together, knowing it could be a vivid masterpiece if she'd let go of the apprehensions keeping her in knots. But he'd never pursued her. For one, they were too young. And two, he had goals he didn't want to put off.

BAM! A swift kick to the underside of his dining chair had August nearly jolting out of it. He cut a glare at Tucker. "What?"

"Dude, I was just saying that we'll help you set up the art exhibit, but you . . ." Tucker mirrored his glare but with a mocking smile as he rose from the table. "Who were you just all googly-eyed over?"

"Huh?" August mumbled.

"Don't play dumb. You just left Driftwood Diner, so

it's an easy guess." Tucker's wry expression remained as he tossed the empty container and swiped one of Zachary's rolled pancakes before returning to his chair.

August, not wanting to say any more than he had to, stuffed a pancake into his mouth, too. The warm apple filling sent him into a groan. The sweet and spicy treat would be well worth the bellyache he was working on.

Tucker swallowed and took a long gulp of orange juice. "Josie's cool. You should see the craft projects she has the kids do in her Sunday school class."

"Miss Josie is my teacher." Zachary bobbed his head and picked a few chunks of shrimp out of the pale gravy. "Her learns me a lot of stuff."

August's smile grew wide, thinking someone needed to *teach* the kid proper English. "Yeah? That is cool." He'd hoped she'd somehow figured out how to follow her dreams. She might not have gotten to see it through the way he did, but his hope was to present her with an opportunity to dream a little or a lot with him.

"You went all googly-eyed again." Tucker rapped his knuckles on the teak table, causing the sound to echo around the spacious dining room. The Bradford beach house was more on the lines of a mansion—clean lines with a minimalistic coastal vibe—but the family's love made it cozy.

August pushed the plate away and leaned on his elbows. "If you're serious about helping me, I could use it."

"Sure. Whatever you need." Tucker tipped his chair on the back legs while twirling his fork.

"Good. I have a few paintings I need to create before the exhibit, but in the meantime y'all need to finish up your breakfast."

"Why?" both brothers asked in unison, both looking expectant.

"We need to head over to the camp and test out the pool for a while." He'd just gotten word earlier that the pool passed inspection.

"Yay!" Zachary squealed. And although Tucker didn't squeal, August could tell his brother wanted to by the way his chair legs suddenly landed back on the floor and the fork stilled in his hand. *Pool* was an understatement for the setup they had at the camp.

The boys cleaned up the table in record speed, grabbed their gear, and headed just inland a ways to where the camp was tucked away on a large piece of farmland. As his truck pulled past the gate and crept up the long driveway, August couldn't help but think about how fun it would be to share the spectacular place with Josie.

Patience, he thought to himself. *Just gotta have some patience.*

By the time the boys had their fill of the pool, Tucker was grumbling about starving and Zachary had set a pretty good rhythm of yawning and declaring he wasn't tired at the same time. August agreed more food was needed, and Zachary didn't protest when August picked him up and carried him to the truck.

August noticed the gray truck crawling up the camp drive as he buckled his little brother into his booster seat. "Tuck, crank the truck. I just need to have a quick word with Uncle Carter," he said while closing the door.

"I have my license. I can drive us, too." Tucker hurried into the driver's seat.

August cut him a firm look. "Not my truck, you won't." He wasn't much on material possessions, but he sure missed his black King Cab while in Europe.

Carter hopped out of the cab while turning his backward hat into the front position. "She in?"

"Nice to see you, too," August said sarcastically.

"We ain't got time for pleasantries." Carter gestured with both hands at the five large buildings sitting in a wide arc—each one already designated to house a specific fine art. "We've got a lot riding on this place."

"I know this." August stared at the large L-shaped art building to their right as he leaned on the side of Carter's truck. His gaze moved around, baffled by the sight before him. "I just can't get over this being the same plot of farmland I left two years ago."

"I sent you the plans and pictures."

August shrugged. "I know, but it's a whole lot different in person." He pointed to the swaying trees that seemed to be welcoming him. "Those palmetto trees in the courtyard are a nice touch."

"I thought so, but we need to get to breathing some life into the rest of this place." Carter hitched a thumb over his shoulder. "I'm hanging a mural in the photography studio and have photos for the other buildings to correspond with each particular fine art. Now it's time for you to get the lead out with the exteriors."

"I'm working on it." August rubbed at the tension collecting against his forehead.

"Two months are gonna be gone in a blink, man. So either get to it with Josie or let me handle it. I don't know why you just can't offer her the position and be done with it."

August raised his palms. "Josie isn't one you can just toss something like this at. Plus, she clammed up as soon as I walked in the diner."

Carter let out a bark of laughter. "She ain't seen you in ages, man. You probably scared her with all that black hair." He reached his large paw over before August could move out the way and mussed his hair. "What did you expect?"

"Whatever." August leaned over to the truck and tapped on the tinted window when he noticed Zachary sacked out. The window whirled down. "Prop little guy's head up or he's going to have one mean kink in his neck." He watched on to make sure Tucker rearranged the boy in his seat properly. "Are y'all cool enough in there?"

Tucker settled back into the driver's seat. "Yeah. I got the AC cranked. It's chill." The window went up, hiding the goofy face he was making.

August shook his head and brought his attention to Carter. "Now that I've seen Josie, I just don't know . . ."

Carter's brow furrowed. "Now that you've *seen* her? Hello! That woman is just as beautiful as she's always been."

August thought about seeing her earlier with all that long white-blonde hair gathered in a messy topknot and the light sprinkling of freckles across the bridge of her nose that were front and center without a drop of makeup to hide them. She was a natural beauty, no doubt about it.

"She's gorgeous, but that's beside the point." August let out a pensive sigh and stretched his hands out between them, showing off the fact that even though he'd spent the better part of the day in a pool, paint still clung to his nail beds. "She didn't have one drop of paint on her hands. None on her clothes—"

"Are you kidding me right now? Maybe not all artists are as sloppy as you." Carter shoved into August's shoulder, causing him to stumble sideways a bit.

He steadied himself and took a half step out of Carter's reach. "No. I'm looking for passion. She used to have it in spades, but if she's allowed it to fade . . ." August shrugged again. "I just don't know."

"What are you going to do about it?"

August glanced at his brawny uncle. With only a few years' age difference, they were more like brothers than not, and they knew each other like the backs of their own hands. "You know me. I have a plan."

Carter fixed his dark-blue eyes on him from underneath the brim of his hat, and August noted the seriousness in his expression. "Don't shell-shock her again. The poor woman has gone through enough."

August huffed. "This ain't going to be easy."

Carter nodded his head and started off in the direction of the music building, where his passion resided. "Nothing in life that's worth it ever is," he said over his shoulder and waved a hand in the air. "Now get to it!"

"I'm on it!" August yelled back as he climbed into the truck, too preoccupied with his thoughts about Josie. It wasn't until they reached the city limits of Sunset Cove that he realized he'd let his kid brother drive.

3

With the sun casting a glittery effect on the sand and surf, the image gave off a perfect depiction of tranquility and whispered a message that all was right. It was the same picture Josie worked diligently to showcase as well over the years to help hide the debilitating fears that were constantly threatening to overtake her. Through carefully placed smiles and keeping to the edges of every situation, she did a good job most of the time, but the unexpected visit from August Bradford had rattled her. She worried it would expose the shadows that continuously lurked just underneath her surface, at the ready to swallow up the light. It wasn't due to the man himself, but the aftermath he would leave in his wake once another wave of an opportunity picked him up and carried him far from the shore of Sunset Cove.

Opal and Sophia prattled in their lounge chairs on either side of Josie. She'd mostly tuned them out as Opal recapped her disastrous encounter with August Bradford at the diner.

"He left his number. How much more obvious could the man be about his interest?" Opal snickered, straightening the top of her crocheted swimsuit that, in Josie's opinion, resembled a doily. Who knew where she was even able to find such a suit.

Josie returned her attention to the shore, but the

only thing she could see was a set of silvery-blue eyes. She didn't care to admit how much August's eyes and the mere sound of his familiar voice tied her up in knots.

Adjusting her oversize sun hat, Sophia giggled for the hundredth time that sunny afternoon. "I can't believe you clammed up, Josie. You should have strutted your pretty self around that counter and laid a welcome kiss on that man and told him it was about time he made his way home to you."

"Oh, my goodness! Wouldn't that have been a hoot! The Knitting Club probably would have all passed out!" Opal sighed. "Too bad our girl could hardly breathe. You would have thought Henry Cavill himself had sauntered into the diner," Opal said as she mimicked Josie's reaction, clutching her chest and widening her eyes. In a blink, her silliness fell away and was replaced with a thoughtful expression. "Come to think of it, August does favor Henry quite a bit, minus the cleft chin. Oh, and Henry's British."

Sophia waved Opal's last comment off with a flick of her prissy hand as a wayward Frisbee flew by her head. Someone shouted an apology, sending her prissy hand to wave that off, too. "That's not French, though."

"Close enough." Opal shrugged.

All three women agreed that August living abroad, spending a good bit of that time in France, was the most romantic thing. Josie often dreamed about being by his side, but she'd never admitted that out loud.

"I can't wait to see him without the blue hair and piercings." Sophia sounded a bit too excited for Josie's liking. "He was a looker even with all those trinkets and hair dye trying to camouflage it. Bet he's drop-dead gorgeous au naturel."

Back in high school, Josie thought his rebellious style

was what made him so fascinating and mysterious, but seeing him with his natural black hair and no piercings in sight, she understood there was no truth to that theory. August Bradford carried himself in such a gracious and respectful manner, it automatically drew people to him. No matter the hair color.

"He still has tattoos," Josie mumbled, feeling defensive all of a sudden. Not many and no new ones that she saw, but still . . .

"Look! Our girl is turning all red again!" Opal pointed as the giggling picked back up.

Josie sucked her teeth. "Hush up, already. Two hours of y'all picking on me is more than enough."

"Honey, we're just trying to get you to lighten up a bit." Opal sat up and placed her hand on top of Josie's fisted one. "Ease up on yourself. It's okay that you like him."

"I don't even know if I'd call it that. In school, I always felt sick to my stomach when he was around. Six years have passed and I still feel sick." Exasperated with herself and mortified by the whole ordeal, Josie flung an arm over her face. She'd caught only a glance here or there of August since he'd moved away, and each time it had released a colony of butterflies in her stomach.

"Oh, you're just too precious." Opal snickered again.

Josie had the urge to reach over and tug on one of Opal's reddish pigtails but chose to keep one hand over her face and the other one balled up. "Leave. It. Be." Josie growled stern enough that Opal finally removed her hand.

"Pass me the sunblock," Sophia requested, ignoring her friends' banter.

Josie dropped her arm and studied Sophia as the self-proclaimed debutante smoothed the matching sarong to her navy-and-white one-piece. Even the giant sun hat

matched her outfit. "You're already wearing at least a gal-
lon of the stuff," she teased as she tightened the string of
her teal bikini, knowing good and well she didn't have
even a slight slope of a curve to fill it.

Her friends always complimented her, saying she had
such an athletic physique, but she knew that was code for
a boyish frame. Even surrounded by greasy fare most days
hadn't done a thing to soften the look.

As if on cue, the succulent scent of fried seafood
wafted from the diner just behind them. Inhaling deeply,
Josie fought the urge to go check on things, but it was her
day off, so she stayed put in her chair.

A few beats passed while the wind shifted. Josie
allowed the lazy breeze to carry the aroma and her self-
conscious thoughts away as she refocused on her prim
friend who was still waiting for the sunblock.

"It's been an hour. I need to reapply." Sophia wiggled her manicured hand toward the bottle peeping out
of Opal's straw bag, her flashy diamond ring sending
sparkles dancing along the bleached sand.

Sophia was the only one out of the trio to jump into
the matrimony part of life as well as motherhood. She'd
been married for three years *and* had the cutest toddler
Josie had ever seen. With both of those major life accom-
plishments and an impressive job at a PR firm that represented several major figures in the professional sports
world, she was one busy lady but balanced it all quite well.

Josie respected Sophia's determination. The Southern
belle with an Italian heritage was intriguing, and her
spunk for knowing what she wanted and going after it
made her admirable. Sophia didn't allow anything to get
in her way when it came to accomplishing her dreams.

Josie, on the other hand, did nothing with her own
dreams but allow them to dim like a burnt-out star.

"Don't forget to head straight over to my parents' house after church Sunday for the barbecue," Opal mentioned for the third time since they'd parked it on the beach.

Sophia scoffed. "Honey, you cannot refer to a sprawling estate as a mere house."

"Call it what you want. Just head straight there after church. I'll be really offended if you don't show up," Opal commented with a good bit of sternness.

Josie and Sophia saluted Opal at the same time, cracking up.

"No need in getting so riled up," Sophia sassed.

"Just wanting to make myself clear . . ." Opal shrugged and let out an odd giggle. "Daddy doesn't have much free time, and . . . I don't spend much time with him . . . and I want to make some memories."

Josie studied Opal, worry kicking up all sorts of what-if scenarios. "Opal, please tell me everyone and everything is okay."

Opal blinked a few times before her eyes rounded. "Oh no! I'm sorry. No!" She giggled nervously again.

"You better not be hiding something important from us, Opal Gilbert." Sophia shook a finger at their fidgeting friend. "You know how aggravated it makes me when you're not being straight up."

"I promise everything is fine and Sunday is all about fun times." Opal nodded and gazed out over the ocean. "You know . . . that surfer looks a lot like our Superman . . ." She pointed to the figure way offshore, sending both of her friends' attention in that direction. All three sat up a little straighter to take in the view.

Sure enough, even from the distance, Josie knew it was him. Many a summer day, even winter days for that matter, while growing up, she had privately watched him own the waves with his surfboard. She should have known the surfer would be back in action just as soon as an unforeseen force kicked up some proper waves.

August only lived maybe a quarter mile from Driftwood Diner. Or he had before moving out from his adoptive parents' home.

"I wonder if he's staying with the Bradfords," Josie pondered out loud before catching herself.

"Wouldn't that just be the sweetest? I bet Zachary and Tucker are ecstatic." Opal clapped her hands.

August's childhood story was one that had drawn a lot of attention around town. His parents lost their parental rights for him and Tucker, and the boys' grandfather was appointed as guardian. Come to find out, the grandfather pretty much abandoned them—staying out of town for months at a time. Thankfully, the Bradfords got wind of it and adopted the boys.

"August!" Opal shouted, drawing Josie out of her thoughts and driving her into a wall of distress. "Here comes our superhero."

Panicked, Josie slapped her palm over her friend's mouth. "Are you crazy?"

Opal shrugged off Josie's hand and shouted again when August began walking out of the surf with his long-board tucked under his arm. Josie searched around like a madwoman for her cover-up, finding the white hem barely visible in Opal's bag. She knew before begging that Opal wouldn't be handing it over, but she tried anyway.

"Hand me my sundress. *Now*," she said through grit-ted teeth, nearly growling. Opal ignored her nasty tone and continued to wave like a lunatic, so Josie went for a softer petition. "Please. If you love me—even just a little—you will hand it over this instant. . . . *Please*."

August slowly raised his hand and delivered a much more subdued wave as he began moving in their direction.

He was only steps away from their three lounge chairs. Not nearly enough time for Josie to make a run for it or to snatch the cover-up from Opal's bag. The only thing she could do was lie there like a dead body waiting for the tide to roll in and carry her away.

"Hi, August," Sophia cooed as August stood before them with ocean water cascading down his long limbs.

"Hey. Good to see you," August replied as he set his board down on the sand. Several wet locks of hair slipped onto his forehead. He slicked them back before settling his hands on his lean hips.

Josie noticed remnants of purple and red paint still clinging to his right hand, evidence of an art project, she suspected. She wondered what it might be.

The thought dredged up old familiar feelings from her teenage years. After school, she used to sneak into the art studio to steal a glimpse of whatever masterpiece he would be working on at the time.

"Josie?" August called out.

Looking up, she muttered in his direction without making eye contact, "Huh?"

August's lips quirked up on one side and caught Josie's attention without her permission. "I was just asking if you've figured out a technique for untying problematic knots yet."

"I think our girl needs a lesson on that matter," Opal answered before Josie could form one. Of course she knew what he was referring to since she'd read the note. The very same note she'd already talked in length about with Sophia at Josie's expense.

If they'd been sitting at a table, the chatty woman would have one bruised-up shin by now. As it was, the only thing Josie could do was sit there awkwardly and put up with her friend's razzing.

"Karma," Josie said out of the corner of her mouth for only Opal to hear, but then Sophia decided to chime in as well.

"From what I've gathered, it takes time to loosen uncomfortable knots. And the best way to allow that to happen is, say . . . a *date*."

Everyone nodded in agreement as though Sophia had just spewed out profound words instead of hogwash.

Reaching her limit on being teased, Josie snapped at Sophia without thought. "Three years of marriage makes you an expert, I suppose." Josie was surprised when the brunette beauty practically cowered down in her chair. "Sophia?"

Sophia shook her head. "I'm certainly no expert in that department."

Opal suddenly tossed Josie her sundress. "Josie, take a walk with August so the two of you can work out the details on that date."

Opal might have been the easygoing hippie of the group, but when the whimsy ebbed from her tone, Josie always knew it was time to take Opal seriously. At the moment, Josie had no other choice but to take a walk. Something was up with Sophia, and they needed to spare their friend some dignity by not airing any of it in front of August.

After pulling the sundress on, Josie flicked a hand down the beach. "Follow the way." Resisting the temptation to slap her forehead—*lead*, not *follow*—she began stomping away without confirming August was even following. The uneasy churning in her stomach was all the evidence she needed to know he was close.

"The Sand Queens haven't changed much, have y'all?" August commented as he appeared by Josie's side, easily falling into step with her.

"What do you mean?" She chanced a glance in his direction.

August shrugged his tanned shoulder and offered a kind smile. "The friendship you three share is quite a special one."

Josie thought he was going to tease her about their quirkiness, so his compliment took her by surprise. Most friendships tended to fade after graduation, but the three of them continued to genuinely enjoy one another's company.

"Thank you . . ." She shook her head. "Hard to believe you probably have an entire group of foreign friends now."

The beach stroll continued as August regaled her with stories about a few friends he'd made during his time backpacking through Europe. She was amazed at all of the traveling opportunities he'd had, as well as the chance to study abroad for most of his college years. August had lived an entire new life so completely different from the docile seaside community life she'd lived since he left six years ago.

"I met my friend Alessio during the International Art Ministry. In between projects, we'd gather some of our friends and go exploring. He's fluent in Italian and I'm fluent in French, so we tried teaching each other common phrases to make traveling a little easier. Alessio thought it was funny to mess with people by mixing the Italian and French languages. It was hilarious to most of us, but the owner of one of the hostels we stayed at outside of Paris didn't find any humor in it."

Josie slid her hands in the pockets of her sundress and searched the sand for interesting shells. "That had to be quite confusing."

"Madame Faure thought Alessio was cussing at her. Got us kicked out on the streets." August allowed a little French flair to enunciate the lady's name before slipping back to his relaxed Southern drawl, completely charming Josie.

"No way! That's crazy." She laughed freely, feeling the butterflies die down in her stomach. She'd forgotten how easy it was to talk to August.

"True story." August grinned while squinting up at the sun, clearly recalling the moment.

"Do you miss Europe yet?"

"*Ça me manque un peu, mais pas assez pour revenir.*" The words rolled off his tongue with little effort, and it took quite a lot of effort for Josie not to swoon. The man was too charismatic for his own good.

"Okay, show-off, translation please?" Josie pushed her shoulder into his before catching herself.

"I miss it some, but not enough to return." August stopped to grab a beach ball the wind was stealing away and returned it to a little girl.

Once he was back by her side, Josie commented, "In both languages, that statement is romantic in such a sad way . . ."

"*Tu manges toujours du sable?*" He cut her a sideways glance. "Does that one sound romantic, too?" His tone was filled with flirty tease.

It most definitely sounded romantic to her, so she nodded. "What did you say?"

August slowed and leaned close to her ear, his heated breath tickling the side of her neck. "Do you still eat sand?"

The shiver he'd elicited forgotten, Josie shoved his shoulder once again. "You're never going to let me live that down, are you?" The glare Josie tried to deliver turned goofy as she joined him in laughter.

The memory of that sand-eating dare flickered through her thoughts as a wave rolled over her toes. That day years ago, a thirteen-year-old Josie somehow managed to shed her shyness long enough to stand up for herself when a group of local boys told her she was too girlie to surf their waves. She told them she'd eat a mouthful of sand if she couldn't outsurf them. If she did, they would have to eat the sand. August, not being part of the challenging fools, remained onshore as she proved her place by owning the waves long after each of her competitors crashed.

"I still can't believe you ate sand." He smirked.

"Sometimes you have to prove a point." She shrugged.

The boys couldn't manage swallowing the sand and ended up spitting it out, so Josie showed them up on that too by taking a mouthful of wet sand and swallowing it. What stood out the most to her about that memory was the awestruck look August had on his face.

"I admire you for that day. You've always reminded me of Nan."

Josie couldn't help but smile at the mention of August's adoptive mom. Nan was known as a spunky tomboy, never allowing anyone to tell her she couldn't do something. "I take that as a compliment. I think a lot of your mom."

"You should take it as a compliment. Nan is a great woman." August tipped his head in a gentlemanly gesture before picking up his pace to continue their stroll down the beach.

Josie found her shoulders relaxing and the tension uncoiling from her stomach as they reached the pier. Without prompting, August led her down the wooden planks before sitting on one of the benches near the end. She tilted her head and watched a small cluster of dolphins play around the pier piles below them.

"Tell me something else about your travels." She kept sight of August in her periphery while scanning the murky water for more glimpses of ocean life.

"Like what?"

She shrugged. "I don't know. . . . Oh, did you eat anything unusual?"

August groaned, causing Josie to sit up and look over. "I went with a group of friends down to Périgord for an art festival. . . . I ate *tête de veau*."

"What is that?" She gave him a dubious look.

August leaned a little closer with his nose scrunched and his top lip snarled. "Calf's head."

She gagged. "Why would you eat that?"

"My friends thought it would be funny to tell me it was chopped-up pork loin."

Josie covered her mouth with her hand, but the laughter escaped between her fingers. "That's awful."

"Tell me about it. I'm not an adventurous eater by a long shot either." His face puckered again before taking on a more curious look. "How about you?"

Her laughter came to a halt. "What about me?"

August nudged her arm with his. "Tell me something new about you since I've been gone."

Josie gazed out over the water, wishing she were eloquent enough to spin some adventurous tale for him, but that was not a gift she had nor was there an adventure to share anyhow.

"Come on, Jo. Don't go mute on me." August playfully nudged her arm again, but it didn't wiggle any words out of her.

There was something on the tip of her tongue that begged her to confess, but she bit down on it until it hurt. Surely August would consider her a nutcase. She wanted to tell him that ever since that day with her mom, a fear had set up in her that was so debilitating, she couldn't go any farther than the front door of the diner some days. That fear constantly told her if she didn't stay by her dad's side, something awful was going to happen to him too.

"I teach Sunday school," she finally blurted when he nudged her the third time.

"That's great," August said, his voice sounding sincere.

Josie blinked away the stinging from her eyes and glanced at him. He actually looked impressed and that reassurance was enough to alleviate some of the stiffness from her shoulders. "I enjoy it."

"Good. You should always enjoy what you do. No sense in doing it otherwise."

Josie looked away, thinking his comment was more on the lines of advice she actually needed, but she had no choice but to disregard it. Circumstances didn't allow her any other choice.

Their conversation faded after that as they took in the happenings around them. A few elderly men were having a lively debate while their fishing lines tangled. Two identical-looking toddlers came bouncing down the pier as a teenage boy convinced a naive teenage girl that the dolphins were actually sharks.

With the warm sunshine and sultry breeze blanketing her while the subtle sway of the pier offered its familiar comfort, Josie's head ended up resting on the firm shoulder next to her before she realized it.

Only a few beats passed before she jolted to her feet in such a spastic manner, it looked like she'd been zapped by an electrical current. "I . . . I'm so sorry."

"No worries, Josie. Only thing you should be apologizing for is you moved too soon." August remained stretched out on the bench, completely relaxed with a small smile toying with his lips. "Why don't you come sit with me for a little bit longer?"

"I'm going to head back." She turned and scurried

down the pier with her flip-flops pattering in an aggressive beat against the wooden planks.

August easily caught up with her, but the anxiety had already erected the walls around her. "Are you okay?"

Steeling herself and taking a deep breath, she nodded. "I'm sorry for acting so silly. . . . It's just . . . talking to you the other day, after all these years, was such an unexpected surprise. I guess I'm still in shock today." A nervous laugh slipped out from her wobbly lips.

"You have nothing to apologize for, so knock it off." August shot her a pointed look. "And to be honest, I'm glad I surprised you by my mere presence." Teasing took over the pointed look as he bit the corner of his lip.

"You still bite your lip, I see."

"Yeah. Thought once I removed the lip ring, that habit would stop." He chuckled.

"Why'd you take it out? And the others?"

"They didn't fit me any longer. It was time to try on a new look." He threaded his fingers through his drying black waves of hair.

"I think both looks fit you well, but this one suits you even better." Josie thought he always carried a distinct grace in each step he took, but there used to be an underlying hint of uncertainty to it. She sensed that he had somehow figured out how to shed it within the last six years. It made her wish she could do the same.

As soon as Opal and Sophia came into view with their heads angled close together, Josie knew a serious conversation was going down. "It was good seeing you again," she said softly to August.

He seemed to pick up on his dismissal and quickly gathered his board. "I'm going to leave you Sand Queens to it, but I'd be honored if you could attend my art exhibit next Friday night."

Opal spoke up. "Your uncle's studio?"

August tipped his head. "Yep. Seven o'clock."

"Fantastic. Sophia lives out of town now, but Josie and I will be there," Opal, always the spokeswoman for the trio, answered.

August waved and gave Josie one last measured look before making his way in the opposite direction of the beach.

Josie let go of the confusing feelings he'd stirred and focused on her defeated-looking friend. "What's wrong, Sophia?"

"Ty moved out."

The three women grew quiet as the delicate hum of beach life droned on with occasional bursts of laughter from sunbathers and seagulls squawking in protests at their intrusion. Josie knew the young couple had had a rocky year, but she'd not realized it had gotten to that point.

Eventually Josie asked, "How is our little guy taking it?"

"Thankfully he's still too young to really know the difference. Ty has always been gone so much anyway." Sophia sniffed and dabbed at the corner of her eye with the corner of her beach towel. "Momma's been staying the last month with us, so that's made it easier."

"Do you mind me asking what happened?" Opal asked just above a whisper.

"Ty doesn't think I respect him," Sophia answered, but Josie had a feeling there was much more behind it than that.

"How so?" Josie prompted.

"Y'all know I'm a decision maker. Always have been." Both friends nodded in agreement. If there ever was a choice that made the girls pause, Sophia was the one to resolve it. "The only decision Ty has ever had to make is when he's on a football field. That's been fine and dandy for the last three years, but all of a sudden every time I make a major purchase or decision for our family, he flies off the handle."

"Aww, babe, maybe all the pressure from his career has him feeling a little helpless," Josie offered.

Opal nodded. "I think Jo's right. Didn't Ty's shoulder injury have him sitting out almost half the season?"

Sophia fiddled with her wedding ring. "Yeah."

"And that rookie got enough spotlight time to shine. It makes perfect sense for Ty to be feeling threatened." Josie nodded her head vigorously, hoping to comfort her friend's worry.

"Marriage is a lot harder than I thought it would be." Sophia's shoulders slumped and a frown tugged her lips way down.

Josie exchanged a worried look with Opal before saying to Sophia, "Well, you're no quitter, so if anyone can handle it, it's you."

Sophia scoffed after a few seconds of silence.

"Have a little faith, my friend. It'll work itself out." Opal pulled on her floral-patterned sundress, promptly sending the other two into pack-up mode.

Sophia folded her lounge chair. "But what am I supposed to do?"

"Give him some space to sort it out. In the meantime, lean on Josie and me."

Josie placed a hand on Sophia's shoulder. "Yes, and several trips to Seashore Creamery for therapy. Doctor's orders!"

Opal paused in packing up, looking dreamy all of a sudden. "Ooh yeah! They have squid praline on special!" She was close to squealing and the other two were close to gagging with their faces set into grimaces.

"That sounds awful." Josie wrinkled her nose.

"It's surprisingly good. You shouldn't knock it until you've tried it."

"No thanks. I'm going to stick to vanilla with hot fudge." Josie scooped up two of the chairs, while Opal grabbed the colossal straw bag.

They made quick work of tucking the chairs inside the small shed off to the side of the diner and began walking up the street to the ice cream shop.

Before they arrived, Sophia broke the silence. "Don't think you're getting away with not telling us about what happened on your walk with August."

Josie sighed and looked skyward. "He's just as charming as he ever was and I'm still just as dorky."

"Oh, but that's part of *your* charm." Sophia wrapped her arm around Josie's waist. "I'll never understand why God didn't see fit to give me just a few of those extra inches of height he gave you." She looked up and stuck out her tongue.

Opal skipped inside while the other two paused by the door.

"Oh, but what he didn't give you in the height department, he made up for in the courage department. Sophia, I look up to you. You know that, right?" Josie offered her petite friend a warm smile before they stepped into the shop, where Opal was already ordering three samples of squid praline.

●   ●   ●

After attending the service at Sunset Cove First Baptist Church, Josie headed inland to the Gilbert estate, still wondering why Opal was in such a tizzy about the barbecue. She drove through the open gate and was relieved to spot only a handful of cars. Normally the Gilbert gatherings had too many guests for Josie's liking. It only took her walking into the giant back garden to have the relief chased away as soon as her eyes landed on one tall, dark, and smiling man.

August was near the grill with several other men. He tipped his head toward her, but thankfully, he didn't head her way.

Face blushing instantly, Josie raised her hand in greeting before turning away to find Opal in the small crowd, already coming up with a plan to say hey and then make a quick exit. Her reaction to seeing him was embarrassing and she feared even if he stayed in Sunset Cove, the hot flash and sweaty palms weren't going to fade.

Given the considerable span of time that they had been separated, Josie couldn't figure out for the life of her why the man lingered in her thoughts. August was like a speck of paint caught underneath her fingernail. Even though it wasn't visible, she knew it was there. Sometimes it seemed natural to have it there as a part of her. Yet at other times, it worried her to death and she desired to be rid of it altogether.

"I can't find Opal anywhere," Sophia grumbled as she walked up to Josie. Little Collin was asleep on her shoulder and looked to be weighing the petite woman down. "You okay?"

Josie shrugged, knowing Sophia could see the effect of being around August written all over her heated face. "I haven't seen Opal or Lincoln. Those two better not have forgotten about the barbecue." She was about to take Collin out of Sophia's arms when her friend's dad hurried over and beat her to it.

"Thanks, Dad." Sophia smiled while rotating her shoulder.

Josie gazed at the exquisite backyard, loving how the

azaleas were in full bloom—pinks, whites, and reds lined the garden. Several fountains blended in with the mur- murings of the guests as they grouped around them. She was admiring the arched trellis dripping with wisteria and ivy when Opal stepped underneath it, still wearing the lace boho dress with flowers pinned in her hair from church, making Josie glad she hadn't switched her floral print dress for jeans she had stashed in the truck.

With a wide grin, Opal waved. "Josie and Sophia, I need y'all to come here."

Once they joined her, Lincoln sidled up next to them, towering over the woman. His long brown hair was pulled back and his beard neatly trimmed. He was also in his church attire, a white linen shirt and tan slacks.

Lincoln winked at Opal and then scanned the group. "Carter? August? Will you guys come here for a sec, too?"

As they gathered around the couple, Opal raised her left hand and smoothed it down the side of Lincoln's smiling face. Josie's eyes widened when catching the glint from a delicate ring on Opal's finger. From the gasp beside her, Sophia noticed it too.

Sophia stepped forward, hands on her hips, suck- ing her teeth. "I knew this wasn't just a barbecue! It's an engagement party!"

Opal giggled. "We are engaged, yes, but this is actu- ally a wedding ceremony."

"You're getting married? Right now?" The couple wore wide grins as they both nodded, which Sophia returned with an exaggerated scoff. "Oh, my gracious! Opal Gilbert, you can't just pop something like this on us!" Her arms were waving around and her foot just a- stomping as she kept reprimanding them as if the grown pair were naughty children.

Carter Bradford let out a guffaw. "Lincoln Cole said

he'd never walk down an aisle. Guess the punk figured getting married in a backyard lets him keep his word."

Before Josie could contain it, joy bubbled out of her in a high squeal as she grabbed one of Opal's arms and one of Sophia's and started bouncing up and down. "Our Opal is getting married!" She giggled as tears spilled down her cheeks. Sophia got over her attitude quickly and joined in. They hugged and laughed and wiped the tears away until Lincoln cleared his throat.

"I'd like to marry my woman before the barbecue gets cold."

"You two stand right there." Opal directed Josie and Sophia to the left of the trellis before disappearing among the crowd.

Moments later, their pastor positioned himself underneath the trellis and asked the guests if they minded gathering a little closer.

As everyone settled into place, Josie snuck a peek at August, still coming to terms with him being there in the flesh and not in one of her daydreams. He was whispering something to Lincoln, so Josie took the opportunity to give him a thorough once-over. In dark jeans and a blue button-down with the sleeves rolled up to his elbows, she thought he looked just as handsome as the groom.

A violin began to softly play, but before Josie could look away, August's eyes connected to hers. The side of his lips quirked as his gaze softened. Not in tease, but perhaps liking the idea of her watching him. Again, the reaction to having his attention on her had the heat crawling up her neck and flooding her face, a war of nerves ricocheting through her body. Wiping her palms down the side of her dress, Josie somehow managed to snap out of the daze and move her focus to find Opal's dad leading her through the parted guests.

As the bride and groom exchanged vows, Josie kept them in her periphery, but like magnets, her eyes collided with August's and remained fastened there throughout the ceremony. It wasn't until the pastor told the groom to kiss his bride that August slowly blinked and moved his attention to them to take in the moment, causing her to do the same.

Lincoln leaned down and slowly placed his lips to Opal's while cupping the back of her head. He was a giant of a man, but he was always so gentle with Opal. What seemed to be a quick peck continued for a lengthy amount of time, but it wasn't raucous or inappropriate. The man was loving on his new wife with such reverence, and when Josie noticed Opal wiping away a tear from Lincoln's cheek, her own eyes flooded with tears.

It was the simplest yet most profound wedding Josie had ever attended. No frills. No fuss. Just two souls in love and wanting to dedicate themselves to each other before God and their loved ones.

When Lincoln placed his forehead against Opal's, the pastor asked, "Are you done, Lincoln?"

A light chuckle could be heard from the guests but hushed when Lincoln began shaking his head.

"No, sir. Not even close," Lincoln replied in a raspy voice before kissing his bride once again. The chuckles transformed into sniffling and soft murmurs of celebration.

Eventually the newlyweds turned to face their guests and allowed the pastor to announce them. Once the intimate bubble dissipated and turned to grins and fist pumps, eating and celebrating followed well into the afternoon.

Josie managed to keep a comfortable distance between her and August, but he seemed to be closing the space by the time the wedding cake was served. She quickly gathered a slice of cake and covered it with a napkin before maneuvering around the guests with hopes of slinking away undetected. Making it as far as the shadowy side of the mansion, Josie thought she'd succeeded.

"Leaving so soon?" The distinct boom of his voice resonated close behind her, sending a shiver to jolt down her spine, and almost caused her to drop the plate. August owned one of those rich voices with a depth one could feel when spoken to, homegrown Southern with the edges of his words more defined to keep the twang from becoming too prominent. No other voice had ever stopped Josie in her tracks as this man's. It was both thrilling and terrifying.

Almost too many moments passed with Josie savoring his voice and acknowledging how deeply she'd missed simply listening to him speak. Taking a shaky breath, she ordered herself to turn to face him and was instantly caught in his silvery-blue gaze once again. "I'm supposed to be spending the afternoon with Miss Dalma. I . . . uh . . . I'm bringing her cake . . ." Clearing her throat, Josie held the plate a little higher before lowering it. "You remember her?"

August's lips tipped upward. "Miss Dalma is unforgettable."

His answer had Josie mirroring his smile. "She sure is. Well . . . she's expecting me . . . so I better go."

August took a deep breath and slowly blew it out, seeming as affected as Josie felt. He reached out and placed his palm on her shoulder, giving it a gentle press before dropping his hand. "It was good seeing you again, Jo."

"You too." Maybe her emotions were running amok because of the wedding, but Josie had the crazy urge to sling her arms around his neck and declare how much she missed him. She took her own deep breath and turned tail to get away from the allure of August Bradford before she made a fool of herself.

4

August chipped away at the flecks of paint clinging to his nails as he studied the drying canvas. He was optimistic that Josie would show up at the studio Friday night and instantly understand what he was trying to express to her through the paintings. It wouldn't be the first time he'd tried capturing her attention in the same exact manner.

Back in high school, August spent as much time in the art studio at the school as possible, oftentimes well past the normal school hours. Josie sneaking into the studio after school to check out his paintings wasn't a secret to him, but she was so reverent about it that he'd let her get away with it.

During their junior year, he put great care into painting her a message, and the teenage girl with her keen eye for art caught it instantly. He would never forget that day her face lit up as soon as she got it, before looking around as if she'd expected him to appear.

They only exchanged knowing looks that day, yet it nagged him over the years if he should have initiated a conversation about the painting. August wondered if doing so would have instigated a pivotal change in their friendship. Good thing he didn't live in the what-ifs.

Smiling at the memory, August focused on adding another subtle hint to the picture before him. The rhythmic strokes of his paintbrush over the coarse canvas were cathartic and began pulling him into the creative spell that wasn't ever easily broken once he was in its snare. Hours, even days, could pass without his awareness, but that wasn't the case today. His mind kept flickering back to that high school art room with the blonde-haired, blue-eyed beauty admiring his artwork while he secretly admired her.

The canvas before him faded as he recalled the private painting in crisp detail, even though he'd not actually laid eyes on it in years. It was for Josie. So after she'd left that day, August took the picture home and hid it away. If she found it odd that it disappeared, never to be presented to the class, she never let on about it. The painting was still in his possession, and when the time was right, he hoped to give it to her as a thank-you for truly under-standing him and his art way back when most overlooked him. He supposed people had a right to be confused by him—a good bit older than his classmates with an out-ward appearance beyond different from most of the fresh-faced beach kids.

After the Bradfords adopted him and Tucker, August worked diligently on being the perfect son. He never indulged in lounging in his room while listening to music or anything else normal boys did. If a dish needed wash-ing or the lawn mowed or a floor mopped, they never had to ask. Nan finally sat him down one day and all but told him to knock it off.

"You're thirteen, August," Nan said that day as they sat on the sprawling deck of the beach house. She kept her brown eyes on him as the breeze danced through her short dark-blonde hair.

"Yes, ma'am," August agreed, itching to draw Nan in that moment to give to Derek as a thank-you.

"Then why in the world are you acting like an old

maid? Seriously, I'm disappointed that I never have to tell you to pick up your socks or not to drink out of the milk carton."

August had promised Tucker he would find them a good family—and promised not to screw it up for them—so Nan had totally stumped him that day. Worried that he'd somehow managed to screw it up, he all-out begged, "I'm sorry. I . . . I can do better. Just tell me what you want me to do and I'll do it exactly like that. Please don't kick us out!" He was about to go to his knees and beg even more when Nan quickly wrapped him in a hug.

"You and Tucker are stuck with us, so there's no sense in even worrying about that. And all I want you to do is be August. Not a robot maid. Listen to your music too loud. Be lazy every now and then, and go surfing with your uncle Carter." Nan presented him with a gift with those words that had a profound effect on August's outlook. She gave him permission to just be himself. No pretenses. No pretending.

"I notice you drawing on every scrap piece of paper you can find, so I thought you'd like this." She handed over a bag brimming with thick sketch pads and several packs of charcoal drawing pencils, yet another gift that would give him the tools needed to become what he was meant to be.

And just like that, August found himself.

Midteens, he rebelled a bit and took to dying his hair in wild colors. A few tattoos and piercings followed and he liked how it changed him, like a blank canvas coming to life. He no longer resembled that scared kid who felt lost after losing his parents. That black-haired kid whose stomach ached from hunger and fright on those nights he held little Tucker, praying God would get them out of the living arrangement with their grandpa Ted.

His early adolescent years had been horrible, but then life made a one-eighty and became something more than he'd ever imagined. Eyes fastened on the art project before him, August hoped he'd see another dream come to be with a woman he'd longed to have in his life. He could only hope that delicate bird was finally ready to fly out of the open cage.

A slow chuckle worked past his lips as he picked up the canvas and walked it to an empty spot by the wall. "Josie will get it. No worries," August mumbled to himself as he worked on cleaning his brushes so he could get started on the next message.

"Talking to yourself now? Is that a European thing?" Tucker said as he walked into the studio with the last of the supplies August had asked him to retrieve.

August ignored the jab and set to squirting bold paints on a clean pallet. "What sessions have you signed up to take at the camp?"

"I'm taking a few music classes with Uncle Carter and was thinking about maybe checking out a drama class." Tucker perched on a stool beside August's easel.

"Not even *one* of my art sessions?" August glanced over with an eyebrow drawn up.

"Nah, man. You know I can't even draw a straight line. God gave you all that skill."

August chuckled while shaking his head. "You just don't want to give me an excuse to tell you what to do."

"Whatever." Tucker rolled his eyes. "So . . . you gonna tell me what's up with these half-done paintings?" He pointed over to the canvas drying by the wall.

"You know all about fishing, right?"

Tucker rolled his eyes. "You know I do."

The guys didn't have much growing up, but they treasured their cane fishing poles and had a perceptive knack for knowing when to gather bait. The best time to collect worms was right after a morning rainstorm, and early evenings were the time to scoop up crickets along the edges of overgrown fields.

August tipped his chin toward the incomplete painting. "That's bait. I'm about to go fishing."

"Sweet." Tucker bumped fists with August as the brothers grinned broadly at each other.

August's heart picked up speed as he focused on the challenge ahead of him.

"I'm out, dude, so you can get to it." Tucker stood and stretched his long, lanky body while releasing a grunt.

"Thanks for helping me out." August ticked his chin in Tucker's direction but kept his eyes on the canvas.

"No worries," he heard Tucker say before the door closed.

Focusing completely on preparing his bait, August cranked the music up on his iPod dock and got to it as his little brother had instructed.

He blinked—that's what it felt like anyway—and realized a day and night had passed without letting him know it. Rubbing the heel of his hand against his eye, August took note of his dwindling supplies.

He unearthed his wallet and keys from underneath a pile of used paint rags and shoved them into his pocket. The paint-stained shirt caught his sight, so he yanked it off. After turning the shirt inside out and using it as a rag for his face and hands, he went on a hunt for a clean one.

August made it to the quaint craft store in town after refueling on fresh donuts and a tall coffee from the local bakery. The much-needed sugar and caffeine were already zinging through his system as he loaded the handbasket with various supplies, making do with what was available until his order came in. He rounded the corner on a

hunt for brush cleaner and came to a halt at the endearing sight before him. There stood little Miss Dalma in
her Sunday best. The pale-pink jacket and skirt suit
were probably brand-new, but the camouflage rain boots
on her feet were caked with mud and far from it. Her
hair was pinned haphazardly with a pillbox hat perched
among it.

"Good morning, Miss Dalma. Is there a special occasion at church today or something?" He couldn't think of
anything that would be going on midweek.

"Nah, honey. I'm just going fishing. Or that's the
plan, but I can't find the bait section. Mr. Growler must
have moved it again . . . ," Miss Dalma said absently as she
rummaged through a bin filled with decorative buttons.
"Darnedest thing . . ."

August had a feeling it would do no good to point out
the fact that she was in the wrong store, so he settled on
asking, "How'd you manage getting here?"

"Umm . . ." She huffed and dumped a handful of
buttons into her basket. Several fell to the floor, making
a pinging racket before disappearing underneath the display shelf. "I rode my bicycle."

August scratched the scruff on his chin and calculated
her house to be at least three miles down the road since it
was one avenue past his family's restaurant. He gave her
another once-over and was relieved to find no signs of a
fall. "Isn't it a little difficult to ride a bike in a skirt?"

"Don't be silly, honey." Dalma began hiking up her
skirt with her free hand before August could stop her,
revealing a pair of plaid Bermuda shorts underneath like
it was perfectly normal.

He bit the inside of his cheek to repress a chuckle.
Never had he met such a quirky character in all his life.
Some said it was because she was getting up there in age,

but he spent a good bit of time with her when he was in high school and couldn't recall a time where she ever fit in the "normal" box. "Tell ya what, Miss Dalma. How about you let me go fishing with you and I'll gather us some bait."

Dalma grinned wide with excitement, showing off nothing but pink gums. "Would you?" When he nodded, she continued, "Then you have yourself a deal, honey." She sat the loaded basket on the floor and started to the front of the store. "I'll meet you at my house."

August rushed after her. "It'll be faster if you let me give you a lift in my truck."

She halted so quickly that the rubber soles of her rain boots squeaked against the tile floor and he nearly plowed her over. "I suppose you're right."

The impromptu fishing trip would eat up most of his day, but spending time with the sweetest yet oddest little lady he'd ever met would be well worth it. He offered her his elbow, she gladly took it, and they headed out.

5

After winding around the avenues of Sunset Cove after work, Josie pulled the truck into Dalma's driveway and parked underneath the stilted beach house.

Movement from the hammock strung from the rafters caught her eye as she turned the engine off. A bare foot dangled over the edge and tapped at the air. It wasn't until she opened the driver's door that she realized the foot was keeping time to the beats of the Beach Boys' song "Good Vibrations" that was playing from an old cassette player. Taking a deep inhale of the pungent air kicking off the inlet behind the house, Josie walked over and peered down at a grinning Dalma.

"I see you finally found your teeth." Josie crossed her arms and also grinned.

"Darnedest thing . . ." It was Dalma's go-to saying, almost like a brush-off for the weird moments she tended to collect. She hitched a thumb in really no direction in particular. "I found them in my tackle box."

Her statement had Josie cringing for two reasons—nasty teeth and fishing alone. Both of which Josie would have helped out with. "Please tell me you washed them before putting them in your mouth."

"I got better sense than that." Dalma scoffed, lacing her fingers and resting them on her midsection. She wore a pink suit jacket, unfastened to reveal an Eagles T-shirt underneath that totally clashed with the plaid Bermuda shorts she paired with it. "I rinsed them off with a can of Dr Pepper first."

Josie stood there watching the silly lady nod her head and hum a few bars of the song. She gave up on the teeth and moved on. "What have we said about fishing alone?"

"That you get to keep all the fish." Dalma giggled like a schoolgirl. "Don't worry, dear. August Bradford accompanied me. Plus, he let me keep all the fish we caught and even cleaned them for me. He's one fine young man."

Josie was relieved but her cheeks still heated at the mention of August's name. "I'll fry them for supper. . . . How'd you end up fishing with August?"

"We ran into each other at Growler's and he offered to go fishing with me. Sure wasn't a hardship to spend the day with that handsome man." She let out a low whistle before raising an arm and wiggling her fingers. Josie took the hint and helped her climb out of the hammock. They quietly headed for the stairs that led to the top floor.

"I don't understand why you don't go ahead and move in with me. There are no tall stairs at Driftwood Dreams," Josie commented when Dalma began grumbling halfway up the staircase that led to the front door. The little lady was stubbornly refusing the inevitable.

"Because you need to be ready to take on a suitor and don't need anything in the way of that." Making it to the top of the stairs, Dalma worked on catching her breath.

"I don't need a man. I'm perfectly capable of anything right on my own."

Dalma glanced over her shoulder. "I never said you did, dear. You don't need one, but I bet the right one sure would complement you."

Josie ran a fingertip over the rigid texture of an upside-down seashell on the sign attached to the stair railing.

She'd fashioned it and several others to look like a ghost when she made it as a gift for her little old friend several years ago. She thought it was quite fitting since Dalma chose to name her house *Coast House.*

Josie left the name plaque and climbed the last few steps. "You wouldn't be in the way even if I had a suitor to complement me." She opened the front door and ushered Dalma inside. The faded-pastel seashell motif found in most inlet homes was prominent, but books stacked in every nook and cranny was outside the norm. Dalma refused to part with even one book and Josie didn't have the heart to make her, but it was beginning to look like a bibliophilic obstacle course instead of a house.

Dalma went straight to the fridge and pulled out a pitcher of tea. She set it on the creamy tiled kitchen counter before turning to look at Josie. "You're right. I wouldn't, but *you* would. And I certainly won't allow you to use me as the excuse to not let a good man sweep you off your feet and carry you off into the sunset."

"You've been listening to too many audio romance books again." Josie narrowed her eyes and smirked, trying to play off the conversation, but by the looks of her thinning lips, Dalma was having a lucid moment and wouldn't be sidetracked so easily.

"God has too many plans for you, young lady. Shame on you for getting in his way." Dalma jabbed a finger in Josie's direction before pulling out two fine china teacups.

Josie filled them with the iced tea, knowing the dainty cups were meant to hold warm tea, but also knowing Dalma did things differently. She handed one to Dalma, took a sip from hers, and then began rummaging around for ingredients. "I'm going to get started on supper."

"Okay, dear. Go ahead and ignore my wise words.

And leave that for later. I just want a snack for now."
Dalma pulled out a heart-shaped box of chocolates from
the pantry. Odd enough since Valentine's Day was two
months ago.

"Where in the world did you get those?" Josie asked
as she started mixing the dry ingredients for the fish
dredge—flour, cornmeal, cayenne, salt, and pepper.

"I found them in a suitcase this morning in my
closet." Dalma popped a chocolate into her mouth and
chewed it thoughtfully. "Still good," she commented and
held the box out for Josie to take one.

"No thanks." Josie waved the candy off.

Once she had everything prepped for later, Josie made
her way through the maze of books to select one, but the
one she was currently working on wasn't where she left it.
After skimming a few other piles, she gave up finding it
and selected another one.

Dalma moved to the back deck with her iPad,
already listening to some historical romance Josie helped
her download. Josie pulled the pouch of colored pencils from the kitchen drawer and followed behind her.
They settled on the daybed Opal had refashioned into
a deep swing with lots of funky outdoor pillows. Josie
used her long legs to keep the bed swaying languidly
and began adding life to the black-and-white pages of
the old musty book while a British voice narrated a tale
about an ornery duke and his lowly maid falling into a
forbidden relationship.

A few hours passed, and Josie knew it was time for
supper and bed when Dalma began talking about having
a meeting at the library she needed to get to. The lucidity
tended to slip away drastically when the little lady became
too tired. It hurt Josie to witness it, but she would bravely
endure it in order to be there for Dalma just as she had

been there for Josie during those dark days that followed after losing her mother.

Looking back on that time, it was Dalma who quietly showed up when others seemed to drift away. She was the one looking close enough to realize Josie's grief had slipped more into a bout of depression and made the appointment for her to see the doctor.

Going through her own battle with depression, which kept showing up in small seasons every now and then, was why Josie helped Theo and Deandrea. It was easy to spot someone battling the same shadows after living it herself. The smile that only touched the lips and had nothing else to do with the rest of the face. The void stare. Even when their eyes were on you, the focus was in a dark place no one could see but them. Head tipped away from the activity of life, only present yet not engaged. Josie didn't know exactly what she could do for Deandrea, except for showing up and offering the woman nudges of help just as Dalma had done for her.

"My husband works too much," Dalma commented, pulling Josie from her worrying over Deandrea and returning it to Dalma.

Josie couldn't come up with a response to that, so she chose to say nothing. She helped Dalma into bed and tucked the quilt around the dear lady.

Dalma settled against her pillow and muttered as her eyes drifted shut, "Will you stay just a little longer until Gerald makes it home?"

Josie swallowed past the lump in her throat and whispered, "Yes, ma'am." She took her book and pencils to the wingback chair in the corner of the bedroom and quietly worked well past midnight. One thing she'd come to understand in her young life was that people left, but she wanted to be the person who could be depended on to stay.

● ● ●

Math was never a favorite subject for Josie, but she had become obsessed with numbers during that week. She kept a tally of how many times she'd watched the diner's screen door and how many times she'd lied to herself about not looking for a certain tall, dark-headed man to show up. Both totals had gotten completely out of hand by Thursday, and she was right irritated with herself and with that certain guy when the sum total of times he'd made an appearance was a big fat zero.

The math calculations didn't stop there. The days before the art exhibit seemed to be subtracted all too quickly, and the pile of discarded outfits added up to a grand mountain in the middle of her bedroom floor. By Friday, she had to use caution in maneuvering around it.

"I can't go," she mumbled into the cell phone and had to yank it away from her ear when Opal's voice rang out at too high of a volume.

"Why not?"

Josie moved the phone back to her ear and scrutinized the mountain of material. "I don't have anything to wear." It sounded like a solid excuse to her, but from Opal's exaggerated snort, it wasn't.

"That's just silliness. You have a closet full of lovely church dresses. Wear one of those."

Sure, Josie had a nice selection of dresses she only wore on Sundays—her preferred choice of attire any other day of the week was jeans and a T-shirt—but she found each one she pulled from the closet lacking in some way. When she hesitated, Opal yammered on.

"Fine. I'll bring you something to wear. I'll be there in ten."

Josie threw her hand out like a stop sign even though

her friend couldn't see it. "No, no!" Suddenly the black maxi dress wedged into the side of the material mountain seemed suitable enough for the event. If it were left up to Opal, Josie would end up wearing a tie-dyed jumper with Moses sandals and flowers woven into her hair. The thought sent a shudder through Josie. She shook it off and yanked the dress from the mountain, causing an avalanche in the process. "I've found something."

Opal snorted again. "Good. I'm on my way regardless, so be ready." With that, the phone clicked off and ended Josie's futile attempt at getting out of the evening ahead.

With no time to fuss over her appearance, Josie left her hair down in the beachy waves it naturally formed into after her shower and pulled on the black dress. After tugging it into place and pushing her feet into a pair of silver sandals, she rummaged through the top dresser drawer that served as her jewelry box. Most of the collection had belonged to her late mother. She plundered around for a set of bangle bracelets, but a beautifully painted box in the style of van Gogh's *Starry Night* caught her attention. Instead of a night sky, it was a beach with brilliant waves. She traced the looping paint strokes of the sea as a hidden memory wiggled loose and came to light.

Math might not have ever been a favorite subject for her, but art certainly was. During her senior year, she was selected to take an advanced art course offered at the high school. The senior project was to research and present an artist or a specific art style to the class. Josie's pick was immediate, pop art. She loved the freedom the style offered and presented several artists and a few canvases she'd created for her project. Opal's passion was already clear at such a young age, so she chose to focus her presentation on the craft of woodwork.

Josie had expected August to present someone famous—Monet, da Vinci, or Donatello—but he surprised the entire class, including the teacher, by his choice.

Needless to say, everyone was taken aback when he presented a handmade necklace fashioned from sea glass. August, never one to skimp on even the minute details, displayed the delicate piece of jewelry on a spindly branch of driftwood. The various blues—teal, azure, indigo— entwined with the delicate silver necklace and stood out dramatically against the bleached wood.

The hour flew by with him telling the class about the history of jewelry artisanship and how he'd apprenticed for several months under a local artisan. With the artisan's guidance, August had created the piece on display.

Josie, along with every other girl in class, fell in love with the necklace. Some even begged him to let them have it or create one specifically for them.

"Sorry. This is the only one I'm making and it was made for someone in particular," August announced to all the girls' disappointment.

The necklace never showed up around any girl's neck at school, so it was thought that he'd given it to his mom. Months passed and the necklace was all but forgotten.

Graduation came and went with the expected news of August moving upstate to attend college. It was the same plan Josie had up until the devastating life storm struck her family and claimed her mother's life. She had no other choice but to turn down her acceptance into the art program and stay in Sunset Cove with her dad.

The day he was to leave, August spent a long time hovering at the counter at Driftwood Diner until finally working up enough nerve to ask Josie to step outside with him. Nervous and confused as she was, she agreed.

Standing underneath the overhang on the side of the

diner, August offered her a stunning, hand-painted jewelry box. "I've wanted to give this to you for a long time now and . . . well . . . I should have given it to you the day of the presentation."

With trembling hands, Josie fumbled with opening the lid and nearly dropped it when her eyes landed on the stunning piece of art inside. August plucked the delicate necklace out of the box, slipped it over Josie's head, and settled it against her plain black tank top.

She gazed down at the necklace he'd just given her through a sheen of tears. "This makes me feel beautiful."

August openly admired her before slowly shaking his head. "No, you're wrong. It's just as I suspected." He reached over and brushed a wisp of hair off her blushing cheek. "*You* make the necklace beautiful."

"Ah, August . . . I can't believe you're giving it to me . . ."

"I made it for you, Jo. I took chips of sea glass and bonded them with the larger ones." He skimmed the pad of his index finger along one of the stones that rested close to her collarbone. "I wanted it to be close to impossible to count how many pieces of sea glass were used to form the piece, because I want you to realize the beautiful parts of your life can be just as endless if you allow it."

Such profound words from a young man, but it didn't surprise Josie. August had already lived more life than most Sunset Cove adults, and that living produced wisdom. And that wisdom had her in tears.

They stood in the shadow of the weathered building, allowing a truthful yet silent conversation to pass between them. Through nothing but meaningful looks, both admitted to the hidden feelings they'd had for each other.

August placed a soft kiss on her damp cheek before walking away, leaving Josie with one of the sweetest yet most heartbreaking moments of her life. The young artist gave her so much in that moment beyond the stunning necklace, yet he took so much more. He walked away with her heart and never returned it.

During his absence, Josie kept busy with helping her dad, but August Bradford had never completely left her thoughts. Now as she gazed at the necklace tucked inside the box, she was ashamed to admit she'd failed at doing what he'd encouraged her to do.

Taking it from the box, she slipped it on and pressed her fingers to the intricate sea glass, whispering, "It's time to remember the beautiful parts of living and to create some of my very own. God, please help me to be brave enough." She picked up her small clutch and pulled the front door open just as Opal was about to knock.

True to fashion, Opal was dressed in a pair of wildly patterned palazzo pants and a flowy top with a silk scarf tied around her head.

"Hello, Mrs. Cole." Josie grinned affectionately at her friend, still trying to come to terms with Opal being married.

Opal played with one of her chandelier earrings that brushed all the way to her shoulders to playfully show off her wedding ring. Her eyes zeroed in on the necklace before a gasp escaped her lips. "August gave that to *you*! When?"

Josie's hand automatically reached up to protectively shield the piece. "Umm . . . before he left for college."

"No way!" Opal moved closer and shooed Josie's hand away so she could admire the necklace. "All this time and you've never told me."

"I've never told anyone." Josie shrugged. "I just . . ."

"I understand, honey. You wanted it to be just between you and August. How romantic." Her green eyes twinkled before giving Josie a hug. "Are you ready to go?"

"Yeah, I've had enough arithmetic to last a lifetime. Art is more my subject." She stepped outside into the humid night and locked the cottage door.

"Do what?" Opal's face scrunched up as she eyed her friend.

"Nothing. Never mind. Let's do this." Josie pointed toward Opal's vintage VW van, where she saw Lincoln behind the wheel. She was ready to get on with it before chickening out on a beautiful part of her life that had been waiting to come true for the last six years.

6

An undercurrent traveled around the dimly lit gallery through hushed conversations as people focused on the canvases artfully arranged along the indigo wall. August took a deep inhale of the lingering scent of paint, one of his favorite aromas, and listened on as his mom talked to the group surrounding them.

"The guy has more talent in his paint-stained pinkie—"

Tuning Nan out, August gave the group a bashful smile before moving through the crowd. His dad, Derek, squeezed his shoulder as he passed by and gave him an understanding look. Nan never tired of bragging about him or his two brothers, but he'd never been able to grow comfortable with receiving such praise. Sure, he loved talking about the art pieces, just not about himself in particular.

His eyes kept sweeping over the crowd with hopes of spotting a certain blonde who should have been easy to catch sight of. Josie was tall for a woman but carried the height with a grace he'd bet she didn't even realize she possessed.

Wildly enough, a head full of golden-red coils caught his attention first. August couldn't contain the grin as he headed Opal's way near the front of the gallery.

"Nice scarf." He eyed the silk material that seemed to

be losing the battle with taming back Opal's unruly hair as he reached to shake Lincoln's hand, who was standing beside her.

She smoothed a hand over it. "Thanks. I found it at a flea market in Woodstock."

"I checked out Woodstock while I was in New York. I went there to gather inspiration for the fine arts camp. Even the light poles in that town are works of art."

"Well, that's probably the best place for inspiration then. I certainly find it to be." Opal nodded her head, sending the curls on a springy bounce.

"Straight up. I could live there." As the words left his mouth, August noticed the blonde beauty standing beside him. She wore a black dress that reminded him of the lining inside an expensive jewelry box, which went perfectly with the significant piece draped around her neck. Seeing that necklace on Josie stirred a deep feeling in his chest.

"You're part of the art exhibit, I see." His eyes flicked from the necklace that the dress showcased exquisitely before settling on her delicate-blue eyes. The light shade always reminded him of the softer-hued sea glass woven into the necklace.

Josie's hand reached up and touched the necklace, but she looked uncertain. "You'd like to move back to New York?"

No form of greeting, but August liked how Josie's need for an answer to her question outweighed pleasantries. Clearing his throat, he murmured, *"Un lieu magique comme Woodstock ne peut être apprécié que pendant les visites, sinon elle perdrait son charme."*

The worry slipped from her eyes as the corners crinkled with amusement. "Now you're just showing off again."

Receiving the desired effect of putting her at ease, he translated, "A magical place such as Woodstock can only be appreciated during visits, otherwise it would lose its charm." He leaned closer, catching hints of Josie's coconut perfume, or perhaps it was her shampoo. Whatever is was, she smelled of summer and sunshine, and he added it to his list of favorite scents. He stole a few more whiffs of the pleasant fragrance before adding, "Also, I'm not leaving, so there's no getting rid of me."

Josie automatically leaned away, but he didn't miss the slight shiver dancing across her bare shoulders. "Is that a threat?" Her voice held a light edge of tease.

"It's whatever you want it to be, Jo," August teased her in return. He noticed Opal and Lincoln slipping away during their playful exchange. Opal gave him a discreet thumbs-up before disappearing into the crowd. He turned his attention to Josie. "Thank you for coming tonight. It means a lot."

"I love you . . ." Josie did her own double take from her word folly. Her cheeks grew to such a lovely pink shade that he wanted to re-create it with paint pigment. "Art! I meant art! I love *art*!"

As tempting as it was to tease Josie on that, August was smart enough to know when to give her some breathing room. This was one of those times. She'd flee if he went there, and he needed her to see his paintings first.

That will probably send her running off Cinderella-style all on its own.

"I love this gallery too," Josie added after a few beats. "I noticed Carter changed the sign out front."

August scanned the space with its weathered wood floors and cream-colored paneled walls. The walls were bare except for his night's showing on the indigo showcase wall. "It used to be a family beach house until Carter had it renovated into Sunset Studio. He changed the name to Sunset Studio and Gallery once I came on board."

"So it was his idea to combine music and art?" Josie tilted her head toward the door, causing a lock of blonde waves to slip across her cheek.

August reached out and tucked the hair behind her shoulder, not thinking anything of it, but she obviously did. Her face warmed in color again. He smiled and nodded his head. "Yeah. Carter was all about it as soon as I agreed to become his business partner here. He and his wife, Dominica, teach music lessons in the back rooms."

"So you're really staying?" Josie skimmed her fingers over the banister leading to the second floor that now housed supply rooms instead of bedrooms. She sounded genuinely interested in his answer, going as far as meeting his eyes.

"I'm here to stay, Jo," August answered her honestly and straightforwardly, wanting her to have no confusion on the matter. "I'm ready to lay down some roots." He wanted to add that he needed her to be a part of his new root system in Sunset Cove, but something told him to keep that part to himself for the time being.

He brushed off the trepidation as best as he could and began leading her over to the indigo wall displaying some of the paintings he had created during his time in France.

Two French countryside landscapes, a realist painting of a French baker, and a black-and-white of the Eiffel Tower. The fifth painting was a cityscape of Belleville. The area captured on canvas was considered Paris's Chinatown and the buildings were vividly dressed in graffiti. It had also caught Josie's attention, just as he had expected it to.

"How fun . . ." Josie walked closer and leaned in to study the image. She gave him a sideways glance before going back to admiring the piece. "You captured others' artwork in your own art piece. That's quite impressive."

"I didn't want to steal someone else's art, so I redesigned all of the graffiti." August shrugged.

"I can't believe you're trying to make light of the fact that you managed to create art inside of art. That's unbecoming of you, Mr. Bradford." Josie lifted a pale eyebrow in a dainty fashion August didn't realize she was capable of pulling off.

It occurred to him then that Josie Slater was in her element. When surrounded by art, the confident woman she normally kept hidden away behind baggy T-shirts, worn jeans, and downcast eyes slipped out. Standing in this gallery, filled with art and promises of more, she shone. It reminded him of one of the pieces he'd created that week. The canvas was one of three that had kept him so busy the last several days that he had not been able to catch one moment with her.

Six years had passed and had revealed that he missed Josie Slater. Only a few days had passed since he'd seen her again, and they revealed a hole in his life that it seemed only she could fill. Time hadn't dimmed those youthful affections he carried in his heart for her. It had only intensified them.

August kept Josie by his side for the remainder of the event, watching her transformation as it unfolded like a rose in bloom. Petal by petal, the true Josie emerged and ended up entertaining him with her vast knowledge of art. She might not have gone to college or traveled abroad to study international art, but she was well-versed in that world. It was another clue that she'd not completely abandoned her dreams.

As the crowd grew thin and the five France-inspired paintings disappeared out the door with their new owners, August sensed Josie preparing herself to leave. "I have some art projects I'd love to get your opinion on

before you go." He tried not to sound as desperate as he
felt. The hidden paintings in the back room were practically begging to be discovered, but they were for Josie's
viewing only.

"Umm . . . I just need to find Opal." Her eyes darted
around.

He pretended not to hear her as a few guests
approached him to offer their congratulations. Once the
group departed, August began discreetly leading Josie
toward the back of the gallery. One step, a handshake for
a departing guest. Another step to the refreshment table
to swipe them each a crab cake. A few more over to the
beverage table for a small cup of punch to wash the food
down. All the while, his eyes were on his goal.

As they reached the rear section of the gallery, now
empty of guests, Josie mumbled, "I don't see Opal and
Lincoln anywhere."

August leaned close and admitted something that
could ruin the evening. "I told them to leave."

Josie's head jolted up. "What? Why would you do that?"

"Couldn't chance you making a run for it." He lifted
his eyebrows, daring her to deny it.

"I-I . . . Wh-why?" The stuttering began breaking the
eloquence she'd spoken in for the last hour.

"All through school, you'd run anytime I got too
close." He took a step toward her and she took a step
back, proving his point.

"N-no!"

"Fibbing is unbecoming of you, Miss Slater." August
tsked, eliminating a little more space between them and
the surprise awaiting.

"August . . ."

He held out his hands, palms up. "Just check out the
paintings before you run. That's all I ask."

She combed her fingers through her wispy blonde hair and looked around, apparently seeking an escape route.

"I'm out!" Carter spoke, catching their attention. "August, you're locking up, right?"

"Yeah, man. Thanks again for tonight." August offered a fist bump.

"It was my honor. See you at the camp tomorrow?" Carter lifted an eyebrow.

August glanced at Josie briefly. "If my plan fails, you'll see me. But if I can pull this off, I'll see you at church on Sunday instead."

Carter let out a raucous laugh, his voice just as deep and gravelly as August's tone. "Josie, good luck!"

"Hey, shouldn't you be wishing me the luck?" August placed his palm against his chest and feigned offense.

Carter and August set out to volley sarcastic jabs at each other, all in good-hearted fun, as August took advantage of the distraction to take the last several steps to the back room. Its normal use was for music lessons, but that night it held the private art showing.

Josie scooted closer and looked between the bickering men before interrupting. "I think maybe I'm just gonna walk home . . ."

"No!" Both men objected in unison as they turned their full attention to the shy beauty fidgeting before them.

"I'm just messin' with ole August. Seriously, Josie, you'll want to check out these art pieces. They're right up your alley from what I've gathered in the past week." Carter winked, looking like he'd just let her in on a secret.

To August's amazement, it worked like a charm. Curiosity began replacing her anxious expression. He glanced at Carter over Josie's head and mouthed, "Thank you." Carter responded with a chin jerk and a smirk before he headed for the exit.

August wanted Josie to feel comfortable, so before the event began earlier, he made sure the lights were fully up and the window blinds open, even going as far as opening the windows so the nearby ocean breeze could offer more easiness.

Front and center, the three canvases were set up to grab her attention as soon as she entered. From the small gasp Josie released, August knew he'd pulled it off.

"I took a class focused entirely on pop art," he admitted, going for a conversational nonchalance.

Josie looked over her shoulder to where he remained by the door, casually leaning against the frame with his hands placed in the pockets of his dark trousers. He wanted to give her space, but she seemed hesitant to move away from him. He freed one hand and motioned for her to go explore the canvases displayed on wrought iron stands.

Taking a deep breath, August tried to lower his usual voluminous tone and began speaking. "This art movement made it to the United States during the late fifties, but the art world tried protesting. Called it kitschy and not true art, but people began falling in love with the abstract expression this style allowed. It became so popular that the traditionalists had to eat their words."

August continued to spout off random history about pop art Josie probably already knew, watching as she stood before the painting that he'd thought of earlier when he'd noticed her shining. Though he was a naturally cool fellow, sweat began to collect against his skin. He unfastened another button of his gray dress shirt and tried to calm down.

What if she hates them? What if she thinks I'm a creeper?

Josie's face remained neutral as she gazed at the side profile of her own face lifted toward the sun. Where each sunray touched her skin and hair, a bold streak of color began spreading like an unfinished rainbow. The bolts of color were only half-complete, as if the sun wasn't allowed to fully shine on her just yet, but he could feel it moving in that direction and hoped she could feel it too.

Finally she stood taller and turned to look at him, a smile gathering on her lips. "Wow . . ."

He took her one-word response as a good sign. Sighing in relief, August returned the smile but said nothing. He nodded to the next canvas and Josie understood this as her cue to continue her picture walk.

The canvas in the middle was fashioned in the block style that was iconic in pop art. The canvas was divided into four blocks. Each one held a handprint. The two larger ones were diagonal from each other, top right and bottom left, and were only outlined, with no color. The slightly smaller handprints were on vividly colored backgrounds, top left and bottom right.

"I guess this is why Opal insisted on tracing my hand this week . . ." Josie raised her right hand and fit it to the vivid red palm, a perfect match.

The same stirring from earlier tightened his chest as he watched Josie move her hand and fit it against his unpainted one in the left corner.

"Your hand?" Josie guessed, looking over her shoulder at him. August confirmed with a subtle nod.

When he didn't elaborate, Josie moved on to the last piece. It was more in the freestyle technique that he recalled she used to favor creating. From the way her eyes lit up as she moved her finger over the painted part of the canvas with the thick black lines and splashes of bright color, it was still her favorite. Unfinished words exploded in the BAM style all over the canvas.

DR____
BO____
SH____

After an unrushed amount of time passed, with Josie going back and forth between the three paintings, she finally circled around and stood behind them.

"They're only half-complete . . . What are you advertising in these pieces?" Her face was high in color, not from embarrassment or shyness, but clearly from excitement.

August recognized the look. It was the same one that overtook him each time a new project was on the horizon. The anticipation of picking up a paintbrush and marrying it with paint in order to create art on a blank canvas was one of the most exhilarating sensations he'd ever experienced. It was all he could do to tamp down the elation wanting to bubble out of him over the eagerness of experiencing that with Josie for the first time.

He chose to stay rooted by the door and smiled at her reference to pop art being used a good bit in advertising and logo designs. "I want to sell you on the idea of partnering with me." He tipped his head to the incomplete canvases. "They need to be completed."

She wrapped her arms around her long torso, shoulders deflating a bit. "You don't need any help."

"I suppose you're right. For six years I've focused on nothing but my craft." He finally pushed off the doorframe and took a step inside the room. "It's been an epic journey, but a lonely one. I'm tired of the loneliness, Jo."

Josie blinked several times and nodded her head. He wasn't sure if she was agreeing to complete the paintings with him or if she understood the depth of his loneliness. He hoped she was agreeing *and* understanding, because he desperately needed to remedy both.

Clearing her throat, Josie spoke in the polished tone she had used earlier in the evening. "What exactly does this partnership entail?"

The tension that had gathered all night in his shoulders finally released as he let out another held breath. "Well, all partnerships should have a probation period to make sure the associates can mesh well."

"That's sound business practice. Okay." She edged out from behind the stands and glanced around as if on a search for something. "If you have a safe place to keep my necklace so I don't get paint on it, we can get started."

He held in the chuckle wanting to slip out as he glanced at his wristwatch. Eleven o'clock was too late to start. "I must commend you, Miss Slater, on your enthusiasm, but I'd rather relocate this project to my studio. We can get started in the morning."

The business facade she was playing around with slipped away as she gaped at him. "You already have a studio space?"

"Yes." He couldn't contain the wry smile over the simple word *space*. *Wait until you see it,* he mused.

"You haven't even been back two weeks."

"I'm not a man to waste time. God has made us a lot of promises, but time isn't one of them. If there's something I want, I get to it." After a moment of silence, he pulled his phone out of his pocket and handed it to her. "How about you give me your number so I can text you directions to the studio?"

Josie programmed it in and handed the phone back. She inspected the canvases one last time before following August out. He could already sense her hesitance on leaving the art incomplete.

Good.

It was exactly the point he was secretly making to her. The subliminal message he'd begun on those canvases had already taken root. August might have been a get-things-done kind of guy, but he also had an abundance of patience he didn't mind using when necessary. He knew one thing for certain.

Josie Slater would be worth it.

7

In the same way mythical sea creatures always eluded explorers on the hunt, so did any rest elude Josie that Friday night. She rolled toward the open window, causing a creak to whisper from the brass bed frame Opal had given her. It was such a comfortable bed, but it wasn't doing her a bit of good at the moment. As the sultry breeze danced with the sheer curtains, she timed her breaths to the harmony of the ocean waves rolling in just outside. Most nights the lullaby was melodious enough to lull her to sleep, or at least soothing enough to settle her down, but the eagerness to have a paintbrush in her hand prevented the enchantment of the ocean from casting its usual tranquil spell.

A friend has asked for help. Nothing more, Josie told herself for the hundredth time as she fluffed her pillow and settled down once again. Life had served her a gluttonous amount of *no*s, so it didn't take a degree in psychology to get why she was unable to ever utter the two-letter word to anyone else. It certainly wasn't a hardship to agree to help August Bradford. As appealing as it was to spend time with him, the tourist season was gearing up and the diner would soon be the only thing she could focus on. So she would enjoy the unexpected blessing with the three paintings and be thankful that

August was generous enough to allow her to be part of such a unique project.

Josie kept her eyes on the lookout for dawn to arrive, reminiscent of a young child waiting on Santa to show up, as she went over the ever-running list of things she needed to take care of: Dalma, her father, a few church committee responsibilities, and delivering some groceries over to Theo and Deandrea.

"Finally," Josie muttered to her phone when the alarm went off. Tossing the quilt off, she hopped out of bed to prepare for the day.

After dressing in cutoffs and an old T-shirt, she worked her hair into a long side-braid and brushed her teeth. Calling it good enough, she slid on a pair of Chucks and left the comfort of her small beach cottage to start the promising day. It took two attempts before her small pickup truck decided to crank, but once it did, she hurried over to the diner.

"You know that ain't the boy's favorite." Jasper narrowed his eyes at her when she said she needed two orders of stuffed French toast, but Josie couldn't hold his stare and turned her attention to filling to-go cups with the freshly brewed coffee. "August always orders the biscuits and gravy," he added like she didn't already know that.

She shrugged her shoulders and pushed the cups into a cardboard carrier. "It won't hurt him to try something new, since he's making me do the same thing." She'd already filled her dad in about the paint project while they got the grill and fryers heating up earlier.

Jasper went into the kitchen, with Josie following, and began dredging the brioche bread in the custard mixture. "You'll be back in time for your shift, right?"

"Yes, sir," Josie answered while dodging a late sous-chef rushing through the kitchen entrance.

"Sorry, boss," Calvin called out as he hurried over to the sink to wash his hands.

"Happens to the best of us, but only happens more than twice to the worst of us." Jasper plopped the bread onto the grill top, sending out a satisfying sizzle and a waft of sweet vanilla, while giving his tardy employee a stern look.

Calvin nodded his head, message received loud and clear, and began rolling out the biscuit dough his boss had already prepared during his twenty-minute tardiness.

Josie busied herself with slicing strawberries and then folding them into lightly sweetened cream cheese. As soon as her dad flipped the toast, she moved over and spread the fruit mixture onto the toasted side.

"This was your mom's favorite," Jasper said absently as he flipped two pieces on top of the others to sandwich the goodness inside.

"I know," Josie whispered. The sadness in her dad's voice made it hard for her to speak any louder. She grabbed a to-go container from the tall stack and held it open so he could nestle the decadent breakfast inside.

A little over six years had passed by since they lost her mom unexpectedly, but it continued to sting like it was just yesterday. One minute Jolene Slater had been flouncing around, joking around with customers in her usual style; the next minute she was on the floor gasping for breath like a panicked fish out of water. A pulmonary embolism stole her from them before they noticed the grease fire in the kitchen that caught during the frenzy. The diner was saved with minimal damage, but the loss of Jolene left lasting wounds on not only the father and daughter, but also the patrons of Driftwood Diner.

Guilt squeezed Josie's empty stomach, sending out a growl of discord. It was the same guilt mixed with obligation that kept her tethered to the dream her parents had shared of owning and operating their very own restaurant. "You need me earlier than eleven?" She set the foam container down, ready to call the whole painting idea off. "Or I can just stay all day."

Jasper seemed to snap out of his own haze of past hurt and narrowed his eyes at his daughter, making the young woman squirm instantly. "Calvin, you know our little girl here has caught the eye of a famous artist?" Calvin was not much older than Josie, but it didn't deter Jasper from referring to her in that fashion.

Calvin looked over his shoulder while slinging round disks of dough onto a buttered sheet pan. "Josie Slater, what have you got to say for yourself?"

Jasper took that as the opening to embarrass her enough to have her edging closer to the door. "*Nothing* is what she has to say. The boy had her so tongue-tied that I think she was close to creating her own language."

"Dad!" Josie's eyes grew round as saucers.

Both men barked in laughter, causing her cheeks to heat faster than the convection oven Calvin was placing the pan of biscuits into.

"I'm serious. I reckon we need to find the girl an interpreter. Calvin, you know anyone else who speaks gibberish?"

"Can't say that I do, sir." Calvin chuckled.

Undoubtedly, her dad had no intentions of hushing until she left, so the flustered woman gathered up her food and coffees and made a run for it. She didn't slow until she was loaded in her truck and hurrying along the normally twenty-minute drive inland. Fifteen minutes later, she parked in front of the address August had texted her last night a little after he'd dropped her off. She pulled her phone out and rechecked the address and found it to match the one before her.

"Humph." As she sat staring at the two-story brick building, a shiny black truck pulled up beside her.

August hopped out and walked over to open her door. His hair was damp and he smelled like a fresh bar of soap, looking well-rested and ready for the day ahead. Josie smoothed her hand over her wrinkly shirt, feeling right frumpy and tired in comparison.

With that easy smile he carried around like a favorite accessory, August said, "Good morning." In the quiet of morning, his deep voice boomed with enough exuberance to wake her.

"Good morning," she parroted.

"So you found it okay?" He held his hand out to help.

"Yes." Josie handed him the coffees. "I have to admit I wasn't expecting this." She glanced over and read the stone plaque embedded among the red bricks. FIRE STATION NO. 40.

She knew the old relic was out here, but as it went with most abandoned buildings, the fire station had been easily forgotten. Leave it to August Bradford to remember it. Seemed he had a knack for such things.

"I needed a space to help feed into my creativity. Derek found it, and as soon as I saw it, I knew this was home."

"Home?"

They began walking to the door that was dwarfed by the two giant bay doors to its left. "We remodeled the top loft into my apartment. The bottom floor is the studio."

"But you've only been back—"

"Yeah, but I've been preparing to return for the past year. Derek handled most of it for me." Pride and respect lit his voice at the mention of his father.

"Where'd you just come from then?" She gave him a once-over as he unlocked the door.

"Tucker and Zachary wanted me to stay over with them last night," August admitted, not shying away from the fact that this could be considered a sissy move to have a sleepover with younger siblings. Josie liked that he never cared to fit into preconceived molds anyway.

Josie's gasp resonated around the vast space as they entered. Rustic with an industrial vibe, the worn brick walls and cement floor invited her to stay awhile and explore. She stared at a row of wooden chairs lining the left wall with hooks behind them.

August followed her eyes. "That's where firemen lugged on their gear when they would get called out for a fire." He walked her closer and brushed his fingers along the bricks around one of the hooks and showed her the hint of soot it left on his fingertips. "This is where they hung their helmets."

She smiled appreciatively while circling around. "It looks ready for the fire trucks to pull in at any moment."

"That's what I was going for. I wanted to keep it as original as possible."

She tapped her knuckles against the brass fireman's pole just past the line of chairs, eliciting an echoing ping. "Does it still work?"

"Oh yeah. Between my brothers and me it's been well tested." August smiled. "You wanna give it a try?"

"No thanks." Instead, she grabbed ahold of the pole and twirled around it while taking in the giant area. "This sure is a lot of space for just painting a picture."

August led her over to a picnic table set up in the back with a small kitchenette behind it and sat opposite her. "I have a fairly large project coming up. All of this space will be coming in handy soon enough."

Josie unpacked the plates and didn't inquire about the big project, worrying she'd lose sight of the painting arrangement only being temporary. *That's all this can be. Temporary.*

August opened the lid of his container and made a face. "I think I have your breakfast."

Josie snickered and showed him her matching container. "Nope. You're pushing me out of my comfort zone, so I've decided to help you expand your palate."

"All righty then, but you'll need to keep this in mind the next time I push a little more." Before she could protest about a next time, August led them in saying grace. He thanked God for the food even if it wasn't what he really wanted, which came close to causing Josie to snicker out loud in the middle of his prayer. But she easily reined it in when he thanked God for the friendship he enjoyed with Josie.

His sincerity caught her off guard, so much so, Josie was barely able to whisper, "Amen," when he concluded the prayer.

"Okay, this is good," August admitted around a mouthful.

"I knew you'd like it. Driftwood Diner serves up all kinds of tasty fare. Not just biscuits and gravy and shrimp burgers." Josie managed all three sentences without one hiccup and was even able to add a hint of tease. Seemed the more she was around August, the more at ease she felt.

"I think you might be on to something." August winked at her as he stuffed another giant bite into his mouth.

Josie took a bite of toast too, and as the tanginess of cream cheese and the juicy sweetness of berries hit her tongue, her eyes drifted shut to savor the goodness, but August's satisfying moan had them popping open.

"Awesome, right?" She pointed to his quickly disappearing breakfast.

"Beyond," August commented on a groan.

As Josie washed the sweetness down with a sip of coffee, she regarded the man enjoying his breakfast on the other side of the table. Sure, August was a ruggedly handsome man—Opal wasn't kidding with her Superman reference—but more importantly he carried a gift of charisma that instantly drew people to him. Josie was one of those people, yet it always intimidated her for some reason. Maybe Opal was also on to something about the intimidation coming from her liking him. Even so, Josie was aware enough to understand it went deeper than a mere crush.

The French toast began churning in Josie's stomach, so she pushed the plate away and stood to shake off the unease creeping over her. "I'm working the lunch shift, so I can only stay until ten."

August looked up, apparently catching on to the sudden change in her tone. "Okay . . . Can you come back afterward?"

"I have to close," Josie blurted, nervousness clamping down on her again. She inwardly chided herself, wishing she could remove the ill-fitting awkwardness as easily as August seemed to have removed his piercings.

"Y'all close at *two*." He lifted a thick eyebrow and took another bite, not letting her shift in mood faze him or rush his meal.

"B-but today is S-Saturday. We clean fryers on Saturdays." Josie wiped her sweaty palms against the sides of her shorts, knowing how lame it was to be using that as an excuse. From August's sardonic expression, he knew too.

August took another bite and chewed thoughtfully. "The paintings and supplies are set up behind that partition." He pointed his plastic fork toward a metal room divider along the left side of the room. "Go ahead and pick which piece you'd like to work on today."

Josie regarded the corrugated partition with rustic hinges holding three sections together. It looked like a piece of art in itself. The entire space seemed to ripple with creative energy, and she'd be a fool not to take advantage of it. Squaring her shoulders, she ignored the nagging trepidation and allowed her heart to lead her behind the partition.

Three easels were set up, each holding one of the unfinished canvases, and a long table was set to the side with any and all supplies she'd need. The painting of her profile was too unsettling and personal to start with and the freestyle piece felt a little too daunting in her current state of mind, but the handprints piece on the middle easel drew her as if it were picking her and not the other way around. It was a simple piece, and for some reason she wanted to paint August's hands with as much care and detail as he'd painted hers. Within minutes, she'd prepared her brushes and paints, and with no hesitation, she began to add color to the canvas.

A little later, jazz music began quietly filtering through hidden speakers right before August appeared beside her. Without conversation, he made quick work of setting up his supplies by the canvas of her face. Josie was relieved as well as uncomfortable with him picking that one. He seemed to see her in a lot different light than she saw herself.

She dipped the brush in the cup of water to clean it and chanced glancing over at August, which was a mistake. Watching him tilt his head one way and then the other while biting down on his bottom lip made it almost impossible for her not to get caught up in the view. She shook herself out of the daze and refocused on her canvas, successfully keeping it there through several song changes. Even though Josie gave it her best effort, she eventually gave in and went right back to admiring him.

August must have sensed it and looked up, catching her staring. He set his paintbrush down and then took hers and did the same, not once unlocking their gazes. After angling them both away from the art easels to face each other, August tilted his head one way and then the other while biting down on his bottom lip just as he did earlier when studying his painting. "You're a rainbow." The deep resonance of his voice echoed around the room, and Josie was just as lost in its tones as she was in the depths of his silvery-blue eyes. He brushed wisps of hair behind her ear. "Pale yellow. So pale, the gold is almost invisible." Releasing her hair, he braced one hand on her hip and skimmed the back of his other hand along the heated skin of her cheek. "Rose gold."

Josie didn't so much see but feel him exploring the pigments of her features. His touch released a chaos of sensations that were irresistible yet unnerving, but she dug her nails into the palms of her hands to will herself just to take in the moment and not be a coward for once.

August traced around the edges of both eyes as if drawing her with his fingertip. "And this blue . . ." He angled a little closer, and when he continued speaking, his breath also touched her skin. "A stunning mix of sky and sea with a delicate hint of lime near the center." His finger slid down the bridge of her nose. "A collection of bronze coins."

"That's a nice way to say freckles," Josie said, some-how managing to squeak it out.

August didn't allow her sarcastic comment to distract him. He remained focused as the pad of his thumb grazed her bottom lip. "Scarlet or ruby." Their gazes reconnected as he traced her jawline, sending a shiver down her spine with a bead of sweat chasing after it. "You're going to have to get used to this, Jo."

She cleared her throat to speak and then had to do it again to wiggle the words loose. "Used to what?"

"Me being this close to you." August tightened his grip on her hip, emphasizing his point.

"Why?"

"Because it's where I want to be. And I'm making plans to stay right here." He held her close for a few more minutes before dropping his hands and putting some space between them.

Josie didn't respond. She couldn't. August's touch was innocent and his words sincere, and both caused her body to malfunction. The technique of breathing was lost on her while at the same time she was close to hyperventilating. Sweating at the same time as trembling. Wanting to trace his features and offer her own sincere words, while also wanting to flee.

To prevent herself from doing either, Josie plucked the paintbrush from the cup and turned toward the canvas as if August Bradford hadn't just shaken her to the core.

8

August could barely focus on the canvas in front of him as his idiocy played on repeat. *Did I just do that? Say that? What happened to the goal of making her feel comfortable and slowly presenting the idea of being more than just friends?* But, man, he couldn't help himself. Just as he'd thought last night at the art show, the woman was in her element in front of that easel. She shone. Yes, he'd promised Carter he'd figure out how to broach the idea to her about joining them at the camp, but he also wanted to figure out how to present the idea of becoming a significant part of his personal life as well.

"I need to head out." Josie spoke, breaking their two-hour-long silence.

"Sure, okay." August dropped his paintbrush into the cup of water, picked up a rag, and began wiping his hands. "Just leave it and I'll clean up."

She ignored him and worked on putting her stuff away.

August looked at the canvas and noticed she'd finished one block. Pop art was a little deceptive. It didn't look like it required much detail, but there were lots of hidden elements that observers wouldn't notice. Had those details not existed, the piece would be noticeably lacking. Josie clearly held the skill needed. "I'm impressed, Miss Slater," he commented, hoping to lighten the mood before she left.

"I, umm . . . I was trying to get as much done as possible—"

"There's no rush—"

"I don't have a lot of time to dedicate to this—"

"Hurrying through life will only rob you of the joy of the journey." August stepped in front of her before Josie had another turn at cutting him off. "Take a breath, Jo." He placed his hands on top of her rigid shoulders and gently squeezed, hoping to put her at ease. The good Lord knew he'd messed up doing that earlier.

Josie's mouth popped open but closed, keeping whatever comment locked inside and taking the suggested breath. He matched her breath for breath for a few beats until the rigidness of her shoulders faded away. His eyes caught on a few speckles of purple paint on the side of her neck. Looking closer, he also found some in her hair. Paint on Josie Slater was one appealing sight, but he bit down on his lip and decided not to point it out.

He tilted his head to the side until her baby-blue eyes met his gaze. "I enjoyed working alongside you this morning. I really hope you'll feel like returning after work."

"I'll . . . I'll try."

August knew that was all he could ask of her, so he placed his hand on the small of her back and led her to the door. Watching the little white truck pull away, he berated himself for the incident earlier that sent her walls up and probably put a padlock on them. He was never one for subtlety, but he knew better than to come at Josie with his heart wide-open. "Danged if I didn't do it anyway," August grumbled under his breath while scraping some blue paint off his thumbnail.

By the time the truck was out of sight, August figured it was in his best interest to go have a talk with the only man he knew who was an expert on subtlety. He closed up shop and headed out.

August parked his truck beside the family restaurant and used his key to get in the side door. Dishes clanged in the kitchen as the staff prepared for the lunch and dinner shifts ahead. August paused long enough to greet a few people before scooting into the dining room. The lights weren't on yet but enough coastal light flooded through, making it easy to find Derek at his favorite booth.

"Hey, Dad," August greeted as he tapped Derek on the shoulder before sliding in the booth and swiping the glass of tea.

Derek looked up from the stack of papers in front of him and smiled. "Hey, you. To what do I owe this honor?"

"I need some woman advice."

Derek dropped his pen and closed the lid of his laptop. "This calls for my undivided attention."

Derek Bradford was the quietest man August had ever met, which was completely opposite of August and Derek's younger brother Carter, but his presence spoke volumes and demanded respect. August had tried to garner as much wisdom from the man as possible over the years and sure hoped to collect some now.

August leaned forward and tried lowering his voice. "I think I messed up today." Making sure the coast was clear, he told his dad how exactly he messed up while drawing swirls in the condensation on the glass. "I left tact at the door, man." He shook his head and waited for Derek to lecture or poke fun at his foolishness. When Derek remained quiet, August glanced up and only found a deep sense of understanding looking back at him.

"You're in love."

August slumped. "Yeah, I am, but I'm screwing it up.

Today was the first time Josie was at the firehouse, and I had to go and act like an idiot."

"Maybe it was a little too soon, but, Son, what you said about her being a rainbow—" Derek shook his head and smiled—"I'm impressed. Bet Josie was too, but she probably didn't know how to respond to that type of forwardness. And even though we're an affectionate bunch, not all people are comfortable being touched or having someone in their space, so be mindful of reading her body language, okay?"

August sighed. "I know . . ." He tossed his hands up. "It just feels natural to hold her hand or hug her or put my arm around her shoulder—"

"Or trace her face," Derek interjected on a quiet chuckle.

August rolled his eyes and snorted. "Or that. Yeah, but I do pay attention. Josie doesn't cringe or flinch away. And you know me, I'm respectful."

"I do."

August propped his elbows on the table and scanned the empty dining area before asking, "You said you had to chase Nan?"

Derek quietly chuckled again. "Yes."

"How'd you finally catch her?"

"You're not going to like the answer." Derek ran a hand through his neat salt-and-pepper hair.

"Lay it on me, man." August drained the rest of the tea and grabbed the small pitcher to refill it. This was something he'd missed while traveling abroad and even up north. Seemed only Southern restaurants supplied tables with their own pitchers of beverages. It sure did make life easier.

"Nan Bradford wouldn't let someone catch her even if they had a gun pointing at her head. That stubborn woman had to finally figure it out for herself whether she was going to relent or not."

August groaned, knowing he had a stubborn one on his hands, too. "Then what did you do until she finally decided?"

Derek's mouth quirked on one side. "I kept quietly pursuing her. Took tons of patience." He glanced over his shoulder before leaning toward August. "I will say this . . . Nan always had an excuse to keep me from getting too close. It was a trust issue on her part, and so every time she'd give me an excuse about something, I would find an answer to it."

August rubbed his forehead. "How so? I need examples."

Derek focused past August, toward the large picture windows that overlooked the inlet. He seemed to be searching for something and found it when his eyes snapped toward August. "One time she told me she couldn't go to a concert with me because she had to do laundry."

August squinted at his dad. "No, you didn't."

"Sure did. I showed up several hours before the concert. Her roommate let me in and I went at it like a Merry Maid until Nan showed up and was too amused to refuse going to the concert with me."

"Josie never says much about house chores."

"No, but has she given you an excuse for something else holding her back?"

"Many." August sighed. "Derek, I just want to give Josie an opportunity to claim her dreams like you and Nan gave me. I ain't forcing her to do any of it. I just . . ." He shook his head.

"I understand your heart is in the right place, Son. Just keep in mind that it is ultimately Josie's choice to partner with you in the art department at camp."

"I know. I'm just hoping to present it to her in a way that makes it too good to resist."

Derek grinned. "If that young lady loves art as much as you say she does, I think she'll choose the partnership. Just be patient."

August snorted. "Then tell your kid brother to get off my back for a minute."

"Carter is too excited for his own good. I'll have a talk with him," Derek agreed. "Now, I need to get some things sorted before we open. Wanna help me out?"

"Sure."

After helping his dad with some busywork, August made his goodbyes and took the back way out and found an unlikely person sitting on the patio. Though with it being their second run-in in such a short time span, perhaps it wasn't all that unlikely. Shaking his head, he skirted around a few patio tables until reaching the one where a sopping wet Dalma sat, cheek resting in the palm of her hand as she gazed out at the inlet.

"Would you like a menu, Miss Dalma?" August asked even though he knew she wasn't there to eat.

"Nah . . ." Dropping her hand, she looked up at him with a pinched expression.

"Wanna tell me about it?" He leaned a hip against the table and crossed his arms.

She hitched a shoulder up, reminiscent of a sulky teenager. "Fell into the inlet while trying to pull in my crab trap . . . darnedest thing."

August lifted his gaze and took in Dalma's dock, directly across the water from the restaurant. Luckily, it was high tide, so her fall shouldn't have been that far, but that also meant she had swum across it. "You didn't get hurt, did you?" He looked her over and found only a soggy mess.

Dalma wiggled her shoulders and then rolled her neck side to side. "Not that I know of." She raised her bare feet, showing off hot-pink nails. "Lost my bedroom slippers, though."

August didn't know whether to be amused or worried by the little lady. Obviously it was time to look into what was going on with her. "Well, if that's the worst to come out of it, I'd say you're a lucky lady."

Dalma tittered quietly. "Lucky enough to get another ride home?"

August offered his arm just as he'd done at the craft store but couldn't resist teasing her a little. "You had enough swimming for one day?"

Dalma stood and curled her arm around his. "I believe I have."

After August found her a towel and helped her inside his truck, Dalma asked, "You wouldn't feel like granting me another favor, would ya?"

"What's that?" He shifted the truck into gear and pulled out of the parking lot.

"The line came loose on my trap. . . . Would you mind fishing it out of the inlet for me?"

August barked in laughter, knowing that trap was probably wedged in the mud and making itself right at home. "You went too far, ma'am, but I know where a spare trap is and I'll be happy to give it to you." He made a note to go by Growler's to buy her a new one.

Dalma beamed. "You're a peach. No wonder my Josie is so sweet on you."

August's brows shot up as he glanced over at Dalma. "Is she now?"

"Don't play coy with me. We both know it. And we both know you're just as sweet on her." She glanced out her window and sighed. "That poor girl has become so skittish since her mother died. Please promise me you'll not give up on Josie."

He pulled into her driveway and put the truck in park before angling toward the little woman sitting there with her hair still dripping and her clothes wrinkling. "Miss Dalma, I'm careful about making promises . . . How about I promise to try my best to talk her into not giving up on me?" He knew he could keep that one.

"I suppose that'll do." She nodded her head once.

August exited the truck and hurried around to the other side to help Dalma down. He walked her inside and surveyed the haphazard mountains of books strewn all over the living room. He'd seen it the other day after they went fishing, but it was still mind-boggling.

"Here." Dalma poked his arm with another book.

"You gave me one the other day. I'm good." August tried waving it off, but she shoved it into his hand.

"Nonsense. You can never have too many books."

"Clearly." His eyes flickered around the room before regarding the book in his hand. This one had a pirate with billowy long hair with his arms wrapped around a hot maiden. "Thank you, ma'am. You okay or do you need me to stick around for a while?"

"I'm fine . . . but are you sure you don't think you could get my trap out of the water?"

"Pretty sure, but I'll drop another one off to you later today. Deal?"

The worry on Dalma's face eased and was replaced with a smile. "Deal."

"Thanks for the book." He held it up and saluted her with it before easing out the front door.

"Be sure to read it!" Dalma hollered as he jogged down the steps.

August just waved before climbing in the cab of the

truck. He popped open the glove box and tucked the book on top of the other one Dalma had given him. It was some gothic murder mystery, which wasn't his taste in reading either. Releasing a brief snort over Dalma's quirkiness, he fished out his phone and made a quick call to another Sunset patriarch.

"What can I do for ya, kid?" Doc Nelson asked after a receptionist got him on the phone.

"Thanks for taking my call, sir. Dalma Burgess took a plunge into the inlet. She seems all right, but I'd feel better if you could stop in and check on her."

"That ole girl ain't got all her soldiers marching in a line anymore." Even though he was a pediatrician, Doc Nelson was known to make house calls to anyone with an ailment. "If it hadn't been for Josie Slater keeping an eye on her, Dalma would have probably burned her house down by now."

August put Doc on speakerphone before backing out of the driveway. "How's that?"

"Josie flips the breaker for the stove when she's not there and has figured out other ways to keep Dalma mostly safe, but Josie's too busy helping her dad, and everybody else in the town who asks, to mind after Dalma all the time."

"I didn't know Jo was doing all that." He glanced at her beach cottage as he passed by, already knowing the white truck wouldn't be there.

"Josie Slater collects people in need like a crazy cat lady collects strays, but she won't let anyone do that for her."

"What do you mean?" August reached over and switched the radio off in order to hear the doctor better.

"Just last winter, she called in and told her dad she was taking some time off and had already scheduled staff to cover her shift. It took Jasper a few days to get his head out of his backside long enough to realize something was up. Come to find out, Josie had the flu. By the time I got over there to check on her, she was on the tail end of it. Ain't that right sad she'd rather endure the flu by herself than to 'inconvenience' anyone, as she put it?"

"Yeah. Why are you telling me all this?" August parked beside the diner and shut the truck off.

"Just stating a fact. Another fact being even though she's tough as a pine knot, it wouldn't hurt for someone to step up and take care of Josie for a change." Doc had always kept a close watch on the goings-on of his patients, past and present, so it didn't surprise August that he had inside facts on Josie.

He wanted to be there for Josie, but August wasn't up for sharing all that with the doctor at the moment, so he changed the subject. "Rumor has it you're retiring?"

"Rumor has it right for a change."

"Wow. What's this town going to do without you?"

"Well, it's not gonna happen for a while yet. But I'll leave ya in good hands. I have my protégé all lined up to take over. He's a big-shot doctor from Birmingham. Insists on having the whole place done over before he comes. Prob'ly take a year to get things up to snuff for that young whippersnapper." He cackled.

"So you'll pay a visit to Dalma?"

"Sure will." Doc Nelson agreed to stop in later in the day after he closed his office.

With his mind a little more at ease over Dalma, August thanked Doc before ending the phone call and heading inside the diner.

9

Saturdays were always hectic with most locals having the weekends off, which left them plenty of time to enjoy the sunny weather at the beach. Driftwood Diner's screen door kept a steady rhythm the entire day as folks came in and out. Today's lunch rush turned out to be more like a sprint than a rush, but Josie didn't mind. It made the day hurry by and left little room for her mind to wander back to the morning she'd spent at the firehouse. Each time the memory of August tracing her face and saying such romantic things came to mind, her cheeks heated to scalding and she couldn't help but smile. So, of course, she spent the shift smiling like a blushing loony.

"You gonna stop daydreaming and take that boy's order?" Jasper asked close behind Josie, startling her.

She looked over at the cash register and saw August sitting in the very same spot at the counter as he had the other day. The reaction to puke and then hide wasn't as strong as last time, but her stomach did the butterfly flutter at the sight of him. He was still dressed in the paint-splattered shirt and jeans from earlier, but his shirt looked damp in a few spots. A few blotches of pink highlighted a section of his dark hair just above his right ear. It made her want to go over and wipe it off, but she managed to stay glued to her spot.

"Guess I'll do it." Jasper grumbled something else underneath his breath that sounded a lot like her needing some "learnings on social etiquette."

She scoffed. Imagine a barefoot chef, with a long bushy beard and enough hippie flair that people mistook Opal for his daughter, teaching *her* anything along the lines of etiquette.

"Hey there, son. What can I get ya?"

August's eyes slid to Josie before settling on her dad. "How about a seafood po'boy and a mess of your homemade chips."

"Ain't it against family code to eat seafood somewhere besides your own family's restaurant?" Jasper leaned on the counter and seemed to be settling in for a chat.

"Well, I just found out Nan has another local artist's work displayed in her office. Seems only fair that I can eat seafood somewhere besides Sunset Seafood House." August stated that with enough disdain to have Josie squirming in her spot at the other end of the counter.

Josie knew what art piece he was talking about—the one that captured the inlet just behind the Bradfords' restaurant that held several childhood memories. She'd given it to Nan as a thank-you for contributing to most of those memories.

"I wonder if you'd be as bold if your parents were here to hear you being so mouthy." Jasper jabbed a finger toward August.

August scoffed with enough tough-guy attitude to have her paying attention. Out of respect, she never stood up to her dad and needed some pointers on the subject.

With his eyes narrowed and arms crossed, August finally answered, "Not on my life would I try such a mess. Nan Bradford would have me strung up by my toes."

Jasper doubled over in such a loud cackle, Josie thought the poor man was close to collapsing.

August placed his paint-stained hand over his heart in a solemn fashion that had Jasper cutting off his laughter to pay attention. "But I've vowed to my family to *never*, and I do mean *never*, eat your seafood for supper." He gave his head a curt nod, sending his dark hair flopping in his eyes and launching Josie's dad into another fit of boisterous laughter.

"We ain't even open for supper!" Jasper had fat tears disappearing into his bearded cheeks by now.

"My point exactly!" August threw his hands up, still playing it up in all seriousness.

"You're a riot, boy." Jasper took several breaths to regain his composure and headed to the kitchen. "Jo-Jo, get our boy a glass of tea!"

She did as she was told and placed the glass and a small pitcher in front of August, who was busy grinning at his phone.

"You seem to bring out the best in my dad." She stood before him, fiddling with the order pad wedged underneath the cash register.

He pocketed the phone and looked up at her. "Your dad possesses a laugh that needs to be freed at any chance. I enjoy him sharing it with me." The purple hints in his eyes glittered with amusement, and she knew without a doubt that August meant it.

Emotion rolled over her in such a sudden wave that it stung her eyes. Blinking it away the best she could, Josie whispered, "He doesn't laugh like that much anymore." The words barely came out as her throat closed in around them.

August reached over and cupped her hand with his

warm one. "Then I think it's time he gets back to it, don't you?"

"Yes." With her free hand, she batted away the rebellious tear that fled from the corner of her eye.

August lightly squeezed her hand. "Does this—and what I did this morning—make you uncomfortable?"

Josie was surprised by his sudden question enough to get the waterworks in check. She blinked a few times before shaking her head. "Not uncomfortable. Just unexpected."

"So you're okay with this?" He squeezed again.

Josie moved her hand so that she could entwine their fingers together. "I'm okay with this, even if it scares the mess out of me."

August's lips tugged up on one side as he angled his head a little closer. "I've heard you ain't living bold enough if it doesn't scare you a little." Tease reflected in his tone just as clearly as it did in his silvery-blue eyes.

Jasper came bustling through the kitchen's swinging door with a fat po'boy sandwich sitting proudly on top of a mountain of homemade chips, scaring a squeaky yelp right out of Josie.

August coughed back a chuckle as he slid his eyes away from her to study the plate of food. "Oh, wow! You've outdone yourself, sir."

"You best keep this between you and me. Don't need that feisty Nan Bradford coming after me."

"Promise." August picked up the hoagie roll that could barely contain the fried shrimp and oysters stacked inside with the homemade tartar sauce and coleslaw working as inadequate but tasty glue. He took a giant bite and groaned around it. After wiping his mouth with about four napkins, he said, "So good. How'd you manage making it taste so light?"

"It's the tempura batter I use, instead of the cornmeal dredge most other places use." Jasper beamed.

"It's a winner." August tucked into the food with gusto.

"Thanks, son." Jasper waved goodbye to some parting patrons and shuffled back into the kitchen.

As Josie kept herself busy with closing down the front, August kept up an appealing litany of appreciative moans and groans until his plate was completely wiped clean.

August gathered his plate as two o'clock arrived and walked into the kitchen. He didn't emerge again until she was closing up. She noticed he was covered in what looked to be grease.

"The fryers are clean," August commented as he walked over to her.

"Okay . . ." She was confused yet grateful about not having to clean the fryers. "Why'd you do that?"

August shrugged. "You're helping me with the paint- ings, so I want to help you in return." He leaned closer with a coyness twinkling in those silvery-blue eyes. "That's what friends do, right?"

"I suppose." She shrugged back, trying to mimic his casualness.

"You ready?" August asked.

She regarded his filthy shirt. "For what?"

"To paint." He held out his hand, and for some reason she wouldn't completely grasp until long after that day, she accepted it.

They loaded up in his truck, and in the confines of the warm space, the scent of grease was a bit overpowering. Wrinkling her nose, Josie let out a giggle. "We stink."

August cranked the truck and rolled the windows down. "I think it's more *me* than *we*." He stared out the windshield in the direction of the ocean waves. "But I have an idea on how we can get the stink off." He shifted the truck into reverse and then into drive. "You'll need a bathing suit."

"We're going to the beach?" Josie wasn't opposed, but she already had her heart set on heading into the country.

"That would work too, but I have a better idea." That's all the answer August would give her, grinning and shaking his head when she asked for more clues.

She gave up on figuring it out and dashed inside her house when he pulled up only minutes later. Josie made quick work of changing into a tankini and loading a bag with a change of clothes and a towel. After covering up with a tank top and a pair of cutoffs, she dashed back out. She was happily relieved when August headed inland.

Once they reached the fire station, August commented, "Did you know there's a pretty steep hill in the backyard here?"

Josie unfastened her seat belt and glanced over at him. "No. An actual *hill* in this flat country?"

"Yep. I think they must have built up the foundation before building the fire station." August shut the truck off and exited with Josie following. "Let me change into my swim trunks and I'll show it to you."

"Umm . . . okay . . ." She had no idea why he was suddenly interested in showing her a hill, but she let it go and wandered over to inspect the paintings in progress while he went upstairs to change. The profile picture of her wasn't even halfway complete but it was already breathtaking. She loved the vibrant streaks of color that touched her face at various angles. The canvas on the easel beside it looked a little hurried when compared to the one he'd been working on. The time clock seemed to be ticking down on the project, but then it occurred to her that was self-imposed and perhaps it was time to slow down a bit and really appreciate the process, as it seemed her painting companion was a pro at doing.

Josie was about to pick up a paintbrush when August walked past the partition, wearing the same blue board shorts he'd worn the first day he visited the diner, minus the shirt, and that was distracting.

A bottle of shower gel in one hand and a towel in the other, he asked, "Ready to get cleaned up?"

Heat flooded her cheeks as she blurted, "I'm not showering with you!"

August bit his lip, but the smirk was unmistakable. "Sweetheart, don't go putting thoughts like that in my head." He tsked and motioned for Josie to follow him, leading her to the side door and then around back.

Sure enough, there was a hill, and when she saw what was draped down it, she let out a laugh. "No, you didn't."

"I did." August walked over to what had to be the longest homemade slip-and-slide she'd ever seen and began squirting shower gel down the length of it. "It's ten feet wide and a hundred feet long."

Josie watched with a good amount of apprehension as August turned on several sprinklers lining the edges, instantly soaking the clear plastic and producing tiny bubbles. It looked dangerous but so, so tempting, just like its creator. Especially when the familiar soapy scent of August's shower gel began perfuming the air around her. "This looks like a broken bone waiting to happen." Even though she was protesting, Josie was already removing her tank top, shorts, and flip-flops.

"No worries. Tuck and Zach came over yesterday and we spent a better part of the day testing it out. Everyone walked away intact." August sauntered over to her and held out his hand with pure mischief lighting his handsome face. "I bet with the shower gel, we'll take off like lightning."

"I don't know . . . I like all of my bones the way God made them and really don't want to chance messing up the great job he did forming them."

August chuckled and gently tugged on her arm. "Come on, Jo. We'll do it together."

Hesitating for only another second, Josie gave in and allowed August to pull her to the top edge. She toed the slippery surface and gave him a sideways glance. "Won't it be complicated to slide together?" She imagined it would be tricky to not bump into each other along the way.

August held her eyes and tilted his head, a seriousness forming in his gaze. "Perhaps . . . That's the case with most anything, ain't it?" He leaned closer. "But I'm willing to risk a little complication as long as you're by my side."

Josie didn't know what to say to that, and August gave her no time to figure it out. In a blink, they were diving down the hill on the slippery plastic. By the time they made it to the bottom, August had managed to do what he did best: he'd helped her overcome her ill-placed fears and live a little. Even if it was on a long piece of plastic and could be viewed as a childish way to spend the afternoon.

By the third trip down the slip-and-slide, the notion of being childish had vanished as nicely as the stench of fryer grease and seafood. It morphed into a heated competition on who could make it to the bottom first. Running starts and horseplay had the two nearly tied in wins and all-out exhausted.

When they couldn't fathom one more trip down the hill, August disappeared inside and returned with a sliced watermelon. They sat side by side underneath the shade of an ancient oak tree and munched on the supersweet treat until the giant bowl was emptied.

Nice and full and ridiculously sleepy, this time when Josie's head ended up leaning on August's shoulder, she left it there and simply enjoyed his nearness. She could have easily closed her eyes and let the day slip into a lazy snooze, but the painting was calling out to her.

"We need to go paint," Josie mumbled but didn't move her head from his warm shoulder.

"Yeah." August yawned. Instead of standing as she expected, he slumped against the tree a little more, wrapped his arm around her, and began running his fingers through her drying hair.

"Seriously . . . we need to . . ." Her words slurred and trailed off.

"Yeah," he repeated again. And again, he did not make a move to stand.

Needless to say, the painting was kept for another day.

10

"This is so sissy," Tucker griped while squinting at the idea August had presented to them.

"Says who?" August asked as he dumped another bag of wooden beads and trinkets on top of the blanket he'd spread out in the shade of the same tree he and Josie had napped underneath the week before. He bit his lip to contain the smile that memory wanted to produce and focused on his brothers. Zachary was already sitting cross-legged and eager to get started.

"The world." Tucker shrugged a lanky shoulder and plopped down beside Zachary, grabbing a spool of jute twine.

"Since when did we start caring what the world thought?" August joined them on the blanket and began fishing out some beads. "Besides, this is for the camp, so man up and start stringing beads."

Tucker rolled his eyes at August but dove into the project with gusto. They were all committed to seeing the camp succeed, and it was no secret that Tucker would do anything to ensure his older brother stuck to staying in Sunset Cove. "Why are you rushing us?"

August gave his watch a quick glance before adding another bead to the twine. "Because Josie will be here in two hours and y'all gotta get lost before then."

"Why? I like her." Zachary grabbed a wooden medallion but replaced it in the pile after giving it some thought.

"I can't chance y'all saying something to run her off or embarrassing me." August gave Tucker a pointed look when the teenager glanced up to dispute him. They both knew he'd be the guilty party.

"You just don't want to share her and that's not nice." Zachary huffed.

"How about you help me knock these out and I'll bring you back over later in the day to play on the slip-and-slide?"

Zachary perked but Tucker didn't look impressed.

"Two words for you, Tuck: shower gel and a boogie board." August waggled his eyebrows.

"That's more than two words but you have yourself a deal." Tucker set in to stringing beads like nobody's business as he and August discussed other ways to soup up the slip-and-slide experience until the task was complete.

● ● ●

It had taken less than two weeks for Josie to complete both the handprint piece and the freestyle piece, and August was impressed as well as disappointed. While she flitted around him, cleaning up her paint supplies, he stood still in front of the freestyle canvas with a wry smirk.

The look he was giving the canvas finally caught Josie's attention, and her busy body came to a sudden halt beside him.

"Why don't you like it?"

"I didn't say that . . ." August tilted his head and studied it from another angle. "It's just different from what I'd imagined."

She scrunched her nose and squinted at the artwork. "How so?"

"The words aren't the ones I was thinking of." He angled his head in the other direction, eyes staying zoomed in on the canvas that Josie had filled with the words DRIFT, BOOM, SHOUT. *Drift* made no sense to him, but he kept his lips sealed on that opinion. It was like she was avoiding the only DR word that made sense.

Josie crossed her arms and huffed. "You said to fill them in however I saw fit."

"I did." August shoved his hands into the pockets of his loose-fitting cargo pants and gave her a sidelong glance as the words DREAM, BOLD, and SHINE came to mind.

"What words were you thinking?" She fiddled with the brush in her hand.

August shrugged and moved over to the table to close a tube of paint. "Doesn't matter now."

"You're seriously not going to tell me?"

"Nope," August answered, hoping to rile her up.

"What is the purpose of these three pieces?" she asked, giving up faster than he wanted her to.

"They were commissioned for a private collection." That's all he was giving her on that subject too. He gestured for her to follow him to the kitchenette, where he began scrubbing the paint from his hands at the sink. "I have another job I need your assistance with."

Josie's eyes darted to the door as they did every time he pushed for a little more from her. "I . . ."

"You handled this project just fine. Chances are looking favorable you can do it again." He leaned near her ear and whispered as best he could, "This next one is *huge*. Please don't leave me hanging."

Josie made quick work of washing and drying her

hands while her head did a jittery shake of protest. "I don't have much time. Especially for a huge project."

August followed her out the door and stepped in front of the truck door to block her escape. "But the project is for the camp. It's a new medium I haven't worked with before, and I bet you haven't either." He raised an eyebrow, hoping it was enough bait to hook her once more.

Josie glanced around before meeting his eyes. "What's the project?"

The plan was to behave and keep his hands to himself, but when she stepped into his space, the idea was nixed. Slowly he reached out to unravel the hair tie from her long braid and then worked his finger through it. "Only one way to find out."

"August." Her exasperated tone was enough to unleash his grin.

"Jo." And his flirty tone was enough to have her huffing.

Josie tilted her head closer, all the permission he needed to continue exploring the silky texture of her hair. "I have to work a double tomorrow."

"No worries. I'll be here working on it. Whatever time you can spare to help will be greatly appreciated. I'm gonna need it. Thanks again for working with me on this pop art project. I'll have your part of the commission by the end of the week." He already had the check written but wanted to secure another reason to seek her out if Josie decided to bail on him. Leaning against the truck, he tugged her against his chest and wrapped his arms around her. The hug was a perfect fit, just like everything else with Josie Slater.

"Okay." On a long sigh, the stiffness of her body transformed to softness as she finally returned the hug.

August recalled a favorite blanket he had as a kid.

It was nothing special, just an old tattered afghan blanket with moth holes, but he always kept it close when comfort was needed. After his parents were taken away, August needed the blanket more than he cared to admit. Holding Josie, he realized she had the same effect on him, and it took great effort for him to let her go when she eventually took a step back.

"I can't wait for you to see what *we* have to do for the camp." He handed her the hair tie and pulled on a playful grin to lighten the moment.

"Okay." It seemed to be the only word Josie could form, but he caught sight of the smile she was failing to suppress. As she climbed into the truck, she reached for the door handle, but August wedged himself in the way. He leaned down and widened his grin into a goofy expression until she cracked and returned it.

"Now that is one pretty picture to leave me with, Miss Slater." With that he stepped out of the way and closed her door.

As the vehicle disappeared around a curve in the road, August let out a chuckle. "Making that woman laugh could easily become one of my favorite pastimes," he mused to himself.

11

"What just happened?" Josie mumbled a mile down the road as the shock finally wore off. She steered the truck to the edge of an overgrown field and put it in park. Placing her forehead against the steering wheel, she sucked in several deep breaths.

You know what just happened! You knew it would if you allowed August Bradford close enough!

One short, exhilarating week of painting and a few stolen moments were enough to have her falling head-first into his appealing world. It was filled with so much alluring whimsy and creativity that she wouldn't mind never returning to her normal life. Knowing that wasn't an option, Josie sat up, quickly rebraided her hair, and shifted the truck into drive and headed to the diner.

She managed to make it through her shift and was back at it the following day to do it all over again. While going through the motions of the diner routine, curiosity over the huge project kept Josie distracted. Surely August was at the firehouse working on it without her, and that just didn't seem right . . .

"Earth to Josie." Opal waved her hand in front of Josie's face.

Josie hadn't realized she was propped against the broom handle instead of using it to sweep the floor. "Oh. Hey." Snapping out of it, she put the broom into motion, each step sending out a faint creak from the wood floor. "They're shutting down the kitchen, but I can get y'all something real quick." She offered Opal and her giant husband a smile.

"I'm just going to swipe us a glass of tea." Opal tucked a set of work gloves into the back pocket of her jean overalls. They were rolled up to just below her knees and were paired with a white tank top and high-top sneakers. After pouring herself and Lincoln each a glass, she scooted over to where Josie was sweeping.

"Y'all out delivering furniture?" Josie asked absently while working on placing a set of chairs upside down on top of a table.

"Yes." Opal took a long swig from her glass.

Josie noticed Lincoln wandering around the smaller dining room, sipping his tea and studying the various wall hangings. She couldn't help but smile. Opal had met her match with war hero First Lieutenant Lincoln Cole. She was still trying to get used to them being married. "I thought you had Tucker Bradford helping deliver furniture?"

"Carter has kept him busy helping to get that camp ready. I thought about asking Theo, but he's too scrawny." She sighed. "I need someone built more so like my Linc to handle the heavy lifting."

Josie snorted while moving to the last table. "There's certainly nothing little about him."

"I heard that," Lincoln said without looking their way.

Opal giggled. "Speaking of tall, well-structured men, how's it going with August?"

Josie's shoulders jerked up automatically. "Fine. We finished the paintings and now he has another project he needs help with. I'm hoping to work on it with him tomorrow." She wished she could go after work today, but there were interviews lined up for summer help that she had to help her dad with.

"I don't mean the work part." Opal sat the empty glass down, picked up the dustpan, and helped Josie collect the mess from the floor.

"What other part is there?" Josie asked as the answer played through her head—the shared laughs, conversations, simple touches that felt anything but . . .

"Don't feign ignorance with me. We're both way too smart for that game." Opal dumped the trash into the bin.

Josie swapped the broom for the mop. Taking a deep breath of the lemony scent of the cleaning product, Josie whispered, "He still rattles me, but it's getting better . . . I'm more comfortable with being around him."

"That's good."

"You scallywags done swabbing the deck?" Jasper called from the kitchen door.

"Aye, aye, captain," Opal answered and followed it with an "Arr!"

"You brought yer own pirate, lass?" Jasper guffawed and waggled a finger at Lincoln as the big guy walked over to them. "He's got all that hair and a limp. Just needs an eye patch."

"Daddy," Josie scolded but was relieved when she heard Lincoln let out a chuckle.

"Oh, and he's right ornery at times. Definitely a good quality for a pirate." Opal giggled and then asked Josie, "Can I help with the interviews? Pretty please!" Opal beamed, giving the impression she was the one asking for a favor, but it was obviously the other way around. Struggling to find solid help was a constant thorn in Josie's side.

Josie propped the mop against the table and turned to wag a finger at Opal. "As long as you and Dad leave the pirate parody at the door."

"Aye, aye, matey!" Opal and Jasper shouted in unison.

Josie rolled her eyes again but couldn't help but smile.

"Well, this pirate is going to go hang out with August." Lincoln's eyes landed on Josie as soon as he said that name.

"Okay, honey. Have a good time." Opal went up on her tiptoes and puckered her lips.

Of course, Lincoln had to go all romantic pirate hero and lift the tiny woman clear off her feet before laying one hot kiss on her. Still holding her, he angled away and asked, "You want me to get August to swing by and pick me up?" Again, he slid his knowing gaze over to Josie.

"No!" Face on fire, Josie quieted her voice and repeated, "No. I'll take Opal home later."

Lincoln arched a thick eyebrow, looking rather smug for teasing her. "If you're sure?"

"Yep."

Lincoln returned his attention to his wife, giving her one more heated kiss before lowering her to her feet and heading out.

Opal grabbed an extra mop to help knock out the floor cleanup as Josie went back at it without bothering to protest. Opal wasn't allowed to pay for food and the Slaters weren't allowed to fuss over her helping out when she had spare time.

As they finished cleaning up, Opal and Jasper broke their promise to Josie and continued spewing silly pirate phrases. It was one long afternoon with those two clowns teaming up against her.

By the time she made it home, Josie was bone-tired. Sleep should have come easily, but she was met with another restless night instead. When morning arrived, her fingers were itching to paint. She wasted little time getting ready before heading over to the firehouse.

As soon as Josie walked past the open bay doors, she noticed August, which wasn't surprising because she always noticed him. But today was a little bit more peculiar than normal since he was stretched out on top of a white school bus.

"What are you doing up there?" Josie asked, her voice and footsteps echoing around the giant room.

"I'm floating on the clouds." August sounded groggy, but he was dressed in his typical work uniform of paint-splattered cargo pants and tee. His bare feet were casually crossed at his ankles.

Surely he hadn't slept up there . . . Hints of freshly brewed coffee from the kitchenette floated by, setting her a little more at ease that he hadn't. But only a little, due to his answer making no sense. "What do you mean by floating on the clouds?"

August propped up onto an elbow and peered down at her. "Come up here and see."

Josie took in the stark-white bus before looking up at him. "I don't know about that." She was more comfortable keeping her feet planted on the ground.

He quirked an eyebrow and, in a challenging tone, said, "Chicken?"

"That's, umm . . . You're really high up there. That has to be against firehouse safety code." She hoped her mocking scold would deflect his challenge.

Instead, he started clucking at her.

Taking a few deep breaths, Josie moved over to the ladder propped against the side of the bus and gave it a few shakes to test its sturdiness. When it stayed relatively in place, she began ascending it. As soon as she climbed high enough to see over the top edge of the bus, those calming breaths whooshed out in surprise. The entire roof had been transformed into a sea of clouds and blue skies.

And sure enough, August Bradford was floating among them, looking like an artistic deity.

"Whoa . . ."

August reached over and helped her onto the top of the bus. "So what do you think of our next project?" His clear eyes twinkled with an excited energy that must have been contagious because Josie was starting to feel the symptoms.

"We get to paint the entire thing?" She placed her hand on a cloud and took in the smooth texture.

"Yep." August mirrored her and ran his hand over the surface too. "Automobile paint goes on exceptionally smooth. Have you ever worked with an airbrush?"

"Ooh. No!" Josie was pure giddy for the chance to try it.

"I've set up an old car hood you can practice on. It took me a few turns with doing that to get the feel for the flow of paint."

"What are we adding to go with the sky?"

"I thought we'd base it out mostly in blues and then add some palmetto trees waving in the breeze. And whatever else we feel inspired to add. Carter ordered a custom vinyl camp logo to go on each side. It's white, so we'll have to paint the background pretty vibrant to make sure it stands out."

"Remember that field near the camp that's always planted in sunflowers each season?" Josie asked.

"Yeah."

"It'd be neat to add our own sunflower field to the hood." She glanced over, hoping to see approval, and was relieved when she did.

"Sounds good to me."

"So that's the plan? Nature?"

"Yep. Once we finish, I have a body shop lined up to complete it with a clear coat. Even sprung to have the windows tinted." August winked at her and began climbing down the side of the bus.

Josie scanned the fluffy clouds one last time before following. After August slid on a pair of shoes, he gave her a tutorial on the airbrush. She set out to practicing on the hood propped against the side wall. Once she felt confident enough, she moved to the bus. August was setting up several small worktables around its perimeter.

"We're going to use these big guys to base out the bus." He pointed to large paint guns and then pointed to the smaller ones. "And these will be used for the fine details." He went over the plan, then pulled his phone out of one of his cargo pockets. Within seconds, lively music began filtering around them.

"We're going from jazz music to hip-hop?" She gave him a skeptical look.

"Jazz was the mellow mood needed for the paintings." He motioned toward the bus as his head began bobbing to the beat. "But this calls for high energy."

Josie bit the inside of her cheek, trying to tamp down her amusement at the charming artist while watching him dance his way over to start adding blue above the taped-up windows. She didn't understand how he wasn't making a mess with the paint or getting tangled up in the hose while dancing around like that, but he managed it just fine. After taking a moment to enjoy the morning's unexpected entertainment, she picked up an airbrush and joined in on the fun.

The morning danced into the afternoon and then moved on to the early evening with the two bringing the white bus to life. Trees boogied in the breeze and sunflowers swayed in rays of vibrant sunshine. Every so often, the mood would hit August and he would break out dancing. He had natural rhythm mixed with just the right amount of laid-back whimsy to have Josie comfortable enough to bob along to the beat.

"I would have never taken you for a dancer!" Josie shouted over the music.

August looked over his shoulder while keeping rhythm. "Feels good to dance," he said simply.

"Yeah, but I thought you'd be too cool for that." She shook her head and watched his hips move to the hip-hop song.

"Nah. Some folks don't know the meaning of cool." He bobbed his head and pivoted around. "Enjoying something like dancing, now that makes me cool."

The more the man talked, the more Josie was becoming enamored with him.

After adding a few more highlights to a palm frond, he set the airbrush down and danced over to Josie. Without asking, he took the airbrush away from her, placed it beside his, and began dancing her around the firehouse.

A giggle burst through her parted lips as a tingle raced all the way to her bones. A feeling of euphoric freedom overtook her and the musical moment carried her away. They danced through at least a half-dozen songs.

"I can't remember the last time I've had this much fun." She giggled again, wiping the sweat from her brow while dancing around in a silly fashion. She kept on until noticing her dance partner had grown still. She looked up and found him watching her. "What?"

August shook his head slowly. "I'm a thief."

Josie froze. "Come again."

"A thief of moments." He took a step forward and skimmed his fingertips along the heated peak of her cheek. "I want as many as I can steal in the time God gives me. Jo . . . will you be a thief with me?"

"I . . . I've never stolen anything." She knew that made no sense, but it was the first thought to pop into her head.

"No worries. I'm a career thief of moments. I can teach you." The serious expression morphed into a mischievous smile as he offered her his hand, clearly giving her the choice.

As one song drew to a close and another began, Josie decided she was tired of allowing fear to hold her captive. Maybe it wouldn't hurt too badly to steal a few moments with him while they worked on these projects. She would have them to reflect on after life returned to the humdrum of routine.

Josie placed her hand into his. A second of gentleness passed along her palm until his grip tightened, pulled her close, and then sent her into a sudden spin.

"Let me explain how this moment stealing works." August twirled her again until they were near the bus's rear, where a palmetto tree looked to be grooving to the beat of the song. Her back to his chest, he leaned close to her ear. "Each time you catch sight of this bus rolling through town and see this tree dancing with the others and the flowers bobbing their yellow heads up front, you'll remember this moment. You'll remember we floated on the clouds this morning and danced among trees by sundown."

Josie knew in her heart he was correct. She'd never be able to look at that bus without remembering the beautiful memory of dancing and creating a mobile masterpiece with him.

They pranced around until August moonwalked to the airbrushes and handed one over to Josie. Hours skipped by with Josie giggling and allowing August to lead her in the enchanting moment of creativity.

By the time the moon and stars were fading into a new day, August had properly taught Josie just how fun moment thieving could be. But there was a problem with that. She wanted to steal lots more but knew it was a terrible idea all the same.

12

August had always heard that two sets of eyes were better than one, but at the moment he wasn't sure that was true. One very opinionated blue set seemed to only be in the mood for glaring.

August glared, too, and pointed at the finished bus. "That's progress."

Carter kept staring at him from underneath the brim of his ratty hat, rocking slowly in the rocking chair. They had each pulled a chair up beside the bus to admire it. "A painted-up bus is not getting Josie on board with becoming a permanent part of Palmetto Fine Arts Camp. Stop playing games with the grown woman and be up-front with her."

August scrubbed his hands down his tired face, cringing when he found a pretty thick scruff on his cheeks. "I'm not playing any games, so lay off." He sighed. "That woman's entire life has been her doing what others expect of her. I don't want this opportunity for her to partner with me in the art department to be another expectation. I want her to decide she *wants to* instead of *having to*."

Carter halted the chair and rested his elbows on his knees, studying the evidence that Josie could handle what they would be offering. "I get that, man, but I need to finalize the staff commitments soon. Time's running out and you're lollygagging instead of getting things ready at the camp."

"Have I ever let you down?" August watched his uncle shrug a shoulder, knowing good and well he hadn't.

"I reckon not, but you've tested my patience plenty enough times." Carter narrowed his eyes before reading an incoming message on his phone. "You check out the bunkhouses yet?"

August blinked, surprised at the conversation change. He was almost too tired to keep up. "Yeah. They're epic. Lincoln and Opal killed it. Those two sure do make a good team."

"Yeah. You and Josie would make a fine team too if you'd quit goofing around about it."

Carter stood and slapped August on the shoulder with enough force to send him swaying sideways. "Get some rest and then talk to Josie about our job offer."

"Yes, sir," August muttered sarcastically as he watched Carter toss a hand in the air while walking out to his truck.

Fatigue warred with August, but needing to check on Josie won out before he dozed off in the chair. Around ten, he pushed through the screen door at Driftwood Diner and caught a glimpse of her looking a little haggard with her hair in a messy ponytail. She rubbed one of her puffy eyes and yawned as she wrote down an older gentleman's order.

"Okay, Mr. Albro. Give us about ten minutes and we'll have those pancakes right out." She offered him a tired smile and handed a passing waitress the order slip as she moved behind the counter.

August gazed at her affectionately, impressed by the kindhearted woman she'd grown to become. Even though she could stumble around words sometimes like an uncoordinated woman in six-inch stilettos, he noticed an understated elegance about Josie . . .

"Boy!" Jasper hollered out, catching August staring

at his daughter. Josie's blue eyes shot up to find him still standing by the door.

August tipped his head to her before sliding his attention to Jasper. "Sir!" he called back with his voice coming out quite hoarse.

"I ort to hog-tie you and beat ya with a tobacco stick for keeping my little girl out so late." The man sounded like he was teasing, but his serious expression didn't seem to match it in August's opinion.

"Sorry, sir. Time got away from us, but I won't let it happen again."

"You best see that it don't." Jasper pointed at him before disappearing into the kitchen.

The owner didn't run him off, so August took that as a sign that he was welcome to stay and walked on inside. He eased onto his usual stool and propped his elbows on the edge of the counter.

"I figured you'd still be sleeping." Josie placed a steaming cup of coffee on the counter in front of him.

"Thanks." August picked up the cup and took a tentative sip, letting the hot liquid soothe his rusty throat. "And I figured if you weren't allowed to sleep, then neither should I."

They both pulled out a long yawn and followed it with a hushed snicker.

"Painting with you is fun and all, but I'm going to run out of steam if we keep this up." She pointed her pen at him before scribbling something on a slip of paper.

"I agree." He studied her over the edge of the mug. "No more all-night paint parties, young lady. I've put you on artistic restriction."

The side of her mouth hitched up. "Oh yeah?"

"Yep."

Before August could continue the teasing reprimand,

Jasper stomped out of the kitchen with an overflow-ing plate of biscuits and gravy. The succulent scent sent August's stomach to growling loudly.

"Ain't no sense in you going for that *starving artist* mess." Jasper jabbed a finger toward the plate of food. "Eat up."

"Yes, sir." August sliced the fork into the biscuit and took an ample bite. "Hmm . . ."

"What exactly were y'all doing until the wee hours of the morning, anyway?"

August fished his phone out and pulled up the photo app, scrolling back to the colorless bus before handing it over to Jasper. "We painted a bus. That's what it looked like yesterday morning. Flip through until you see what it looks like now."

Jasper slid his finger over the screen and flipped through the pictures a few times while August continued eating. He let out a low whistle and glanced over at Josie, who was starting a fresh pot of coffee. "My little girl help do this?"

August pointed to the picture he'd captured of Josie working on her sunflower field. "There's your evidence. You have one talented daughter, sir."

"Humph." Jasper appeared to be genuinely stunned by this fact. His brows pinched as he scrutinized the pictures. Finally he handed the phone back and blinked several times. "I'm gonna let Jo-Jo call it a day in about another hour, but you need to let her rest today."

August nodded, sensing the man had something weighing heavy on him all of a sudden. "That's the plan."

Jasper reached over and clamped him on the shoulder but kept his eyes averted. "Good." Scratching the side of his beard, he wandered into the kitchen as he mumbled something August was unable to catch.

By the time August finished polishing off the colossal portion on his plate, he could barely hold his eyes open. Somehow, he managed to settle his bill and head outside to set up an afternoon of R and R. Once that was complete, he shuffled back inside the diner just as Josie was untying her apron.

He held out his hand and asked, "You ready?"

"I thought we already decided no painting today." Josie stared at his hand instead of taking it. The tips of his fingers still held speckles of blue sky, but he knew that wouldn't deter her from holding it.

"No painting. Promise." August was too tired to be patient, so he grabbed her hand and led her outside to the lounge chairs he'd set up on the beach underneath a large umbrella. Each one held a fat, fluffy pillow and a thick beach towel that looked so inviting he could hardly stand it. *I'm getting too old for these all-nighters . . .*

"Wh-what's this?" Josie blinked with quite an exaggeration that August was surprised her eyelids managed to reopen.

"A time-out." He waited until she stretched out on one of the chairs and snuggled under the beach towel before doing the same.

As his eyes drifted shut with the languid hum of the ocean coercing him right into a heavy stupor, August vaguely thought about how he had more than just the task of showing Josie an adventurous side of life. He had to show Josie, as well as her father, that he'd take good care of her in the process. He knew he had failed a little, but after a good long nap he planned to start doing a better job.

Josie's soft snores joined the soothing melody of the beach and invited August to join in with his slightly louder snore.

13

Pop . . . crunch . . . chomp. . . . Pop . . . crunch . . . chomp. . . .

The pattern of sounds kept pulling at Josie until the sweet scent of apple joined in to finish waking her up. Blinking several times, she finally managed to keep her eyes open and found a redheaded fairy watching her.

"What are you doing?" Releasing a long yawn, she stretched like a lazy cat.

"Waiting for the two of you to come back from the land of Nod." Opal looked at the nonexistent watch on her wrist. "I've been waiting a long time." She took another noisy bite of her apple and smacked while easing her eyes over to August.

Josie did the same and noticed that the racket Opal was making hadn't disturbed his slumber in the least. Arms slung over his head and one foot dangling off the side of the lounge chair, he was still out for the count. He looked right boyish with his distinctive features relaxed.

Tearing her eyes away from the man too handsome even in slumber, Josie glanced at the watch that was actually wrapped around her wrist and had to do a double take. "It's four."

"Yes. Your daddy says the two of you have been out here sawing logs for the better part of the day."

"We worked on painting an entire bus yesterday and didn't stop until it was time for me to go to work this morning." Josie sat up, took a second to get her bearings, and then retied her fallen ponytail. "I think we overdid it."

"He's quite peaceful, isn't he?" Opal crouched down beside August's chair and studied him as if the man was an anomaly. Close to his ear, Opal took another loud bite from her apple. August didn't budge. "Maybe I should pinch his nose. Think that'll wake him?"

Josie playfully popped her friend. "Leave him alone."

Opal glanced over her shoulder. "Now what would be the fun in that?"

The goofy woman came close to jumping out of her skin when a large hand snatched the apple from her tiny one and stole a bite as both women let out a surprised yelp.

"You've teased me with this apple long enough," August said around a mouthful before taking another bite and continued munching away until only a thin core remained.

"You sure do know how to play possum," Opal commented in awe.

"It's a required skill when you have younger brothers." August raked his hands through his messy hair, only making it stand up worse. "Let's find some supper."

"Ooh! I've just tried out a new soup recipe. It's warming in the Crock-Pot. Y'all come eat with me." Opal clapped her hands as a breeze sent her curls into a springing motion. "Lincoln is out of town to help his dad with something and the man doesn't give me much kitchen time . . . and well, there's plenty!"

Josie caught August's attention and wrinkled her nose while shaking her head.

He shrugged his shoulder. "Soup sounds good to me."

Josie shook her head one last time. *You've been warned, big boy.* "I need to head over to Dalma's, but y'all enjoy."

"You sure? I can bring you a bowl by later," August

asked, completely oblivious to what he was getting himself into.

"Nah, that's okay. I'm supposed to have supper with Daddy." She offered a pleasant smile, knowing her steak would be grilled to perfection. That soup . . . not so perfect.

With a hankering for some fresh fruit, Josie swung by the produce stand and grabbed a basket of strawberries on her way to Dalma's. Routine had them out on the back deck with an audiobook playing while Josie worked on adding color to one of the old books. Today's audio selection was a romantic comedy about a sassy bakery owner who hired a ruggedly handsome yet moody handyman to help fix up a small bed-and-breakfast her late great-aunt had left to her in a will that had some sort of marriage stipulation.

"Could this book hit one more romance cliché?" Josie snickered while adding a teal swirl to the pattern developing on the page.

Dalma's response was to shush her, so she went back to adding more color to the design she viewed as intricate doodles. Dalma refused to get rid of any books, so Josie thought it was safe to use them as sketch pads. She even found quite a thrilling satisfaction in allowing herself this small creative outlet and keeping it hidden in plain sight.

Just as Josie was about to flip the page and begin another design, the narrator said something to catch her attention and followed it with a sultry moan. Josie whipped her head around and pinned wide eyes on her friend, who was raptly listening. "Dalma Jean Burgess! What do you have us listening to, young lady?"

Dalma shrugged her narrow shoulder. "The blurb said romantic comedy. Guess that little baker likes to add some spice . . ." She tittered.

"You're incorrigible." Josie scoffed, playing it up. "You've offended my delicate sensibilities." They both burst into a fit of giggles, but when the narrator began describing body parts, Josie plucked the device out of Dalma's lap and turned it off. "That's enough of that. . . . It's time for us to head over to Daddy's. He's grilling."

"Sounds good." Dalma held a hand up for Josie's help in standing. Once she got to her feet, she straightened her muumuu and scooted inside. "Just let me put my teeth in and grab something I have for Jasper."

Josie followed her into the bedroom. "What do you have for him?"

Dalma removed a bag from her closet and gave it to Josie before shuffling into the connecting bathroom.

Josie peeked inside the bag and squinted. "Why on earth would you get my daddy auburn hair dye and beard wax?"

"It was on sale." Dalma shoved her top dentures in and wiggled her mouth around to adjust them, looking rather silly.

"So?"

"So . . . I thought that color would suit him better than the grayish blond." She gathered her long white hair into a messy bun that any teenage girl would envy.

"And the beard wax?"

"Wouldn't hurt him to use it."

Josie gave up, knowing both products would go unused, and led the amusing lady out the door.

* * *

A loud knocking kept up a hasty repetition on Josie's door the following day as she sorted laundry. She had the entire day off and was catching up on chores that needed to be done around the house. The last two weeks of running in and out the door seemed to have stirred up an interior tornado. Clothes and shoes had been strewn all over the place and the mail had scattered on the top of her dining table with a few letters somehow winding up underneath it.

Tossing a load of darks into the washer, she called out, "Be right there!" Setting the machine to do its thing, she hurried to the door and opened it.

"You couldn't warn a guy?" August's hands were braced on the top of the doorframe, showing off his natural casual air, but the frown on his face didn't fit.

"About?" Josie opened the door wider and beckoned him in.

August dropped his hands and followed her to the spotless kitchen that smelled lemony fresh. "Opal made me eat frog stew."

"Frogmore?"

"No. *Frog*. As in the amphibian." August's face puckered. "And she was so excited about it that I had no choice but to choke down an *entire* bowl of it." He rubbed his stomach and shuddered.

"But I did warn you."

"When?"

Josie wrinkled her nose and shook her head in the same style as yesterday.

"I thought that meant you didn't want soup." August rubbed the side of his neck.

"I'm going to give you a pass this once on your lack of perception and blame it on you being half-asleep, but keep in mind a wrinkled nose and a headshake is your warning from here on out. And FYI, *never* eat anything Opal cooks. She is a genius at a lot of things. Cooking ain't one of them."

August sighed. "Got it."

"How about I make it up to you with a treat?" Josie batted her eyelashes playfully, causing August's puckered face to smooth out.

"Depends on how you define *treat*. If it's anything like Opal's definition, I'll have to pass on it." He gave her an uncertain look, but she could tell he was just teasing her.

"Trust me, Opal and I have completely different definitions of the word." She moved over to the fridge and pulled an artfully arranged platter of white chocolate–covered strawberries from the top rack and turned to show them off to him.

"Oh, now this is a treat I can get behind. Very creative, Jo." August took the platter from her hands and studied the little pieces of edible art.

"Thank you. I swirled drops of food color into the white chocolate before I dipped the berries."

August turned the platter this way and that, tilting his head as he regarded the treats. "It reminds me of stained glass. Almost a shame to eat them." He finally selected one and bit into it; a guttural moan followed. Clearly they had the same definition of *treat*.

"The idea actually came to me in a dream." Josie took a seat and reveled in the fact of August Bradford being in her kitchen.

August settled at the table and began munching his way through her artful treats. Her plan was to present the platter to Dalma, but he was enjoying them so much, she decided not to mention it. Plus, it gave her a perfect excuse to create some more.

"I like the way you dream, Miss Slater. You dream in color." He took another bite and winked at her.

To stop grinning like a fool, Josie grabbed up a strawberry and took a bite while keeping her head cast down. Her teeth popped through the chocolate shell before sinking into the juicy fruit. The mix of creamy sweet with the crisp tartness was such an indulgence for the palate that she wondered why she had never made them before now.

As August sat there munching away, he took in the cozy kitchen and seemed to appreciate its beachy vibe. It was designed with lots of subtle blues and beiges with coastal accents. "I'm digging your house."

"Thanks . . . I inherited it from my mom." It had been Jolene's family's beach cottage. Her parents left it to her and it was passed on down to Josie after she died. "She decorated it and I just can't bring myself to change any of it." It was slightly outdated and probably seemed kitschy to guests, but she didn't have the heart to change what her mom had fashioned for the space.

"It's perfect just the way it is, so no worries." August offered her a sympathetic smile as his silvery-blue eyes held her watery blue ones. "I like the name, too. Driftwood Dreams suits it."

"Thank you." A mental picture of the name plaque popped in her head. Another project with her mom. They'd fashioned it out of actual pieces of driftwood they found on beach scavenger hunts. She let out a deep sigh, missing those hunts as much as her momma.

"Did you name it after the diner?" August asked.

She blinked the memories away as best she could and focused on August's handsome face. "No. Actually it was the other way around. My parents named the diner after the beach house."

August nodded, seemingly impressed. He finished off another strawberry and asked, "Would you like to go see the camp?"

Josie tamped down the heaviness of missing her mother and pulled on a smile. "Yes, please. I've driven by, but all you can see from the road is the rooftops of the buildings." The community had been abuzz about the camp ever since the plans for it hit the local papers. It had been featured on the news several times.

August pulled an envelope out of his back pocket and handed it to her before swiping one last berry. "I almost forgot. Here's your cut for the pop art job."

She placed it on top of the now-neatly stacked mail and began following him to the door. "It almost feels wrong to get paid to have fun, but I feel like a real artist now."

August halted and turned around, revealing a deep scowl poised on his handsome face as he finished eating the strawberry. There was a smudge of white chocolate at the corner of his lips, but before she could point it out, his tongue slipped out and licked it away. "Let's go ahead and get you straight on something right now." His hands went to his hips, and then he leaned close enough to her that she could smell the sweetness of his breath. "You're an artist. Period. No paycheck and no one's opinion weighs in on that truth. Got it?"

Josie fidgeted under his scrutiny, but she nodded her head and muttered, "Okay."

"But you should be paid for your work. I'll have your check for the bus job by tomorrow."

"No." Now it was Josie's turn to scowl at him. Even though his nearness was doing crazy things to her heart, she held her ground.

"No?" One of his dark eyebrows arched way up.

Josie felt like a doofus when she tried to mimic his overly dramatic eyebrow arch. Clearly, by the smirk twitching at August's lips, she failed. Shaking off the silliness, she straightened her shoulders and declared, "I don't want to be paid for the bus. It's my contribution to the camp."

"But—"

Josie held her palm up. "That wasn't work. In fact, I recall it was a night of thievery, so don't even think about stealing my gift to the camp."

August's grin matched hers as he tipped his head. "Okay. Thank you for your gift, ma'am."

"You are quite welcome."

"Even though I think you just got that thievery example mixed up." There went that eyebrow arch again, but this time August also bit the corner of his lip.

Josie huffed, trying not to let his tease and handsomeness fluster her. "You know the delivery of it sounded kinda cool even if it didn't make any sense."

Laughing, he said, "True. Now. How about we go check it out."

Josie needed to put some space between them before she did something silly—like hug him or kiss the fool out of him—so she scooted around August and headed for the door to slide on the flip-flops she kept on the porch.

August walked her to his truck, where he opened the passenger door for her. After she was settled and strapped in with the seat belt, he closed the door and walked around to the driver's side and climbed in. Minutes later they were leaving the seashore behind and entering into woodland and plats of farmland.

"I absolutely love the idea of a camp solely focused on children's creativity and giving them the needed tools and freedom to explore it." Josie knew she was rambling but just couldn't help herself.

"Me too. I think we've managed to cover a lot of areas." August started ticking off a remarkable list. "This summer there will be classes in photography, art, music, dance, and drama . . . But we're keeping the possibilities open to expand in the future. At the end of each week, there's going to be a fine arts fair and a performance night. A lot of area businesses and colleges are participating in it."

"I think that's just wonderful." Josie fanned at the heat rising along her neck and tried blinking the burn from her eyes as the overwhelming excitement for the camp kicked up a notch. It was exactly what the area needed. "Public schools seem more focused on scholastic testing anymore and the fine arts programs are being pushed to the side."

August glanced over at her before refocusing on the road. "You're really passionate about this."

Josie sat up a little taller. "Absolutely. It's why I teach my Sunday school class through arts and crafts. Not everything needs to be taught through a computer or a textbook. Creativity allows you to experience what you're learning. Just ask your little brother. I bet he remembers what we learned about this past Sunday."

August chuckled. "He does. I stopped by there last night after that mess of a supper with Opal. Zachary had to show off his mosaic rainbow and told me all about it representing God keeping his promises."

"See!" Josie couldn't contain her proud grin.

"You do realize you're preaching to the choir on this." August turned off the main highway onto a narrow country road.

"Yes. I just can't help but get worked up over it."

"I think you'd make a great art teacher."

Josie's heart hiccuped at him mentioning her unconfessed dream. A dream that had bloomed while sitting in those high school art classes but died that day right along with her mom. Her hand shot up to rub the pain from her chest. Thankfully, August didn't notice. He was focused on driving through an open gate. The truck crept down a winding gravel road lined with trees as the tires crunched along. The trees gave way and the area finally opened up to reveal several bright-white buildings sitting in a wide U shape.

"Welcome to Palmetto Fine Arts Camp, ma'am." August parked beside a mud-splattered gray truck.

They sat there for a moment and took in the buildings. "It's . . . ," Josie began.

"A blank canvas." August pointed to the L-shaped building on the far left. "That's the photography building. The next building is music. The wide building in the middle is the mess hall. Over to the right of it is the auditorium and dance studio. And the one on the front right is the art studio. It's divided into two parts like the photography building. One part will be set up with several rows of easels, and the other room has tables and supplies for sculpting."

"This is really impressive . . ." Josie leaned forward and took in each building. "Is that stucco on the exterior?"

"Yep. It still has some texture, but I asked for a surface we could paint on."

"You're painting each one?"

"Well, I hope *we* will be painting each one." August hopped out of the truck and hurried around to help Josie out. "The idea is to outline a mural in a specific art style on each building and let the campers help paint them in."

"Oh, I love the idea of making the camp an actual art project."

"He's good for something every now and then," a raspy voice commented.

Josie turned and saw Carter and his wife, Dominica, walking toward them from the music building. "Hello."

"Hey. Josie, you remember Dominica, right?"

"Of course. Dominica is an honorary member of the Sand Queens, even if you keep her too occupied to hang out with us," Josie teased. "She's the only one in your family I know who orders something besides biscuits and gravy."

The beautiful Cuban woman grinned, and it reminded Josie of sunshine and tropical breezes. "They don't know what they're missing out on by not trying the other goodies on your menu."

"I'll have you know I've become more adventurous with their menu. She made me try something different just the other day," August piped in, nudging Josie from her musings. "The stuffed French toast is outrageous."

"It is." Dominica nodded. "I'm proud of you, August." Her faint accent curled around each word, making Josie smile.

"Hey now. I order shrimp burgers all the time." Carter threw his hands up.

Josie glanced around. "Carter, I assume you and Dominica are teaching the music classes."

"Yes. I guess we can handle it." Dominica leaned into Carter and they exchanged meaningful looks. That look conveyed just how enamored the newlyweds were with each other.

Josie shook her head. "This place is going to be awesome. Do you have other instructors lined up?"

"Pretty much," August answered rather quickly.

"Yeah. We've just gotta work out some commitment issues with one in particular. Once we get that buttoned down, I think it'll be a match made in heaven," Carter commented as he glanced at his wife and winked, clearly an inside joke of some sort.

Dominica giggled and August grumbled and Josie didn't understand any of it. Before she could question Carter on what he meant by that, August grabbed her hand and started leading her away from the sudden awkwardness.

"Let me show you the rest of the camp," August said, making a quick getaway.

Dominica let out a small gasp from behind them. "Aww. He's holding her hand."

"*Taisez-vous!*" August growled over his shoulder and sped up into a clipped pace past the mess hall and through a small patch of trees.

Josie didn't know much French, but she was pretty sure he just told Dominica to shut up. His calloused hand tightened around hers and she reveled in the claim it exhibited. When they emerged on the other side of the wooded area, Josie gawked at the unexpected sight.

"Oh, my goodness. This looks like a scene right out of the *Swiss Family Robinson* movie. Opal told me about it, but I had no idea y'all went all out like this."

"We thought the kids would get a kick out of the cabins being set up like tree houses. Opal and Linc have quite the imagination."

Josie nodded in wonder. She angled her head back and gazed up at the rustic cabins resting on top of stilts that were fashioned from thick tree trunks. From the thatched roofs to the vines weaving around the windows, the cabins looked enchanted.

"There's a dozen in all. Six female cabins with bunk beds enough to hold ten apiece. And six male cabins holding the same amount," August said.

"So you can only accommodate a hundred and twenty campers at a time?" Josie let go of August's hand and hurried up a winding set of wooden stairs with him on her heels.

"Yeah. We wanted smaller groups. Too large and someone will get overlooked."

"Y'all have really thought this through." She peered inside a window, taking in the bare mattresses sitting on top of the cedar-wrapped bunk beds. Off to the right of the room, a twin bed was set up beside a desk for a camp counselor, she guessed.

"Several years in the making, actually." August's hand skimmed over the tree limb that was fashioned into a deck railing.

Josie gave him an impressed smile and then began roaming around the top deck. It was lined with wood tables and chairs. Just past the thick foliage a splashing sound had her ear inclining in that direction. "Is that water?"

"Yep." August guided her down the stairs and through the small wooded area to the right of the cabins. This time when they emerged past the trees, a lagoon-style swimming pool greeted them. A waterfall languidly trickled into one end of the deep-blue pool from several stacked boulders, and a cabana made from tree branches and vines sat on the opposite side.

"I'm blown away. . . ." Josie shook her head as she let go of his hand and started wandering around the stone path weaving alongside the pool.

"To the left of the cabins is an outdoor amphitheater."

Josie bent and tested the water temperature, finding it to be a refreshing cool. "How many acres of land is the camp?"

"Roughly two hundred."

She stood up and gaped at him. "Seriously?" When he nodded his head, she shook hers. "I had no idea . . . I thought y'all were converting a field into a small camp. . . . I'd never have guessed all this was hiding back here."

"It's Carter's land. Derek and I invested into the project." August shrugged, but it did nothing to downplay the impressiveness of what they'd achieved on a large piece of farmland.

"A family operation. I like that."

"Me too." August climbed on top of one of the large rocks and sat down.

Once Josie explored the pool area, where she found a hidden bathhouse and a water fountain, she joined him on the rock. "I want to be a kid again so I can attend this camp."

"You and me both. Too bad we're too old . . ." August casually pushed his shoulder into hers. "What would you say if we were to offer you another way to be a part of the camp?"

"How?" She looked at him guardedly.

"I have some short travel commitments and other obligations that will conflict with the camp season, so I need another art instructor." August glanced away before meeting her eyes. "I can't think of anyone better to fill the position than you."

Her stomach dipped at the same time her heart began galloping. The offer was exciting yet unattainable. "August . . ." She shook her head.

"Just give it some thought. In the meantime, could I ask for your assistance in another short-term project?"

"I don't have much time, and I have other responsibilities."

"I understand, but we'll do better at scheduling this go-around. And no more working past dark." He held his hand up. "Promise."

A hint of rebellion clattered around inside her. "I'm not a child. I can stay out past dark."

"Not on this project, you won't." August looked sideways and grinned. "I've sketched out the murals on paper already, so we just need to draw them on the buildings. Can't do that in the dark, now can we?"

"Oh. I suppose you're right. All we have to do is the outlines?"

"Yes. Please say you'll help me out." He continued watching her, but the grin softened with sincerity and expectancy.

She sighed and glanced away, knowing she should decline. "I can help some, but you're not paying me."

"Now that makes no sense. You should be paid for the work." August bowed his head in an effort to catch Josie's attention, but she wouldn't look at him.

"Please let me do this as a thank-you." She cast her eyes to the water glittering below them. "This is beyond anything I've ever thought I'd get a chance to be a part of, and I'm so honored." She motioned around. "This is a *want to* and not a *have to*, so don't rob me of that with a paycheck."

"Jo, I hope you realize your life should be filled with *want to*s and not just *have to*s."

"I know. You have no idea how happy these last few weeks have made me. I really appreciate you allowing me to be a part of these opportunities." The water below began to blur, so she blinked the tears away and finally looked at him and offered a careful smile, even though it wobbled with emotion.

"Well, you've been doing me a huge favor. If you're not going to allow us to pay you, at least let me do you a favor in return." He crossed his ankles and reclined on his elbows. Eyes closed and face up to the sun, he emitted such a serene peace about him.

Josie watched August, wishing she could sketch as well as he could so she could capture the moment. Instead, she listened to the waterfall flowing into the lagoon, promising herself every time she heard a sound resembling that, she'd remember August allowing her to be a part of the amazing place they were currently hidden inside.

He cracked an eye open and caught her staring. "What?"

"I'm just practicing my moment thieving."

His eye drifted shut. "Good, good. Now what favor can I do for you in return?"

"Let me think about it and get back to you."

"Okay. Whatever you want, Jo, I'll give it to you." Between his deep voice and the sun glowing against his tan skin, August was warmth conveyed in sound and sight.

With her eyes focused on him, she memorized each contour and angle of his handsome face for far too long. She knew basking in his warmth a minute longer would probably produce a permanent sting when he left again. He was too talented to stay tied down in a small town for too long.

Josie brought her focus back to the pool and broke the silence. "This pool is so extravagant."

"Yeah, that's Carter for you. The guy's imagination can get carried away." August let out a languid yawn and sat up.

"Nothing wrong with that."

"I guess. He had some fancy pool company come in. One minute it was an old cornfield and then the next it was this over-the-top lagoon with giant rocks and waterfalls." He patted the stone they were sitting on and rolled his eyes. "This is a fancy *grotto*."

Josie peered over the side and watched the waterfall from the rock below them cascade into a curtain in front of the small cavern. "He must really be into pools."

"Nah. Carter wanted it to look like a resort he and Dominica visited a while back."

Josie sighed. "Aww. That's terribly romantic."

"Don't tell Carter that. It'll go straight to his head." August nudged her leg.

"How exactly did you become so close to Carter and Dominica, other than the obvious?" Josie looked over, quite curious about the three of them and their tight bond.

August smiled. "Carter is like the big brother I never had. He taught me to surf and how important it is to serve others through ministry. The summer after I turned sixteen, Carter offered me a job helping out with their praise and worship band during my summer breaks. It was the first time I got a taste for travel." August paused and let out a grunt. "I was hooked after that."

"And what about Dominica?"

"One summer, her praise band merged with Carter's band and that's when we met Dominica. She was the bass player, but I was drawn to her for more than her musical talent. The guys razzed me for following her around like a puppy the entire summer, but it wasn't like that. I knew Carter and Dominica were made for each other. Just took a while before they caught on."

Josie grinned. "You played matchmaker?"

August winked. "Sure did. And we see how epic that turned out." He hopped down and wiped his palms on the sides of his shorts. "You ready?"

Josie laughed again. "You realize you ask me that all the time?"

"I'll *always* give you a choice, Jo." He held his hand out, presenting her with another choice.

For the first time, she didn't second-guess the choice but accepted it. Holding that man's hand and allowing him to lead the way felt right and safe at the moment, so she left her fears by the lagoon and followed her heart for a spell.

Too bad she couldn't figure out for the life of her how to allow her heart the freedom to lead all the time.

14

Draw it on the side of the building, he said. *That's it,* he said. Josie seemed set on their situation only being temporary, but his hope was for it to be a more permanent one. Both with the camp and with him.

Josie was all about their new project in the beginning and had taken it upon herself to outline almost the entire art building with the intricate lines and shapes. August knew that would be her favorite of all the buildings since he settled on an art deco design for it. Even that was intentional. He allowed her liberties to change it up a bit when Josie mentioned a few ideas. The changes complemented the entire design, leaving him quite impressed with her eye for detail.

So, yes, it was great at first, but when a couple weeks slid by with Josie barely showing up to help outline the murals, he knew she was withdrawing from him and the time might never be as right as it was two weeks ago.

"No cute helper again today?" Carter asked as he offered August a bottle of water.

August placed the paintbrush in a bucket and downed the entire bottle, wishing he had another. May was heating up with record temperatures. "Nope. Now I'm wishing we would have begun with this project before it got so hot and she was more willing to help." He mopped his

long, damp hair off his forehead and moved to the corner
of the building.

Both guys propped themselves against an unpainted
section of the wall that held a little shade.

"What did you do to run her off?" Carter crossed
his arms.

August's shoulder jerked up. "I have no idea, man.
She seemed on board at first, but now not so much." He
knew that was a fib. She'd probably hightailed it because
the job offer had finally sunk in, but he didn't feel like
listening to Carter give him lip about it.

"What are you doing to get her *back* on board?"
Carter's tone bordered on too gruff and demanding and
was already irritating August.

August wiped a smudge of paint off the side of his
hand onto his baggy shorts and took a deep breath, but
the humid air did nothing to cool his temper. "Nothing
at the moment." He hitched a thumb behind them at
the wall. "There's too much to get done around here."
He shoved Carter as he passed him and picked up the
paintbrush, feeling smug when his effort left the big guy
stumbling sideways a bit.

"Okay, you just keep on sulking around here with
your paint kit." Carter walked by and shoved him back,
but August knew it was coming and braced himself. When
their shoulders crashed together and neither Neanderthal
budged, Carter let out another snort and walked off, muttering, "Punk."

An hour passed as August finished the outline of
a massive treble clef on the side of the music building.
Words such as *HARMONY*, *MELODY*, and *MUSIC*
would join the musical notes to create a graffiti style that
would eventually wrap around all four walls. He heard

before he saw a vehicle flying up the driveway. It was eating up the gravel and spitting it out all over the place.

He hopped off the ladder just as the small pickup truck barreled through the parking area. It came to a sudden sideways stop. Josie jumped out and ran over to him, not even bothering to shut her door.

"I'm so sorry!" Her face was flushed and she looked close to tears.

August scratched the scruff on his cheek and squinted at her. "For what?"

"I had no idea." Josie flung her arms around him, her body pure trembling.

August liked having her in his arms but not the part where she was upset. He rubbed his palms up and down her back, hoping to soothe the worry away. "Jo, what's wrong? You can tell me."

She leaned away and looked at him, her blue eyes swimming in tears. "You should have told me the truth. I wish I didn't have to hear it from Carter."

Suddenly Josie's odd behavior made some sense. Cringing, he asked, "What did Carter say?"

"It's okay, August. There's no need to be embarrassed . . ." She sniffed and wiped under her nose.

August huffed as his arms dropped to his sides. "What. Did. He. Say?"

"He told me about your accident last year in Rome. Don't be mad at him. Like I said, there's nothing to be ashamed of—"

"What accident?" August crossed his arms as his patience grew thin.

She gestured to his right shoulder. "With your arm. Carter told me it was severely injured when a runaway grandma plowed into you on the sidewalk with her moped." Josie stepped forward and gently touched his arm. "I had no idea you were struggling to paint."

"Is that all he said?" August wished he had used that *injured* shoulder a little more forcefully when he shoved Carter with it earlier.

"More or less. He said you really need me here. I'm sorry . . . Something has been going on with my dad and I'm worried and I'm trying to get him to open up to me and he won't . . . I just don't know what to do. . . ." She grew more and more flustered as she kept rambling. Her face was flushed and her hands waved around as she spoke.

August scrubbed his palms down his face, knowing he was going to have to fluster her some more. "There's nothing wrong with my arm."

"Don't downplay it. From what Carter said, she nailed you good." Josie shook her head, still looking distraught.

He hated to think what all Carter might have articulated to her. "You ever heard of a Carter calamity?"

"Daddy's mentioned that a time or two." Confusion replaced the pity she was carrying in her pretty features.

"And what did he tell you about them?"

She hesitated to answer, clearly realizing Carter had pulled a fast one on her. "They're elaborately made-up gibberish." Confusion fell away faster than the pity as anger tightened her jaw. August could see the muscle flexing. He found her even prettier in that moment.

"Exactly." August took a step closer to her.

Josie countered by taking a step back. "Why would Carter do that?"

August took another step and placed his hand on her slouching shoulder. "Don't take it personal." He breathed out a quick chuckle. "Shoot, most folks find it to be an honor if Carter takes the time to spin a tale for them."

"Makes me want to pinch him." Josie crossed her

arms and huffed. "I was in the middle of preparing my craft project for Sunday and he comes to the house acting all concerned over you. Guilt-tripped me right into hurrying over here." She sucked her teeth and narrowed her blue eyes. "Boy, is he good."

August grinned, realizing Carter had used *him* as bait, which in turn revealed just how much Josie truly cared for him. He didn't know if he wanted to punch his crazy uncle for that or hug him. Yeah, definitely hug. All her wishy-washiness was beginning to bruise his ego.

"It's not funny."

August grinned wider. "It kinda is."

Josie fought it, but the smile worked its way loose anyway. "Ugh! I don't have time for this foolishness."

August swept a hand in the direction of all the unfinished buildings. "Neither do I. So how about telling me where you've been while we work on this for a little while?" He pointed to the letter *H* he'd outlined earlier to gauge where to put the treble clef.

Josie surprised him when she picked up an extra paintbrush without hesitation and looked around. "Where's the design sketch?"

August grabbed the notepad from the top of the ladder, flipped it open, and placed it on the small easel by the bucket of black paint. "You mind working on the rest of the word *HARMONY* and I'll do the stuff higher up?"

"Okay." She dipped her brush and set out to outlining the *A*.

As August climbed the ladder, he asked, "You gonna tell me why you ghosted?"

Josie sighed, her shoulders hunching forward. "I've just had my hands full with Daddy acting weird. And I need to figure out different arrangements for Miss Dalma. She left the water running in her sink and flooded the kitchen last week. Plus, I have a friend, Deandrea, that I think I overstepped with on trying to get her some help and now she won't talk to me. And . . ."

August stared down at her as she kept rattling off a long list of people and their situations, baffled as to how she even managed to handle so much. What was even more baffling was why she felt it her duty to take it all on. Thinking it was in his best interest to keep those thoughts to himself, he asked once she hushed to take a breath, "What's up with your dad?"

"He won't tell me. He's stewing on something, like suddenly he has a lot on his mind." Her brush stilled against the wall as she sniffed. "I think I must have done something to upset him."

"He's a pretty straightforward guy. If you did something he wasn't happy about, he'd let you know it."

"I guess." She shrugged and dipped the brush into the paint. "It's just . . . he's been acting like this ever since I've started helping you."

August looked below and watched her take great care in drawing each giant letter. He remained quiet until she finished the *Y.* "You can't let your life revolve around him." He delivered the statement in a gentle tone, but it somehow set fire to her. After tracking the paintbrush flying across the yard, his eyes darted back to Josie.

"You don't know what we've been through. My dad and I . . ." She planted one hand on her narrow hip and pressed the other against her chest. "We're all the other has had since my mom passed away."

Knowing he'd opened a can of worms that a lid wouldn't fit back onto, August set his brush down and hopped to the ground. "I'm not trying to say I know what y'all have gone through. I'm just saying he has to know you deserve to live a life that makes you happy. A life filled with *want to*s."

"Daddy has always provided for me. Always took good care of me." Her bottom lip trembled.

August raised his hands, thinking he should have just cleared up the Carter calamity and sent the emotional woman on her way. "I'm not saying he hasn't, but you're a grown woman."

Josie brushed a wayward strand of hair off her forehead, leaving a smear of paint that August didn't have the heart to point out. "My dad needs me and it's the least I can do to be there for him."

"What about you and your dreams? You're just willing to set aside what you want?"

"A small sacrifice I'm willing to pay for the sake of my dad."

From the rigidness of her body to the harsh set of her lips, August knew arguing with her would be pointless. He pointed over to her truck, where the door remained ajar. "Then it's probably best you get on back to him. Thank you for the help, but I think I'm good." He didn't wait for her reaction before gathering his sketch pad and walking inside the building to get away from the stifling humidity and his bitter disappointment in how things were turning out.

August peeped out the window and watched the truck drive away much more slowly than it had arrived, as if she really didn't want to leave. *Why does she have to be so dang stubborn?* He wanted to push Josie to chase her dreams, dreams that he hoped included him, but he wasn't willing to get between her and her dad to make it happen.

After sulking for a while longer, August loaded up and headed toward the coast to go see a woman who might have some insight. Well, that was if she was having a clear day. By the time he pulled into the driveway and noticed the little old lady almost dangling off her dock, he had his doubts. He hopped out of the truck to see what she'd gotten herself into this time.

"You all right?" August asked, hurrying over to where Dalma was grunting and wiggling against the dock rail. One bare foot was in the air while the other seemed wedged between the railings.

"Darnedest thing . . . The crab trap is stuck." Dalma grunted some more before letting go of the rope and climbing down. She smoothed her silk pajama top that she'd paired with jean capris. "You reckon you can unstick it?"

August moved around her and glanced over the rail, finding the rope wrapped around the pilings underneath the dock. "I can try." He kicked off his shoes before climbing over the rail and down the side.

Dalma giggled from above him. "I got my very own Tarzan!"

"More like a monkey." August grunted. Leaning a little too far, his grip slipped, sending one foot to take a dip in the cool water. Grumbling a few sentiments underneath his breath, he gathered all of his upper body strength to shinny up a little to avoid going for a swim.

It took a good bit of effort and a good-size scratch along the inside of his arm, but the fruit of his labor paid off with a trap filled with good-size blue crabs. Once he wrestled it out of the water and onto the dock, August braced his hands on his hips and took a minute to catch his breath. "That's our supper, right?"

"I like how you think, young man." Dalma patted the top of the trap and began walking toward the house. "But I'm gonna have to get you to do a little breaking and entering first."

"I'm not much on breaking the law, Miss Dalma." August lugged the trap over to the outdoor sink, where a giant pot sat ready to be filled.

"It's my property, so no law will be broken." She led him to the storage closet underneath the house and pointed at the padlock. "I'm not sure where Josie has hidden the key and the propane tank is inside. Can't have a crab boil without it."

August scratched the scruff on his cheek while running through a few ways to go about the problem at hand. He was still too aggravated at Josie to just call and ask where she hid the key, but he didn't want to give Dalma any ideas on how to go about it when he wasn't there either. After regarding the door a few more minutes, he turned his attention to the little lady, who was searching underneath the flowerpots scattered around the space.

"How about you go gather up some Old Bay seasoning, a roll of paper towels, a big spoon, and maybe make us a glass of tea. I'll be there in a few to help bring everything outside."

"What about the door lock?" She put a flowerpot down and cleaned her hands on the sides of her pants.

August waved off her concerns. "I'll take care of it. No worries." He waited until she was halfway up the stairs and out of sight before jogging over to the truck to retrieve a hammer and screwdriver. The door hinges on the closet came loose much easier than he expected and so he was able to get the propane tank out and hooked up to the outdoor burner before Dalma even had the tea poured in the glasses.

Within an hour they were seated at the newspaper-covered table in the yard, munching away on freshly boiled blue crabs.

"You seem to have something on your mind," Dalma

commented while tossing another crab shell on the growing pile in the middle of the table.

August licked the salty liquid from his thumb before selecting another crab. "I can't figure out Josie Slater to save my life." He shook his head and cracked open the crab claw. The messy meal had him sticky all the way to his elbows, but it was worth it.

"Women . . ." Dalma scoffed, making August chuckle. "What happened?"

"From what I can gather, she's put herself on the back burner since her mom passed away." August tore off a section of paper towel and handed it to Dalma. "All I want to do is offer her a chance to do what she loves. She's too talented not to shine as the artist she's meant to be. God wouldn't have given her all that talent otherwise."

"She's hiding her light under a bushel basket," Dalma said before popping a saltine cracker into her mouth.

August picked up another crab and pointed it at Dalma. "Exactly, but try explaining that to her. For everyone to describe her as passive, she sure is one stubborn woman." He grunted, cracking the shell. "She ain't got me fooled."

"I know," Dalma agreed around a mouthful. She washed it down with a swallow of tea.

August leaned his elbows on the table. "Did you know Jo goes around secretly helping all kinds of people? And just the other day, the Knitting Club cornered me at the store and felt it was their business to tell me all about Josie adding Mr. Otis Franks to her list now that he's broken his arm. They say she spent the day mowing his lawn and even changed the oil in his truck. They also insinuated she was shopping him for her sugar daddy."

"Those women are busybodies, but they normally tell the truth."

"Is Jo shopping for a sugar daddy?" He snorted at the absurdity.

Dalma laughed. "Wouldn't that be a hoot, but that was added in there to get you riled up."

"Jo riles me up just fine on her own. I don't need those women adding to it." August watched Dalma dunk a chunk of crabmeat in a bowl of melted butter, waiting for her to fill him in some more, but she continued eating instead. "You have any advice for me?"

She chewed thoughtfully, head tilted to the side, while studying the inlet water. Her cloudy-blue eyes darted back to his. "Oh yes. Only eat local oysters in a month that ends with the letter *r*." She gave her head a swift nod and began to clear the table.

August should have known it was a bad day to ask any advice when Dalma tried melting a block of cream cheese earlier instead of the butter. He gave up and helped her clean. Once the outdoor table was washed down and the kitchen inside squared away, August decided to call it a day.

"I'm heading out, unless you need anything else," he told Dalma as she plundered through one of her stacks of books. He turned to leave when she didn't answer.

"Whoa. Wait a minute. I have the perfect book for you." She wiggled a book from the stack and August was impressed when it didn't cause an avalanche. "Here."

August took the book offering and glanced at the couple holding hands on the cover, figuring it was another romance. He'd acknowledge the humor in that if he wasn't in such a foul mood. One thing was for certain: Josie Slater wasn't easily wooed. "Thanks. I probably need to read this for some pointers," he joked.

"You do that," Dalma advised in a serious tone. "You never know what an unassuming book may reveal."

"Yes, ma'am." August gave her a one-armed hug and left well enough alone. With the glove box filled to capacity with books, he had to shove the new one underneath the seat. If Dalma kept it up, the cab of his truck was going to start resembling her living room.

15

Josie scanned the dining room table scattered with the tissue paper flowers she'd prepared for Sunday school. "Her children arise and call her blessed" was written on the leaves. She'd been working on folding them yesterday when Carter knocked on the door to deliver a serving of his hogwash, which sent her dashing out to go help August.

Still aggravated over yesterday's epic fail, she began packing the flowers into a tote bag and made the mistake of glancing in the mirror behind the dining table. Puffy eyes and a red nose reflected back at her, showing off that she'd spent most of the night in tears. She was missing her mom, worried about her dad, and apprehensive about allowing August any closer.

She glared at the mirror and muttered, "You can check that last part off the list." August dismissing her yesterday was like a punch to the stomach. She'd been naive to think that he'd just keep putting up with her flightiness. "Serves you right."

A tapping echoed through the house. Josie took in her blotchy skin and tangled hair and debated on whether to answer the door or ignore it altogether. When she couldn't work the knots out of her hair by brushing her fingers through it, she chose to ignore the visitor and keep packing the supplies for class while mentally reviewing the Friday and Saturday work schedule. She had the lunch shift today and had to place inventory orders afterward, so the rest of the day would require her to get her act together. She actually had Saturday off, and that should have been a relief, but it left her feeling unsettled. Her dad was cutting her hours and that was something else that needed to be addressed if she could make the ornery man get still long enough to discuss it.

The persistent tapping wouldn't stop and so after a few more minutes, Josie gave in and cracked the door open enough to catch a glimpse of who was standing on her porch.

Dominica smiled and held up a basket. "I come bearing apologies."

"You're not who I expected," Josie mumbled, not having a clue who to expect anymore. Her door had picked up on the visitor roster lately. "But you don't have anything to apologize for. It's your fibbing weasel of a husband's fault." She tried to sound mean, but when Dominica's golden-brown eyes twinkled and she started giggling, the meanness disappeared.

"True. Carter tends to pull one over on people. He's even done it to me a time or two." She held up the basket again. "But the stinker felt so bad about it that he had a very special lady whip these up especially for you. They're still warm." Dominica pulled the blue gingham napkin back to reveal a bounty of golden nuggets of goodness.

"What do you have there?" Josie leaned in and stole a whiff of the sweet and spicy aroma. She knew they were apple fritters from one of the ladies from church who was famous for her homemade donuts. It was also common knowledge that the old lady didn't make the fritters for just anybody.

"Are you going to let me in?" Dominica held up the basket again.

Giving in, Josie opened the door and led Dominica into the kitchen. She poured them both a glass of milk and grabbed a handful of napkins. Without pause they dug into the treats, savoring the crunchy exterior of the fried dough that gave way to a soft, gooey texture inside.

"These are so good," Josie moaned out while popping another into her mouth.

"Good enough to forgive Carter?" Dominica looked up with hope lighting her face.

"I guess, but I just don't get why he thought he needed to come up with such an elaborate story like that." Josie shook her head. "Seriously, he said August had been in an accident. That's not something someone should joke around about."

"You're right." Dominica set her glass down and grew serious. "One thing you need to understand about Carter is that if you're blessed to be loved by that man, there's nothing he wouldn't do for you."

"Even coming up with elaborate fibs?" Josie crossed her arms, not buying the excuse Dominica was selling.

"You know August's story. The guy has survived an awful lot of bad and chosen to rise above it. He and Carter have this bond that I've never witnessed before. August has jumped through some pretty big, selfless hoops for Carter. He's the reason why I'm with Carter in the first place. So to answer your question, yes, Carter would tell you hundreds of far-fetched stories if it meant making August happy."

"Carter could have been straightforward instead of fibbing, though." Josie tightened her crossed arms, trying to gather some defense.

Dominica brushed it away as easily as the crumbs from the front of her shirt. "Go ahead and have yourself a hissy fit. Carter deserves it, but don't take it out on August."

Josie's arms dropped, realizing Dominica knew more to the story than just the fib Carter told.

"I was working in the music building when you came up yesterday . . . You were pretty loud." Dominica offered an apologetic smile.

Feeling foolish, Josie closed her eyes and let out an uneven sigh. "Oh."

"It's none of my business what's going on with you, but since it deals with a very special person in my life, I can't help but get in the middle of it."

"I'm good with Carter. Just tell him to keep his stories to himself from now on." Josie rose and began clearing the table. She'd had enough of the visit and wanted to go back to sulking alone.

"I'm not talking about Carter."

Josie placed the glasses in the sink and looked over at Dominica where she continued to sit. She didn't look to have any plans of being rushed out the door. Josie stayed silent, waiting for the woman to explain.

"Can I share something with you?" Dominica asked.

"Sure." Josie didn't think she had a choice in the matter, anyway.

"If you're as important to August as I suspect, then you can count on being important to Carter, too." Dominica motioned toward the basket. "He doesn't do something like this for just anyone."

"Why is Carter so adamant about me helping with the camp?"

"Do you know about my sickness?"

"Some." In Josie's eyes, Dominica was the picture of health, except for her slower movements and her low weight.

"I have lupus and it's set off several other health problems. One being, I'm unable to have children."

The sudden heaviness of the conversation had Josie returning to her chair and plopping down. "Oh."

"Due to the limitations with my autoimmune disease, I feel like it wouldn't be fair to adopt a child and have them stuck with a sick parent."

"Aww, Dominica, you shouldn't look at it that way." Josie's heart hurt for the woman sitting across from her.

Dominica raised a palm and released a sad chuckle. "You sound like Carter, but this disease will progress and so . . ." She took a deep breath and let it out on a long sigh. "We've participated in summer ministry programs for years now, helping with praise services. Before my diagnosis, I had already reached the point where I couldn't keep up with traveling any more, but I missed working with children so much. I told Carter, and the next thing I know that man is building a camp." Her laughter was filled with amusement this time.

"The camp is for you?" Josie's eyes began to burn with tears.

Dominica nodded her head. "We love working with children, and this passion project has become Carter's heart and soul, so of course, it's August's heart and soul. And if those two want you to be a part of that . . . I don't want to sound arrogant, but I say this with humbleness and respect that you should be honored. I know I'm honored to be included in being a part of this camp. Both of those men are rough around the edges, but you won't find two more loyal men."

Dominica quietly left after that, leaving Josie with a lot to think about.

Dominica's words nagged Josie the entire shift at the diner and followed her home that night, where it continued. Josie didn't understand why she somehow ended up mattering to August, much less Carter and Dominica, but it was humbling and intimidating all at once. She worried she'd already messed things up, though.

August's last words to her played on a reel every time she awoke that fitful night.

"Thank you for the help, but I think I'm good."

By dawn, Josie knew for certain that she wasn't good with being done with whatever mission he was on. August simply needed an art partner and had graciously asked her to be a part of designing the camp, and she showed her appreciation by taking her hurt and frustration out on him.

"Talk about a drama queen," Josie muttered to herself as she slipped out of the rumpled bed. As painful as it was, she knew what she had to do. By the time Josie was dressed, the sky had opened up and let loose a thick rainstorm. Tossing on a raincoat and a pair of galoshes, Josie set out in the direction of trying to right her wrong.

She parked the truck in the spot she already considered her own in front of the firehouse and spotted August sitting in a rocking chair by the open bay doors. She sat in the truck for a moment, watching him stare out over the fields. When he finally looked her way, she worked up enough nerve to flip the hood of the coat up and make a run for it.

Without a word, August stretched out a long leg and hooked it under the leg of another rocking chair and pulled it close beside his, a silent invite to sit. Josie shrugged out of the dripping wet coat, tossed it on the cement floor, and sat down. They rocked in an amicable silence and watched as the thick curtain of rain cast a foggy haze to the world just past the firehouse.

From her periphery, Josie noticed a soggy bag of boiled peanuts on one of his jean-clad thighs. True to form, a smear of white paint marked near the left knee of the pants. She wondered if he owned a single stitch of clothing that didn't have at least a speckle of paint on it. She watched as he lifted the glass bottle of cola that was wedged between his legs and took a sip. "Breakfast of champions?"

After August cracked open another shell and popped the peanuts into his mouth, he reached down beside his chair and produced a plastic container of plump red strawberries. "Got these too. Balanced meals are important, you know."

His light tone gave no hint of the hurt he had shown two days ago, so Josie decided to pretend it didn't happen as well.

"Looks like someone made a trip to the farm stand up the road this morning."

"Reminds me of backpacking around Europe. I either stayed in hotels or couch surfed, so I never really had access to a kitchen. Just went out and picked up fresh food from town vendors and open-air markets when I got hungry. Makes me appreciate that benefit here now."

"Are you sure you don't want to go back?"

"Yeah. Country living is for me. That's why I didn't find a place at the beach." He motioned to the only neighbors he had for miles, the trees and fields. "God's beauty is the kind of inspiration I need to feed my creativity. The silence out here whispers to me all the time."

"What does it tell you?" she asked.

August tilted his head toward the open door. "Listen for a while. You'll see."

They shared the breakfast of boiled peanuts as the pattering of raindrops effectively drowned out the world beyond the bay doors. *Or maybe that's just the effect from being in August's company,* Josie thought. She reflected on her time with him and found that to be closer to the truth.

Smiling, she swiped another handful of the warm peanuts and began opening the shells. August even allowed her a few swigs of his cola to wash the salty goodness down before indulging in the fresh strawberries.

"You can almost taste the sunshine in these berries." Josie licked the red juice from her fingers and moaned.

"Mm-hm," August agreed. He ate a few more before placing the container between their chairs. After a few more languid rocks of his chair, August spoke again. "I have a memory for you."

Excited to have him share anything with her, she dropped the green top of an eaten strawberry into the paper bag holding the peanut hulls. "Okay."

"Playtime at the inlet behind Nan and Derek's restaurant."

That simple statement set free a deluge of memories that poured out faster than the rain clouds above them. "Oh, I love those memories."

"Nan giving us treats and sweet tea."

Josie snickered. "Momma and Daddy were always scolding me for ruining my appetite from eating too many treats."

"Ah, now this is where the memory is different for us."

Josie looked over, confused by his statement, and found August wearing a somber expression. "How so?"

"That was never a snack for me and Tucker. We depended on that for a meal." He glanced briefly in her direction before going back to staring at the rain.

In Josie's childhood memory, she only saw a bunch of local kids goofing around the inlet, chasing after crabs and being offered a little treat from the restaurant. His admittance had the memory looking completely different all of a sudden. "August . . ." She didn't know what to say.

He shrugged. "My parents had a nasty drug habit,

among other things. They got tangled up in something awful, and when they were arrested, my mom's father was given custody of us. He made it clear he didn't want us, told me to take care of Tucker and stay out of his way. I did what I had to do to make that happen. Tucker was starting the Head Start program at the elementary school and our schools had different times, so I had to drop out for a little while to make sure he got to go. I'd do odd jobs like mowing lawns or picking up garbage while he was at school to make some grocery money, but sometimes it wasn't enough."

The whooshing of rain kept time with the roar in Josie's ears as her eyes began to sting. Without pause, tears formed to wash it away. They rocked in silence for another short spell as she understood the importance of him sharing the memory from his side of life.

The other day, she kept insisting he didn't understand her duty to her dad and why she had to make sacrifices. Now she realized just how foolish she'd been with her thinking.

Clearing his throat, August said, "That's why I was twenty years old when I graduated high school. I felt awkward being so much older than the rest of y'all most of the time, but not enough to let my dreams get thrown away because of it. Life has given me moments I wish weren't mine, but I've never allowed them to define me or prevent me from living beyond the memory of it . . . Perhaps you should try doing the same."

She reached over and entwined her fingers with his where they were gripping the arm of his chair. "I admire your tenacity, truly. I'm really sorry for taking my issues out on you the other day. That wasn't fair."

"Can we have a redo?" August flipped his hand over and gently held hers.

"How?"

"Tell me what's really bothering you."

She focused on the ribbons of water pouring down in front of them. "Tomorrow is Mother's Day." That one admittance had more tears flowing. "I know it's been six years and I should be over it—"

"Jo, losing your mom is something you never get over." His grip tightened around her hand and he allowed her to cry for a while before asking, "How do you normally spend Mother's Day?"

Josie swallowed, trying to regain her composure. "I teach my class and try to get them to understand how important it is to appreciate their moms and to show them how much they love them." She hitched a shoulder up. "Then I normally bring Miss Dalma a gift before going home and hiding under the covers the rest of the day." She waited for him to balk at that and reprimand her for hiding, but he only nodded his head and kept watching the rain come down in heavy sheets.

"Can I share another memory with you?" August asked.

"Okay."

"As you know, Tucker and I had a messy childhood. My parents would wander off days at a time or have shady people over." He looked over and met Josie's eyes. "I'd sneak Tucker out and we'd go fishing. If the weather was nice, we'd camp out on the bank and pretend life at home didn't exist. It was a sad and scary time, and after my parents were incarcerated, it got worse, so I would tell Tucker we could fish our blues away."

"You want to take me fishing?" she asked even though her heart was aching for what he just shared about his and Tucker's childhood.

"Not this time. This time we are going to dance." Without releasing Josie's hand, August stood and pulled her to standing with him. "Josie, I'm not saying there won't be times where you'll feel sad, but I'd like nothing better than if you'd allow me to dance that sadness away." He didn't wait for her response before pulling her into the shower of rain.

Josie squealed as the cool rain soaked them immediately, but she didn't pull away. Instead, she allowed him to dance her around in the rain. The first part of the dance, she buried her face against his neck and grieved for her mother, thinking perhaps she'd never allowed herself to do that properly. The tears flowed until the rain and August's comfort washed them away with a peace replacing the mournful trembling of her body.

August seemed to sense when the heaviness left her, which was about the same time the rain eased into just a drizzle. He began stepping up the pace of the slow dance, transforming it into a familiar dance she hadn't witnessed in years.

"You know how to do the Carolina shag?" Josie watched him in awe.

"Of course. We live on the Grand Strand, don't we?"

"Yes, but I don't know how."

"No worries. I'll teach you." His lips curved into a broad smile as he swung them around in the lazy six-count dance pattern until Josie got the hang of the steps.

"You are full of surprises." She giggled, taking a wrong step but correcting it quickly. The man managed to be her sunshine in the midst of the heavy clouds, making her long to just bask in it indefinitely.

August pulled her close and lowered his voice even though it still rang out in a sturdy timbre. "Every time it rains, you're going to think about this moment—you wrapped in my arms as the rain washed away our blues and painted our day with the lazy motion of the Carolina shag."

Water trickled from the tip of his nose and his grinning lips as he gently swept a lock of wet hair off of her cheek.

Before she allowed herself to overthink it, Josie reached up and placed her equally wet lips against his, briefly but long enough for the warmth of it to reach her tender heart.

"And when you see the rain, you'll remember the day Josie Slater wasn't too chicken to take the kiss she'd been wanting for a really long time." She smiled at him as August concluded their dance.

August's grin dropped as he focused on her lips. "It took you long enough," he said in a matter-of-fact tone as if he'd been waiting on her all of those years as much as she'd been waiting on him.

Josie's thoughts were fleeting, and before she could manage to wrap her mind around them, August's hands reached over and cupped her cheeks as he closed the gap and took his own kiss, adding the flavor of sweet strawberries and optimism to the memory.

16

Stealing shouldn't be so fun, so addictive, and there was no denying the fact that August had no intentions of stopping anytime soon. He sat rocking long after Josie drove away, contemplating ways he could pull off stealing that woman completely. Their moments were beginning to not be enough. He wanted her permanently by his side—in her rocking chair beside his, at her art easel to the right of his, on her side of his bed . . . If Josie wouldn't totally freak out, there'd already be a ring on her finger and August would be beating a path to the courthouse.

August let out a low chuckle and shook his head. "I'm getting a little ahead of myself."

A deer darted from the field across the road, but August barely noticed. His thoughts were still captured by Josie's boldness earlier. He ran a thumb over his bottom lip, grinning against it, as he recalled the tremble of hers as she kissed him. He hit replay on the memory, remembering the nervous determination set in her baby-blue eyes as she leaned forward and finally claimed something she truly wanted. Just a soft, brief kiss. It might have seemed simple enough, but man, did it mean so much more.

With the grin still in place, August plucked his rain-soaked shirt off. Heading upstairs and changing into some dry clothes, he thought about his dad's advice to look for solutions to problems Josie presented as road-blocks between them. He'd discovered today that not all roadblocks included him, yet he wanted to find her a solution to them just the same. Tomorrow's would be a little tricky, and he'd have to be extremely careful not to upset her in the process, but he was up for the challenge.

The sun had shoved the rain clouds away and was like a beacon, beckoning him to get on with an idea that had sparked from their conversation. He grabbed his keys and wallet and made his way out to the truck. He popped open the glove box to retrieve a pair of shades. One of the books crammed inside fell out and plopped onto the floorboard. He reached down to pick it up and was stunned when catching a glimpse of a colorful page.

"Huh?" August sat up and began flipping through the book, astonished at the artwork he'd been carrying around unbeknownst to him. Curious, he pulled another book out of the glove box and found it filled with color-ful beauty as well. Eyes focused on a page that should be on display in an art gallery, he leaned over and fished the book from underneath the seat that he'd all but forgotten about. Opening it, he discovered it held hidden art just like the others.

Placing the books on the seat with a newfound respect for them and the clever little lady who slyly gave them to him, August added another art project to his to-do list.

● ● ●

"You're coming over after church, right?" Nan questioned August the next morning as he loaded up in the truck once again. "You know our tradition."

He adjusted the phone and cranked the truck. "Yes . . . I may have a guest with me."

Nan laughed. "*May*? Why are you having such a hard time catching this girl? You losing your charm or something?"

The fresh memory of dancing in the rain with Josie yesterday flickered through his mind, so he knew without a doubt he still had an abundant supply of charm. "Don't give me a hard time." He shifted the truck into gear. "Now, let me go so I can be the responsible man you raised me to be and not talk on the phone while driving. Be sure to have the kid ready to hand over."

"You're mouthy today. You better watch it," Nan scolded.

August smirked. "Learned from the best. Happy Mother's Day." He ended the call before Nan could mouth off at him again.

He swung by Growler's Bait and Grocery to pick up a few supplies needed for the day ahead. The store had a small grill that served breakfast and lunch sandwiches and always had a small crowd gathered at the back tables. August inwardly groaned, knowing he had to pass those tables to reach the cooler. Taking a fortifying breath, he hurried past them, but not before a strident voice called out.

"August Bradford, we know you were taught better manners than to walk by without speaking." Bertie Matthews tsked. Her ornery sister Ethel sat beside her with two other hens sitting across from them. Paper cups of coffee and sandwich wrappers littered the table. All of the ladies had teased-up bouffants in various hues of purplish gray and were dressed in their Sunday best.

All of them, that was, except for Dalma, who sat at the end of the table smiling warmly at him. Today's attire was a pair of black leather pants and a green hunting jacket. After taking a second glance, he caught sight of the

camouflage rain boots on her feet. At least the jacket and
shoes matched. He tipped his head and grinned at her as
he moved by her chair.

"Good morning, ladies. Sorry, but I'm in a bit of a
hurry to make it to church on time." He tipped his head
to the rest of the table, using every bit of the manners
he most certainly had but sometimes chose not to pull
out. "Y'all having a *prayer meeting* before Sunday school?"
From their narrowed eyes, he knew they caught his jab.
Some folks liked to dress up their gossiping by calling it
"prayer requests," but August just called it uncouth.

Bertie waved his condescending comment off with
a flick of her wrinkly hand. "How's Josie Slater doing?"

Ah, the ole gal had her own subtle way of making a
jab. Too bad for her and the other hens he wasn't in the
mood to take it. Instead, he slid the cooler door open and
grabbed two cases of Cokes. The mini glass bottles were
his crowd's favorite.

"I heard you two have been spending a lot of time
together," another hen clucked, but he couldn't recall her
name.

Again, he pretended no one had spoken to him. He
set the soda on the counter and rushed over to the snack
aisle for packs of square crackers, packs of peanuts, and
snack cakes. Derek was supplying the sandwiches, so
August was pretty sure he had all he needed to complete
the picnic lunch. He grabbed a few tubs of bait from
another cooler and set it all down on the counter.

"I'll need two bags of ice," he said to the cashier as
the older gentleman rang him up. August leaned over
the counter and swiped a paper sack to hurry the process
along by bagging his own supplies.

"That girl ain't ever going to leave her daddy's side,"

Ethel commented from her post beside her sister. "Not even for some highfalutin artist as yourself."

Heat crawled up August's neck as he handed over the money to the man behind the register. He knew good and well they were just goading him into speaking, but it still stung that they knew right where to aim. Those two sisters liked to play good cop and bad cop. Bertie tried wiggling information out with a kind smile and sugary sweet comments. Ethel would scowl and snap off words like an irritated bulldog.

Once he was sure he had himself in check, August slowly turned toward the nosy women. "I'm sorry, ladies. I didn't hear you." Bertie opened her mouth, but he spoke over her. "Oh, did y'all hear about that estranged couple expecting a baby?"

It was the first thing to pop into his head, but it was mighty effective. All four of their denture-wearing mouths went to flapping in the manner of a starving fish. Dalma continued grinning and gave him a subtle wink. Despite being called the flighty one of the group, August considered her the wisest. With the hook set, August grinned wide, picked up his bags, and moseyed out the door. A bevy of shouted questions followed him outside.

"Who?"

"What couple?"

"They live here for very long?"

"August Bradford, you better get back here!"

Chuckling to himself, he made quick work of loading the cooler in the bed of his truck, hoping that they didn't have time to round up their canes and charge out the door.

Shortly after, he pulled up to the church and parked beside Nan and Derek. As he stepped out of the truck, his family began piling out of the SUV, but his eyes were on the youngest member.

"Are you ready to go to Sunday school, Zachary?" August offered his hand, and the little guy took it and began pulling them both in the direction of the church building.

Derek narrowed his eyes at August as they passed by. "I'm not sure how I feel about you using my kid to get in the door."

"The boss already okayed it," August said over his shoulder and gave his dad a mischievous wink, causing the crowd he loved dearly to laugh. He bent slightly and asked Zachary, "You got any pointers for me about class?"

"Raise your hand if you got a question. And use a tissue, not your finger. Miss Josie keeps a box in our room."

It took a minute for the last part to make sense, but when it did, August chuckled. "Good advice, little man."

Zachary scrunched his nose. "I always use a tissue."

17

Josie busied herself with setting out craft kits on the long rectangular table in front of each chair, but her thoughts were still tangled in the unexpected time she had spent at the firehouse. After dancing a good portion of the day away yesterday until both she and August were a freezing soggy mess, she went home and warmed in a hot shower. That warmth stayed with her the rest of the day as she came to terms with a few things.

For one, she needed to openly grieve her mom more often rather than just keeping it bottled up inside. For another, August Bradford was an exceptional dancer and friend. And the kicker of it all was that she was absolutely falling for him. The nervous crush that had begun in high school was developing into something much more mature. And as scary as that was, it felt right.

She had just delivered a pair of scissors to a kit on the table and turned to retrieve more when she halted. Standing at the door in a white button-down shirt and navy trousers was the man who was stealing more than just moments from her.

"Good morning," she managed to say without stuttering.

"Morning, Miss Josie. Can my brother come to class with me? I went over the rules with him already. He'll behave, I promise." Zachary nodded his head adamantly.

She looked at Zachary and found him similarly dressed

to August, but his chocolate curls had been tamed down while his older brother's black hair was styled in perfect disarray. "I could always use another helper. As long as he behaves." She smiled at them both as a few more children skirted around them to take seats at the table.

"Great. Just let me know how I can help." August's warm smile was so open and welcoming that Josie had to refrain from leaning over for a hug.

She moved away to put some distance between them for good measure. As soon as the table was filled with four- and five-year-olds, she introduced the new addition to the class. "Today I have a helper. This is Mr. August."

A chorus of "Hey, Mr. August," rang out.

His smile broadened as his deep voice boomed out a reply. "Good morning."

Josie didn't think the guy could pull off talking in a low tone if his life depended on it. The timbre of his voice was like a rich cup of cocoa on a chilly night. One you just wanted to savor. She dismissed those silly romantic notions before getting too sidetracked by them and focused on her students. Each one was dressed to the nines and their hair combed neatly.

"Today is a special day to celebrate, so let's open with prayer and then we will get started." As soon as Josie said this, each little head bowed without being told a second time. She prayed and then launched into instructing them on how to form a flower out of the tissue paper. As she showed them with the prepared samples, Josie explained how God had created them just as he created the seeds that formed the flowers. She went on to tell them that their mother's love and nurturing helped them bloom into the individuals God created them to be.

August listened intently, nodded his head at certain points she made, and helped anyone who needed it. She was impressed that he never took over the lesson or the craft project.

As the last child exited with a colorful bouquet, Josie walked over to where August was collecting the scissors and placing them in a container. "You were a great helper, sir."

August looked up and smiled. "Glad I could be of assistance, ma'am."

Josie collected a handful of paper scraps and tossed them into the trash. "I think I've decided on my favor."

He looked over at her. "Oh yeah?"

"I'd like your assistance on Sundays."

"I'd be honored . . . but now I need to ask yet another favor." His expression turned thoughtful.

Josie shook her head. "That's not how this favor thing is supposed to work."

"Yeah . . . I don't like doing things the way people expect. There's no fun in that." His mouth curved up on one side.

Josie snickered. "Okay, then. What favor do you need in return for returning your favor to me?"

August stood up straight and looked baffled for a moment but then impressed. "First off, I must commend you for getting that complex question out correctly. I do believe you've worked the knots out of that tongue of yours finally." He winked teasingly before growing serious. "As for my favor, you have to agree or I may not make it through the day."

"Seriously?"

"Yes. It involves Nan and me going head-to-head. She can be scary when she needs to be, and today I'm scared."

"No. I think today you're being just a tad bit dramatic."

"Just say you'll do me this solid and help me out."

Josie hesitated. "What if I have another favor I need in return for returning your returned favor?"

August chuckled. "Anything. You earned it after those two sentences in a row."

"I'd really like to help you finish the projects at camp."

He dipped his chin. "Done. Now let's get into worship service before people start wondering where we're at." Without hesitating, he entwined their hands and walked Josie into the sanctuary.

An hour or so after church, Josie found herself on a sandbank in the middle of nowhere, eating a ham sandwich, with Zachary sitting beside her on the beach towel. The afternoon was sunny and warm, and that usually had a calming effect on her, but not today. She took another bite of her sandwich and watched guardedly as August and Nan bickered about which fishing pole belonged to whom.

Josie leaned toward her towel companion and asked, "Do we have to do this? I don't think it's safe." She glanced at Zachary, thinking he looked too cute in his fishing hat and colorful life jacket.

"That's why my partner is Daddy. We stay out of their way." Zachary took another bite just as Nan tossed a dip net into the inlet, sending August running after it.

"Playing dirty is the only way you can win?" August shouted at Nan as he waded out of the water with the dip net.

"And you messing with my pole ain't dirty?" Nan landed her hands on her hips and glared at him. The spitfire was casually dressed in a baggy pair of navy cargo cutoffs and a tank top with a ratty trucker hat shoved low on her head, but boy, did she look intimidating.

Just as Josie finished the last bite of her sandwich, August walked over with the dripping wet net and thrust it in her direction. She took it with a good bit of apprehension. "What?"

"This is my lucky net. You're in charge of it today,

partner. Don't let Nan anywhere near it." August's chin
jerked up before he headed over to his tackle box and fishing pole. He was being genuinely serious, but it was hard
for her to take him that way. Gone were the nice dress
clothes from earlier and in their place were board shorts,
a brightly colored T-shirt saying *Got Art?* across the front,
and a floppy boonie hat.

As everyone scurried around, Josie noticed that Derek
and Tucker gave August and Nan a good bit of space.
Apparently, they were wise to the situation at hand.
Josie wished she'd been wise enough to it earlier to have
declined returning the favor.

It was briefly explained to her about the flounder fishing competition. This year Josie was the lucky one to be
partnered with August. Tucker would be with Nan, while
Derek and Zachary would partner. Whoever caught the
most flounder would have the meal prepared and cooked
for them while they got to laze on the beach the remainder of the day. The losers had to clean and fry the fish and
prepare the fixings.

"Let's go!" Nan shouted while loading up in the flat-
bottomed boat.

"Just be glad there's a time limit," Derek told Josie as
they headed over to the boat. "The pain of watching those
two go at it only lasts two hours max."

"Good to keep in mind, I suppose." *What have I gotten myself into?* With a long sigh, Josie climbed in for the
craziest fishing trip of her life.

Derek made good with his promise of only two hours,
and that was more than enough time for the shenanigans.
By the time they had the boat reloaded and were heading
back to the Bradford beach house, Josie was still in tears.

"It ain't funny." August huffed as he pulled his truck
in behind Derek's.

"It kinda is." Josie threw his comment from a few days ago at him as she wiped her eyes and took in the waterlogged, fuming man while he steered the truck with a good bit of force.

August slung the truck into park. "She cheated and pushed me off the boat. Now we have to clean a cooler full of fish *and* cook them. You shouldn't be laughing."

"It'll be okay. I've cleaned my fair share of fish at the diner. We'll get through this." Josie giggled. One thing she'd learned for certain in those two hours: Nan Bradford was not a woman to be fooled with. She'd watched with caution as Nan messed with August's pole or hid his bait or *accidentally* knocked him into the water a time or two. At one point the son and mother went at it in a round of chase, jostling the boat every which way. "It's a wonder we caught any fish at all with how wild you two were being."

August grumbled something under his breath and climbed out of the truck. Even in his soggy, aggravated mood, he didn't forget his manners as he hurried around and opened the door for Josie.

By the time August had changed into a set of dry clothes, his mood had brightened, and Josie found cleaning fish to be quite enjoyable for the first time. She shared a few tips of the trade on how to fillet the flounder and even whipped up her dad's secret dredge for the fish. Once they had them fried to a golden brown and the table set, two surprise visitors walked up the steps of the deck to join the Bradford family.

"Dad! Miss Dalma!" Josie stood and offered Jasper a hug, feeling the gathering was complete all at once by their arrival.

Jasper wrapped her in his signature bear hug. "I heard there's some fresh fish I need to sample." He grinned at Derek.

"Only seemed fair since your daughter is sharing your recipes with the local competition." Derek stood and pulled out a chair on the other end of the table and gestured for Jasper to take a seat.

"She better not." Jasper scoffed playfully.

"I brought a Jell-O salad," Dalma interrupted, holding up a plastic container filled with something red, but Josie instantly knew there wasn't anything sweet and tasty inside it.

"I'll take that," Josie offered, but before she could, Dalma pried the lid off and made a face.

"I think it's gone bad." Dalma sniffed the gelatinous mixture again and was about to stick a spoon into it, but Josie stopped her in the nick of time.

"This is stink bait." Josie quickly put the lid on and handed it off to August to put away. The stench would only ruin everyone's appetite for the feast set before them.

"Well, that's the darnedest thing. I'll have to have a talk with them at the grocery store. No sense in putting stink bait in the salad cooler." Dalma scoffed and settled into a chair, looking as baffled as the group gathering around the table. "That's just asking for it."

"She was at Growler's this morning," August answered, clearing up the confusion.

After a few blinks and quietly mumbled *oh*s, everyone let it go and began passing the tea pitcher.

"Looks like the flounder were biting good today," Jasper commented after taking a healthy swig of tea.

"Yes, but we'd have even more if August hadn't cut my line a few times." Nan pointed a fork at the offender.

"You really want to go there?" August lifted a surly eyebrow from the other side of the table.

"How about we say grace, so we can eat this food before it gets cold." Derek grabbed his wife's hand, causing her to drop the fork and sending every hand at the table to find another.

After the prayer, the crowd set into devouring the bountiful spread and added an abundance of seasoned conversation to send the get-together well into the night.

It wasn't until Josie was snuggled in her bed later that she realized what August had successfully pulled off. It was the first time since her mom's passing that Josie had felt she was actually able to survive Mother's Day. Her mom's memory nudged her a few times during the day as she watched Nan interact with her three sons, but each time an appreciative smile graced her face from those private reflections.

Her phone buzzed on the nightstand with an incoming message. She rolled over, held it up to read, and smiled. **Each time you see a flounder, you'll be reminded that I am king of the fishing pole and Nan is a cheat.**

Smiling, she replied, **Each time you see a flounder fillet fried to a golden brown with a side of my mom's famous slaw, you'll remember how grateful I was that you helped me through Mother's Day without my mom. Thank you.**

Dots started up on the screen followed by another message. **I really enjoy moment thieving with you. I'm the thankful one. Good night.**

Josie placed the phone on the nightstand and watched the moonlight dance on top of the ocean just outside her open window. She thought perhaps the wild fishing trip had actually been a favor to her from August, instead of the other way around, so she was pretty sure she owed him another one.

18

A new morning broke midweek with only a few clouds to mess up the sun's perfect shine, but August had a feeling they wouldn't be lingering for very long. And that was a good thing, because he had an idea that needed testing. He gathered the necessary supplies and headed out the door.

A smile tipped up the corners of his lips as soon as he turned in to the parking lot at the camp and saw that a familiar pickup truck was already there. After checking a few of the buildings, he found a figure hunched over a bucket of paint on the right side of the auditorium. A fairy from *A Midsummer Night's Dream* was already dancing above her.

August knew Josie wasn't comfortable with drawing human figures, but when he explained to her that they would be painting that building in the expressionism style, which would give her freedom in the details, she seemed persuaded to give it a try. He couldn't help but be awestruck as he watched her add a wing to the fairy.

"Looking good, Jo," he commented as he walked up behind her. When she didn't respond, he realized she was wearing earbuds.

Instead of disturbing her, August stood off to the side and took a moment to just appreciate her painting. She bobbed her head and hummed along to a tune with a slight familiarity to it. He kept listening and watching until she turned to gather more paint on her brush and caught him.

Eyes rounded, she let out a little squeak as her body jolted. "You scared me." She pulled the earbud out of one ear and pressed a palm to her chest.

"Sorry." He smirked, tilting his head. "What are you listening to?"

"Why?"

"Clearly it's inspiring." He gestured toward the fairy. "Nicely done."

"'Fly to Your Heart.' It's from *Tinker Bell*," she admitted.

August chuckled. "That's why it sounded familiar." When Josie looked at him inquisitively, he explained, "Never tell Zachary I told you this, but the little guy was obsessed with that movie for a while. He's into the princess movies, too."

"Oh." Josie smiled. "That's too precious."

August winced. "You need to forget I told you."

"I'll try my best. What's with that?" She pointed to the mason jar in August's hand.

He tossed the jar filled with blue paint up in the air and caught it as if it were a baseball. "I've got an idea."

"An idea for what?"

August tipped his head in the direction of the center building and began walking that way. "Let's go make a *mess* in the mess hall."

Josie dropped her brush into a bucket and followed him inside the pristine building. White bathed the entire room in stark brightness with the windows, light fixtures, vents, and doors taped up with sheets of plastic.

Biting his lip, August stopped in the middle of the room and turned in a complete circle before rearing his arm back and pitching the jar. In a loud pop, the jar collided with the wall and blue exploded against it. Shards of glass rained down with sprinkles of paint onto the cement floor. Both stood still, eyeing that paint-splattered wall and then the glass on the floor.

Rubbing the day-old scruff on his cheek, August muttered, "Maybe I didn't think this through enough."

Josie rolled her lips inward to stanch the laughter, but August noticed, so she let it bubble out. "Great concept, Bradford, but poor execution."

They lapsed into a pondering mode for a few beats until Josie snapped her fingers and headed for the door. "Clean up that glass while I'm gone."

"Where are you going?"

"I have a better idea" was all she offered before skipping outside.

August managed to get rid of the glass fail while he waited for Josie to return with her idea. Time crept by, and he began to think her idea had been to make a run for it. He was sitting cross-legged in the middle of the room with his chin propped in a hand, trying to figure out how to make a safer mess in the mess hall, when she appeared at the door holding the rope handles of a giant plastic tote. He hurried over to help her and peered inside as he lugged it into the room.

"Water balloons?"

Mischief swept along her lovely face as Josie leaned close and whispered, "*Paint* balloons."

August was already leaning in to steal a kiss, so he did just that before grinning. "Why didn't I think of that?"

A pretty flush eased onto her cheeks and he hoped his kiss was the reason. Clearing her throat, Josie muttered, "Safer and less to clean up after we make a mess." She grabbed a purple balloon and hurled it in the direction of the blue splatter, sending a vivid burst of yellow to join it. Both adults giggled with excitement, sounding like children.

August set the tote down and followed suit, throwing his balloon with enough force to send splatters of purple all the way to the ceiling. They set into an exuberant pace of tossing the balloons close enough to each other that sprays of paint coated them as well as the walls, ceiling, and floors. By the time the tote was empty, the room as well as the two artists were a hot mess of paint splatters in every color imaginable.

"Umm . . ." Josie turned in a circle. "We have a problem."

August looked around, trying to see what his paint-speckled partner in crime was looking at. "What's that?"

"We've literally painted ourselves into not just a corner, but the *center* of the room!"

"You're absolutely right." August flipped the plastic container over, careful not to disturb any splatters, and gestured for her to have a seat with him. "Let's give it a little time to dry and then we'll try to tiptoe out of here. We're due a break, anyway."

They sat with their backs to each other and took in the now-lively space. Josie's body relaxed against him. August loved how comfortable she'd become with him. They'd come quite a long way since that day he'd first walked into the diner.

"The Knitting Club came in for breakfast yesterday," Josie said after they'd been sitting in silence for a while.

"Yeah?"

"Yep. Miss Bertie insisted that I ask you about an estranged couple and a possible pregnancy."

August tilted his head and let out a roar of laughter. "They don't waste any time, do they?"

An elbow landed in his side. "What'd you do?"

"I made up some hogwash so they'd get off my back about you."

Josie's body went rigid against his. "What about me?"

No one liked to be the focal point of the Knitting Club. Smiling to himself, August decided to goad her. "Oh, they were just implying that you'll never go for the likes of someone like me." He expected her to get flustered and start wiggling around, but he was pleasantly surprised when she did none of that. Instead, she reached behind her head and began combing her fingers through the hair along his neck. He was pretty sure she could feel the goose bumps rising along his skin underneath her touch.

"I do believe we've proven their ridiculous implications wrong already."

August couldn't contain the grin as she continued to comb through his hair. "I like proving those old broads wrong . . . They might have said something about you being too chicken to kiss me good and proper each time I visit you at the diner . . ."

A playful smack tapped against the side of his head. "Now you're pushing it, buddy." Josie snickered, clearly amused by his flirting.

Man, did he love making her laugh. Life could divvy out too many frowns and way too many tears, so he always viewed laughter as a gift that one should take advantage of as much as possible. If Josie would let go of some of her apprehension, he'd happily spend the remainder of his days supplying her with that gift and more.

"Humph," Josie said on a huff.

"What?" He glanced over his shoulder at her and saw her pointing toward the kitchen doors.

"I just realized there's things taped on the walls."

"Oh yeah. They're removable vinyl stickers. After the paint dries, we'll remove them to reveal different shapes and words underneath. I think it'll look pretty killer. A paint company is going to come in and seal the walls and floor afterward. That way the mess we made today will remain a mess."

"Humph," she repeated. "I'm impressed by the thoughtfulness you've put into the details for this place."

"The glass jar was lame though."

"Just a technical hiccup we solved rather easily." She pushed playfully against him.

August returned the push but with less force. "We make a pretty good team, don't ya think?"

"I agree. What are the images and words, by the way?"

"Now *that* you are just gonna have to wait and see." He inhaled the favorable scent of wet paint and gazed at the intricate mess they'd pulled off, excited to see the finished product himself. "How's your dad doing?"

"He's about the same. Standoffish, doing more and more of my duties, and snapping at me if I try doing them myself." She released a pensive sigh. "I just don't get it."

"Maybe he feels like he's put too much on you."

"I keep trying to get him to talk to me, but he just keeps brushing me off." Josie sighed and leaned heavily against him.

August really liked the idea of being her strength, so he held his back a little tauter to be the support she needed. He also wanted to be so much more to her.

Time, gotta give her time, he reminded himself.

"That Jasper can be one stubborn man, like most men, I suppose," August mused. "Just give him a little space. I'm sure he'll come to you when he's ready to share what's bothering him. In the meantime, I'd like you to help me test out an art project I want to do in one of my art sessions this summer."

Josie's posture stiffened, but it eased away almost instantly. "Okay."

August reached over his shoulder and ran his hand through her soft hair, feeling a damp spot here and there, knowing they'd both have a time getting rid of all the paint that had attached to their bodies during the paint balloon explosion. He didn't mind it, though. It was a way of life for him and he knew he'd be bringing traces of paint with him to the grave one day. "I sure hope God lets me paint in heaven."

Josie stiffened again. "Where'd that come from?"

"I don't know. It just came across my mind. I love painting so much that I just hope it's something I'm allowed to do for eternity."

Her head came to rest on his shoulder. "As long as you honor and worship God with it, I don't see why he wouldn't allow it in heaven."

"I honor and worship him with every art piece he allows me to create here on earth, so maybe I'm golden on it for heaven, too."

Josie's giggle pressed against his spine, and it instantly became his most favorite feeling in the world.

"I'm sure you are *golden*." She giggled again and the feel of it embraced his heart.

August wanted to tell her he was falling good and hard in love with her but asked instead, "You close tomorrow, correct?"

"Yes."

"Since you don't have to be up with the chickens in the morning, do you think you could stay out after dark for a little bit tonight?" A long drip of blue paint crawled a little farther down the wall in front of him, catching his eye.

"Yes, but not too late," she replied.

"No ma'am. Not too late. Meet me here around eight."

They sat there and watched paint dry for a while longer, neither seeming to be in a rush to be free from the other. Eventually, they took their shoes off and followed a winding maze of unsplattered floor out the door on their tiptoes.

Not wanting to let her go quite yet, August bumped his hip into hers as they strolled through the courtyard side by side. "You want to be let in on a secret?"

A twinkle flashed through the blue of her eyes. "I have something I need to do here shortly, but I have a little time to spare, so sure."

"Hold tight." August jogged toward the art building. "I just gotta grab some of the secret." After scooping up a handful of clues, he grabbed a pen and the map he and Carter were using to log in the secret locations. He turned and found Josie by the door, looking on with curiosity.

"What are you up to?"

August held up the baubles and trinkets dangling from leather cords that were made up from stones, wooden medallions, feathers, and other similar whatnots. "I need your help hiding some clues around camp."

Josie took a step closer and surveyed the booty in his hand. "Where'd you get these?"

"Tucker and I made them. Zachary helped some, too." August took one and rubbed the wood medallion over a glob of orange clinging to the shoulder of her shirt. "Now we have a signature Josie clue." He winked at her and wrapped each one around her neck. Even though her lovely face was camouflaged in flecks of the rainbow, he noticed the pink blooming along her cheeks. "I want to kiss you."

Josie blinked slowly and murmured, "Okay."

August didn't linger long, just placed a sweet caress on her warm lips before taking a step away from her.

She giggled and pointed toward him. "You have blue paint on your bottom lip now."

A deep groan worked its way loose from his throat. "I never want to wash it off. Nothing better than a painted-up kiss." He winked after delivering the tease and decided it was time to put some space between them before he lost control and tried to swipe some more blue paint. He stepped outside into the bright sunshine. The more time he spent with Josie, the more vivid life became.

"What exactly are these for?" Josie asked as she followed him toward the woods.

August stopped at a low-hanging tree branch and handed her the map and pen and then pulled a trinket from around her neck. "We hide them throughout the camp. Campers have to identify at least six of them either by marking them on a copy of this map of the campgrounds or by snapping pics with their phones." He reached up to pull down a branch and tied the clue securely around it before letting it spring skyward. He tapped the map. "Will you put an X right there?"

Josie placed the X in the rightful spot and asked, "And what is the prize?"

"Random stuff. Camp T-shirts or hoodies, hats, phone cases, lanyards, drawstring bags . . ."

They moved past the tree house cabins and ended up at a small chapel that resembled a kid's playhouse.

Josie gasped. "I had no idea this was out here. Y'all have treasures hidden everywhere." She hurried inside with August following. The mini chapel held only four pews, but it was spectacular.

"That's the whole point in the hidden clues. It's to motivate the campers into exploring the campgrounds instead of hanging out in the cabins during downtime." August moved out the back door and tied a trinket over the doorframe.

Josie watched him before making a note on the map. They did this for most of the next hour, moving from the chapel to a flower garden with a gazebo in the midst of it. After they left a clue underneath the vine-woven roof, August led her to a veranda that covered a nice-size cement slab. Giant plastic containers full of chalk seemed to be waiting for someone to wander along and doodle on the slab. Of course, Josie couldn't resist grabbing a piece of chalk, and August couldn't resist watching her as he tucked a clue in a shrub. She hummed out some unfamiliar tune while she drew dancing sunshine with orange-and-yellow swirls. He wanted to pick up a piece of chalk and join her, but the day was beginning to slip by too fast.

"All right, young lady, I'd say we're done for the day." August folded the map, tucked it into his back pocket, and held his hand out to her. A thrill worked through him when Josie took it willingly.

"I love all of the understated details y'all have put into this place," Josie complimented once they returned to the art building.

August gave her a warm smile as he put away the map for safekeeping. "All part of the plan." He led her to the parking lot.

"What plan?"

"To make people fall for us." August winked, placed a kiss on her paint-splattered cheek, and tucked her inside the truck. "Hurry home and get washed up. We have big plans for tonight."

"August, you have more charm than one person needs. You know that, right?" she teased, making him laugh.

"All part of the plan." He waited for her to ask what plan, but Josie was too smart to fall for that. Besides, he had a feeling she'd already figured out his plan by that point.

19

Shielding her eyes from the sun with one hand while the other was settled on her hip, Josie hollered, "You are not Zacchaeus! Get down off that roof this instant!"

"I can't!" Theo hollered back, clinging to the crooked weather vane with a rooster on top.

"Why not?" Josie began climbing up the ladder that was leaning against the white clapboard house.

"I'm . . . I'm scared. . . ."

Grunting, Josie made it to the top and sat on the sloped roof beside a frightened Theo. "I told you I would be by today to patch the roof. Why didn't you wait?"

"You say I ain't Zacchaeus! Well, you ain't Jesus. You can't be everywhere at the same time." Theo cut her a knowing look.

Josie was taken aback by the truth of his statement and had to just sit there in the sweltering heat for a few beats, staring at the sandy yard below. There wasn't much grass but she could see where Theo had freshly mowed it. Taking a deep inhale and huffing it out, she looked over at him and cringed when noticing the puckering skin along his cheeks. "Oh, Theo, you're sunburnt to a crisp. We've got to get you down."

"I ain't white like you. I don't get sunburn."

"That's incorrect. Doesn't your face hurt?"

He scrunched his face and cringed. "Yeah."

"That's sunburn." Josie looked around, finding a scattering of tools, a stack of new shingles, and a small bit of rope tied to the hammer. She'd prepared all that and left it on the porch earlier before heading to the camp and wished that's where Theo had left it. She undid the rope and wove it through his belt loop and then hers, tethering them together. "Okay, Theo, this is how we're going to do this. I'll start down the ladder first and you will follow me."

"I . . . I don't know . . ."

"I'll be right behind you. Plus, we're tied together, so no way can you fall. You'll be safe. Promise." It was only a one-story house, so she felt confident in the promise.

It took many agonizing minutes to talk Theo into it and that many more before they both made it to the ground in one piece. Josie hurried Theo inside, and after directing him to have a seat at the kitchen table, she plundered through the medicine cabinet and came up empty-handed. Deandrea's bedroom door was closed, and that always meant she was having a bad day, so Josie chose not to bother her. Instead, she searched through a few more cabinets before finally remembering there was an aloe plant on the porch. She rushed out there and broke off a section of it and moved back inside.

Josie showed Theo the green plant with the clear liquid beginning to ooze from the end. "I'm going to apply this to the burn. It'll help soothe it. Then I'll call Doc Nelson and see what he thinks—okay with you?"

"You're covered in paint," Theo pointed out instead of answering her.

"I was working at the camp this morning," she mumbled, focusing on carefully applying the aloe on his cheeks and forehead, inwardly cringing with knowing the poor guy had to be in pain.

"Paint looks good on you, like you should be wearing it all the time." Theo tried to smile but stopped short and winced.

"How long were you up there?"

"For a while. I dunno." Theo shrugged.

"Promise you won't do something like that again."

"Okay." He sighed. "It's still hurting."

Josie made Theo a glass of ice water, worried he might be close to dehydration as well. "Let me give Doc a call."

It took a spell to get Doc on the phone, during which Josie chanced a peek inside Deandrea's room. Finally she heard Doc's voice. "Sorry about the holdup. We're as wide-open as a Case knife."

"That's okay," Josie reassured him, before quickly filling him in on Theo's situation.

"I'll call in a prescription for Silvadene, but in the meantime, give him a dose of Benadryl and tell him to take a rest on the couch."

"Benadryl will help?" Josie asked, not thinking about that.

"It'll help the boy get still somewhere for a little while. And if he's resting, then he won't be hurting," Doc explained.

"Oh. Okay. Thanks, Doc."

"No problem. How's Deandrea today?"

Josie sighed and glanced at the closed door. "Not good. She won't get out of bed. What can I do?"

"I've seen depression climb on somebody like the plague. Let me make some calls and see."

"Okay. So I can head to the pharmacy to pick up the prescription?"

"I'll call as soon as we hang up."

"Thanks again."

"You're welcome."

After hanging up, Josie rummaged through the cabinet once again and fished out two pink tablets. She put a DVD on and sat with Theo until he dozed off. Once he was settled, she hurried into town and picked up the ointment and some other supplies. After that was taken care of, she took care of patching the roof.

It had been a long day, but Josie made herself a cup of coffee to refuel for the night ahead before washing off the paint and grime.

As twilight settled in and began toning the day down, Josie arrived back at camp in a fresh set of shorts and a T-shirt after scrubbing for close to an hour in the shower. A few stiff spots in her hair told her she hadn't quite been able to remove all the paint.

"You ready?" August reached for her hand and began walking toward the wooded area behind the main buildings.

Smiling at his persistence in giving her a choice, she said, "Sure."

He led them in the direction of the amphitheater and skirted around it to where the camp opened up to a large recreation field. There was just enough light glowing from the night-lights near the cabins and the amphitheater to illuminate the quilt and two blank canvases set up in the midst of the open space.

August didn't stop until they stood at the edge of the blanket. "Have a seat and I'll explain this idea."

Josie did as he instructed. After she crossed her legs, he placed one of the canvases in her lap and handed her an open pen.

"One of my sessions is titled 'Design through the Senses.'" He pulled a folded bandanna out of his back pocket. "The idea is to create an art piece without the use of sight. May I?" He lifted the bandanna.

Josie nodded her head and closed her eyes as the soft fabric covered them. "Eyesight is considered the most important sense to an artist."

"Yes, but I want my students to understand that you need all of your senses to create art. And leaning too heavily on just one of them is careless. I want them to feel the art. To listen as their pen moves across the canvas."

After the bandanna was secured, he took her hand and settled it against the canvas. To Josie's disappointment, he moved away from her and took his warmth with him. "Don't leave me."

"I won't. I'm sitting in front of you." His shoe nudged her knee, giving her some comfort in knowing he was near. "I'm tying on my blindfold . . . Okay. Let's draw."

"This is weird," Josie muttered, unsure about what to do.

"Just picture the image you want to create in your head and allow your hand to free it on the canvas."

"Easier said than done."

August chuckled but said nothing else.

Josie's thoughts went straight to her companion, unable to focus on anything else. She'd been on a few casual dates over the years, but none of them left a lasting impression. No connection was made with any of the guys. Either they didn't get her or she simply didn't get them. But this man sitting in the dark on the quilt in front of her truly understood her. When she wasn't with him, she was thinking about him. Life before his return was dull in only subtle shades of gray, but now everything burst with color and vibrant movement.

With Josie's thoughts centered, she suddenly heard the pen scratch against the surface of the canvas before realizing she was drawing. The texture of the canvas tickled against the side of her palm as the pen created who-knew-what. She decided not to worry about what it should be or what it couldn't become, and just let the pen go in whatever direction felt natural . . .

"Are you about done?" August's deep voice broke the trance.

"Didn't we just get started?"

"About an hour ago."

Josie's hand moved over the canvas a few more sweeps before stilling. "Okay. I'm done." She was about to reach up and remove the blindfold when she sensed the warmth of August's presence just before his breath tickled her lips. She waited for him to move to do what, she didn't exactly know, but minutes passed with only his breath mingling with hers. It wasn't a kiss, but in her opinion it was quite possibly the best kiss she had ever received.

Josie took in a deep inhale. "You always smell like a masterpiece," she blurted and was surprised by her words. From August's quick intake of breath, he was also. She sensed him moving closer until his soft lips pressed just beside her parted lips.

"A masterpiece?" He spoke the two-worded question against her skin, making her shiver.

"Yes. That unique smell of paint and crisp new canvas." She tilted her head to the side and edged forward until she found the warmth of his neck. "And something completely unique to you . . . a masterpiece . . ."

"I could get lost in you, Josie Slater. Lost in every way." August pressed a tender kiss to her lips as the blindfold loosened and slipped away from her eyes.

Blinking a few times, Josie found him staring at her. They remained silent as her eyes cataloged the moment. The sultry air was bristling through his thick hair and the moonlight highlighted the seriousness on his handsome face. Slowly he leaned forward again, but before he made much progress, a long streak of water came from out of nowhere and nailed him between the eyes. A forceful slap of water hit Josie in the shoulder as she spotted Tucker darting across the field wielding a serious-looking water gun.

"Attack!" Carter yelled from somewhere in the dark.

August growled as he pulled Josie to her feet and started sprinting toward the patch of trees. Several more pops of water nailed them before they could find cover.

Heaving, August yelled, "It's not fair to attack a man who can't defend himself!"

Water pelts continued to whiz by them, some making contact, as Josie clung to August's arm. Something buzzed through the air and landed at her feet. Another one clattered close to it.

"These aren't even half the size of theirs!" she whined but picked the water guns up and handed one to August, anyway.

"Beggars can't be choosers." August was all business as he jumped out from behind the tree and charged toward the field, hollering like a wild man as he went.

Josie stayed rooted by the tree, giggling at the hilarity of the grown guys going at it with water guns. Much to her relief, she wasn't left alone for very long. "How did they know we were here?"

"Because the idiot told us!" Carter unleashed his water gun on her as Josie unleashed a scream.

Having enough, a jolt of adrenaline had Josie taking off through the darkness in hot pursuit after Carter. "Don't hide from me now, Mr. Fibber!" She caught up with him and set out to emptying her water ammunition on him as they lapped the shadowy field.

As she hurried to refill the gun at a conveniently placed water hose by the small storage building, she heard Tucker shout out, "That's my gun, punk!"

"Not anymore, *sucker*!" August's boisterous laugh rang out over the field as Tucker started squealing like a little girl.

The water war continued until all four were drenched and quite winded. Without much ceremony, Tucker and Carter slunk off into the night just as stealthily as they had appeared while Josie helped August gather the canvases and quilt, which had somehow managed to make it through the attack relatively unscathed.

"This place is creepy cool at night with it being so deserted." Josie gazed around the dark woods as the constant crackling of leaves and little twigs gave way underneath her shoes.

"Except for water gun–wielding ninjas," August interjected.

"Of course." Josie snickered just as a loud splash interrupted the near quietness. "They're swimming now?"

"Probably. We've been sneaking out here most nights. Gotta make sure the pool is decent enough for the campers, ya know. That's why I warned them we'd be here tonight." August chuckled. "Guess the attack was my fault."

"It's okay. The water felt good with it being such a humid night." Josie pulled the collar of her drying shirt away, not enjoying how it was already growing sticky from the heat.

August pulled out a key and unlocked the art building. "Let's see what these canvases hold." After flipping on the lights, he dropped the quilt so he could conceal the canvas behind his back. "You first."

Blinking a few times to adjust to the sudden light, Josie turned her canvas so they could inspect it. Heat crawled up her neck and onto her cheeks, but August smiled warmly at the confession doodled all over the piece.

August reached a hand out and traced the letters with his index finger. "You wrote my name . . . and I like the hearts all around it." He looked up and met her nervous gaze. "But I think the wings are my favorite." Several sets of wings, resembling the ones she drew on the fairies earlier, were scattered around the canvas.

Josie dropped the canvas to her side, but August tugged it out of her grasp. "Ugh. I feel like a silly schoolgirl doodling her crush's name." She rolled her eyes and shook her head.

"When I drew on that postcard and left it on the counter, did you think of me as some silly kid passing you a note in class?" He raised his dark eyebrows.

"No."

He lifted the canvas slightly. "There's nothing silly about your drawing, Jo. I really like the idea of me being in your thoughts enough that you'd pour it out on this."

She huffed. "At least show me yours so I don't feel so weird about mine."

Without hesitation, August pulled the canvas from behind his back. Stunned, they both stared at it with pinched-up faces. August handed Josie her canvas and ran his fingers over his. "I can't believe I forgot to open my pen."

"Invisible art." Josie snickered.

August held up a finger. "Maybe not. Let's see if I left a hidden message." He walked over to a supply cabinet and pulled out a piece of charcoal and began running it softly over the top of the canvas. Slowly an image emerged.

Josie gasped as a slightly obscured image of her laughing appeared.

"See. You're on my mind, too." August gazed at Josie for a spell before clearing his throat. "Okay, young lady, it's getting near your bedtime." He led her outside and placed a tender kiss on her cheek before tucking her into the truck. "Good night."

"It has been. Thank you."

August tipped his head and closed the door.

Josie drove home with thoughts of her wish still fresh on her mind. Those wings were her expressing the desire to be free to follow after the dreams and goals she'd allowed to grow dormant. August Bradford had persistently dared her to allow them to reawaken in the last few weeks. Only problem was she couldn't figure out how to set it all free while still remaining grounded in her duties to her dad and the diner. And she was still avoiding the dreadful conversation she was going to have to have with August about the job offer. Sure, she managed to balance the small projects and work, but anything more than that seemed impossible.

• • •

"Honey, you're looking a little rough today . . . and is that paint in your hair?" Opal reached over from her lounge chair and tried working out the dried clump but only managed to pull Josie's hair.

"Ouch!" Josie leaned out of her reach and glanced at her watch. "Just leave it. I'll try to get it out after work."

"I wish you didn't have to work today. I've missed you," Sophia commented as she lathered sunblock on her son's shoulders while the toddler tried wrestling free from her grasp.

"I know . . ." Josie fiddled with the unraveling hem of her shorts. "How's things going, Sophia?"

Sophia said nothing until Collin wandered over to the shore. In a lowered tone, she said, "Ty moved back in last week on a trial basis."

Opal perked up. "Oh, that's wonderful news."

Josie squinted at Sophia. "There's a *but* in there."

"Some photographs of him dancing at a club with one of the cheerleaders from his team made the gossip rounds. The PR team suggested we give the marriage another try, for Ty's career image. Dumb reason, I know, but I only agreed for my son's sake." Sophia shrugged.

"Aw, honey. What does Ty say about it?"

"Ty doesn't say anything. He's focused on workouts and getting in shape for training camp," Sophia mumbled, sounding anything but optimistic about a reconciliation. "And those photos . . ."

Josie pulled her phone out and did an internet search that quickly offered up the photos. Shaking her head, she said with confidence, "This is a team event. Really, there's nothing amiss in this pic that I haven't seen hundreds of times before with Ty. . . . I recall pictures going around about two years ago of you dancing with one of the tight ends and all the gossip that broke loose about the two of you. Remember how silly that was?"

"Josie's right. The media twisted that about you and now they're doing it about Ty. Don't let gossip win, honey." Opal stood and wandered over to the shore, where Collin was scooping up shells.

"It's just been so stressful." Sophia's words escaped on a heavy sigh.

"I bet." Josie watched Collin and Opal walk the shore with brightly colored sand buckets in hand and slightly stooped over, like detectives on the hunt for clues.

"How about you? How are things going?" Sophia asked.

Josie understood the desire Sophia had for changing the subject. She also understood her worries seemed trivial compared to her friend's struggling marriage. Rather than whine about what was truly bothering her, Josie chose to tell Sophia all about the unexpected adventures she'd been on as of late. By the time she had to leave for work, Josie had her friend in stitches.

"That fishing trip and water fight are just too hilarious." Sophia laughed some more.

"Yeah. That family is something else." Josie couldn't contain the affection she felt for the entire bunch that made up August's world. "Okay, friend, I'm off to work now." Josie stood but bent over to give Sophia a hug. "Hang in there."

"I'm trying my best." There was no missing the anguish in Sophia's voice.

Josie squeezed one last time before walking up the beach and into the busy diner. The counter was lined with customers, and several more were waiting for a turn. She quickly washed her hands, tied on her apron, and got lost in the lunch rush. She held a smile firmly on her face, but there was no denying the fact that her heart just wasn't in it anymore. Busy as they were, Josie didn't think the clock would ever move to closing time.

On autopilot, she locked the door at two o'clock and began stacking chairs on top of the tables as one of the waitresses finished washing them down. Just as they finished closing down, August emerged from the kitchen.

Blinking, Josie asked, "Where did you come from?"

"The kitchen." He smirked while hitching his thumb over his shoulder.

"How so?"

"I offered to clean fryers, so they let me in the kitchen entrance without further comment."

Josie leaned into him and took a sniff. Sure enough, a greasy aroma masked his normal, more appealing, scent of fresh soap and paint. "Why exactly are you cleaning fryers again?"

August reached over and brushed a wisp of Josie's

blonde hair from her forehead and then briefly cupped her cheek. "I've made plans with a certain Slater. Very important plans."

Before she could ask what the plans were or simply swoon, her dad came bustling out of the kitchen.

"This ain't gonna be purty," Jasper told August with apprehension scrunching his features.

"No worries. It's just like riding a bike. You never really forget."

"I may not have forgotten, but my body may not *allow* it."

Josie noticed both men were wearing board shorts, which sent her adventurous spirit plummeting quicker than her dad probably would plummet off the surfboard.

"Meet me out back in a few. Gotta see a man about a fish real quick." Jasper headed outside, still grumbling about surfing being a bad idea.

August ignored his griping and turned to Josie. He reached out and playfully pinched her protruding bottom lip. "You're too cute when you're pouting."

"No, I'm not." She scoffed.

"Not cute or not pouting?" He tilted his head and gazed at her warmly.

"Both." She cut her eyes at him. "Don't let my daddy get hurt."

"Yes, ma'am." August glanced around before leaning down and giving her a quick kiss. "I'll see you in the morning at church."

"Oh, that reminds me. I want to collect on a favor."

"I'll give you another kiss, woman. No need to use up a favor for it." August leaned in, but Josie angled away and giggled.

"No, I need something else," she clarified. "Remember me telling you about Theo while we painted the other day?"

"Yes." He nodded.

"Do you think it's possible to find him a job at the camp? Maybe one where he can stay there during the summer session? I think it would do him good and—" Before she could continue rambling or start begging, August quieted her with another kiss.

He remained in her space and said, "It wouldn't hurt you to use a favor for yourself just once. It's always all about everyone else with you, but, Jo, you're just as important."

"I . . . uh . . . but I'm fine." She began to fidget. "So do you think finding Theo a job is possible?"

Shaking his head, August chuckled. "Let me talk to Carter and see what we can come up with." He pressed his lips to her forehead and added, "Your heart is too beautiful, Miss Slater." After a subtle wink, he sauntered out the door.

It took a few moments of standing frozen in the middle of the dining room before Josie could collect herself enough to finish out the day. Once everything was clean and put away, Josie saw the few employees out and then settled on the deck to watch the two men who meant an awfully lot to her. They spent more time frolicking in the ocean than surfing due to the fact that Jasper couldn't manage to stay upright on his board. Eventually August must have given up as Josie watched them move past the waves and straddle their boards instead of riding them.

Josie caught herself giggling a few times as she focused on August. He seemed to be having a lively conversation with her dad. His hands animatedly waved around as he told Jasper all about something she couldn't hear. Shaking her head at the idea of them becoming buddies, she decided to leave them be to have their fun and head over to spend some time with Dalma.

20

"I need you."

That's all it took for Josie to agree to help August once he filled her in on what exactly he needed from her. He smiled, relieved that she was finally coming around, as the special guests arrived at the camp for a weekend retreat.

"Only three more weeks before this scene blows up ten times bigger." Carter rubbed his hands together as the colorful bus pulled into the parking lot.

August stood beside his uncle, equally excited. "Yeah, man. This is going to be one epic adventure you've gotten us into. Thank you for letting me be a part of it."

Carter slapped him on the back. "No way would I do this without you. Come on. Let's go welcome them." He set off in a hurried pace with August by his side.

As the bus doors opened, Josie scooted down the steps first, followed by Dominica holding hands with the camp's guest of honor. The young lady with lopsided glasses and a whimsical smile had stolen their hearts a few years ago and never returned it. Emma immediately let go of Dominica's hand and made a beeline for Carter.

"I like this place. Yes, I really like this place." Emma nodded, sending her wispy strawberry-blonde hair to dance around. "Carter, Dominica said we are making music. Lots and lots of music. I like that. I like that a lot."

Carter patted her on the shoulder. "Of course. We

can't do this without music. I hope you're ready to play me a song on the new keyboard we have in the music room."

The eighteen-year-old began chatting away about a new song her piano teacher was teaching her back home in Charleston.

Josie walked over to August with a wide grin on her face as about a dozen other young people filed off the bus, most with a parent or a shadow. "This is a great way to open up the first session of camp."

"I think so too," August agreed before moving over and helping with the luggage.

"August, we're making music!" Emma hollered out.

August turned around to look at the sweet angel who taught them all to appreciate the uniqueness of autism and that nothing was off-limits as long as you believe in it. "Yes, but I'm going to be offended if you don't make art with me too."

Emma looked around and seemed to ignore August's tease. "You made the walls into a coloring book. Your coloring book needs to be colored."

"That's the plan." August chuckled as he and Josie watched Emma walk off with Dominica, quietly rambling as they went.

"She's chatty compared to your other guests," Josie commented while a few other campers, whose ages varied from late teens to early twenties, stayed glued to their shadow's side with their eyes cast to the ground.

"Because she's comfortable around us. Carter and I actually met her during a summer ministry program several years ago and we've kept in touch ever since, but Dominica is her favorite now. Emma and her parents made a few trips to the camp while it was being built, so I think that's helped her being at ease here already." August started walking toward the cabins with an armful of suitcases.

"Really? That's pretty neat." She glanced over her shoulder at the campers again. "I hope the rest of them will have a good time."

"We had a specialist who focuses on autism meet with us a few times. She gave us a lot of advice on how to help them get the most out of the weekend. The itinerary has been catered specifically for them to have a good time."

A little over an hour later, they entered the mess hall with its vividly painted walls that revealed a large camp logo with palmetto trees along the left side wall and a giant fork and spoon standing guard at the kitchen entrance door. Josie looked appreciatively at the newly revealed white images that had been previously hidden underneath the splatters as the new aroma of spicy marinara and garlic took over the previous paint scent.

"Pretty cool, Mr. Bradford." She nudged August on the arm as they went over to the buffet table to select their pizza.

"We did good, Miss Slater." He nodded his head to the campers, who were gazing at the colorful paint splatters. Their faces lit up in awe. The weekend ahead was looking quite optimistic.

Early the next morning, the art studio was filled with wary-looking campers. August took in the project at hand, hoping he'd kept the complication out of it. The specialist warned them to never overwhelm the special-needs campers. "This morning we printed off the photos you took yesterday. We are going to take the photos and glue them to iPad cases."

Josie handed each camper their bundle of pictures. They let the young adults take their time flipping through them. Bowls of glue and sponge paintbrushes were placed on each table, waiting to be used to transform the black cases into individual works of art. August took a moment to explain decoupage and a few facts about the technique, but no one took the initiative to start.

"May I?" Josie asked Emma, pointing to the pictures spread out before her.

Emma handed her a photo and the other campers seemed to lean in that direction to get a better look. Josie smiled enthusiastically before tearing the edges of the black-and-white photo Emma had taken of the pool. Once the edges were artfully jagged, she slathered glue on the back of it and then pressed it onto the case.

"If you brush a layer of glue on top, it'll seal the photo," Josie advised as she offered Emma the paintbrush to do just that.

Emma scanned Josie's face for a moment as if making her mind up about her. "You have freckles like me." Emma tapped the tip of her nose, where a few pink dots added character, and then reached up and tapped Josie's tan freckles on her nose. "We match."

"Yes, we do." Josie gently tapped Emma's nose, and August could do nothing but smile admiringly from where he stood at the front of the room. "Are you ready to add another photo, Emma?"

Emma went to it and the next thing August knew, others were beckoning Josie over to show them how to tear the photos. After watching in astonishment for a moment, August moved over and helped out. They set no time limit on the class, as advised by the specialist. That way those who tired of the project could freely go on to something else, while the ones who might have wanted to spend the entire day on the project could do so without feeling any pressure to finish.

After two stragglers finally made it out the door hours later, Josie helped August clean up.

"That was a hit." Josie playfully bumped into him with her hip as she passed by.

August brushed a pile of photo scraps into the trash bin he was holding. "Yeah, it was after you broke the ice. Now they all have a custom case that they personally designed."

"How'd you even know to do iPad cases? What if someone doesn't have one?"

"No worries. Carter bought each camper one."

Josie dumped a bunch of sponge brushes into a bucket filled with water, causing a small splash. "Say what?"

"He used their camp registration fee to purchase the iPads."

"You say that like it's no big deal to blow your earnings on the campers." Josie scoffed.

"This camp isn't about making money. It's about making a difference." August moved over to gather up the bottles of Mod Podge glue, but Josie stepped in his way. "What?"

She gestured for him to lean close, and when he complied, Josie placed a slow, sweet kiss against his lips. With her blue eyes locked on his, she broke their connection and said softly, "You, August Bradford, are making a difference. More than you know."

He didn't know about that. He sure did hope he was, but even being unsure on the matter didn't keep the grin from his face. She'd just made him feel like a million bucks.

The two-day retreat went off with only a few hiccups, but nothing major in August's opinion. All the special-needs campers seemed to enjoy themselves after settling in to the atmosphere. And boy, did Josie shine, just as August knew she would. She was a natural teacher and helped out with the other two art sessions, where they focused

on freedom of design so that none of the campers felt
overwhelmed with learning something too unfamiliar. He
caught himself several times just watching her, thinking
how she belonged in the midst of the happenings at camp.

By the time the small group departed Sunday afternoon, August realized it was time to have a talk with Josie
about accepting the job offer. He just hoped it would be
the answer he was seeking.

• • •

The following week, Carter gave August his final ultima-
tum about holding off on interviewing someone else to
fill the art instructor position. Hesitant to say one way or
the other, he left his uncle at the camp and headed to the
diner around closing time. Josie was behind the counter,
a frown on her beautiful face, and was focused on her
laptop screen.

August leaned over the counter and tried to catch her
attention. "Have dinner with me."

She glanced up from the laptop. "Tonight?"

"Yes. I know you have to open in the morning, so I
promise not to keep you out late. How about six at the
firehouse?"

She hitched a tired eyebrow up, and he knew he
should leave her alone to get some rest, but he'd started
to grow selfish with wanting as much time with her as
possible. Plus, there was a certain conversation he couldn't
put off any longer.

After keying something else in, she moved those soft-
blue eyes to him. "Okay."

"Great." He tapped the countertop and stood. "I'll
see you then." With that, he rushed out the door on a
mission.

21

Releasing a drowsy sigh, Josie parked in front of the fire-house and climbed out of the truck. She took a second to stretch her tired back before moving to the side door. She raised her hand to knock, but before her knuckles connected to the surface, the door swung open.

Standing on the other side of the door, August stared at Josie with happiness lighting his handsome face, and she could have sworn there was a glow in his blue eyes. Each time she was face-to-face with him, it was like finally getting to the head of the line for the most thrilling roller-coaster ride imaginable—one she was equally excited to participate in as well as unsure if she could handle.

As she debated on whether to step out of line and pass up her turn, August grasped her hand and pulled her inside. "I've got an art exhibit I'd like to show you before we eat, if that's okay."

"Okay," Josie mumbled, feeling she really had no choice in the matter as he began leading her up the set of wrought iron stairs that led to the loft. "All this time and I've not gone up here once," she mused out loud.

"Ah, but it was for your own good. It would have been too tempting to lock you in my tower and never let you go," August teased and followed it with a menacing laugh.

Josie couldn't help but join in with a tired snicker. "Have you been watching Disney princess movies with Zachary again?"

August gave her a side-eye glare. "Thought we discussed the importance of never mentioning that."

"Which one did you watch with him this time?"

"Woman." His deep voice boomed, but there was a
playful expression fighting to break through his feigned
scold.

As Josie moved her attention away from the man who
was too cute for words and saw the sitting area upstairs
for the first time, she choked on air.

"It's a fine exhibit, don't you think?" He plowed on
quickly, not giving her time to question him or flee.
"Allow me to explain them."

"August—"

He took a few steps to the brick wall and halted in
front of the profile painting of her. "You light up when
you paint. When I watch you get lost in your art, there's
no denying that's what you were created to do." He ran
his fingers down the pink cheek on the canvas, close to
the same shade her cheeks carried most of the time when
in his presence. "This is exactly what you look like when
you teach Sunday school and how you looked when you
helped me teach the art sessions this weekend . . . Jo,
you *shine*."

"Les rêves peuvent se réaliser." She slowly spoke the
words that were painted at the bottom of the piece, knowing she was butchering the beauty of the language, before
looking over at him for an explanation.

August repeated with a much smoother cadence, *"Les
rêves peuvent se réaliser.* Dreams can come true."

"What dreams does this picture represent?" She
motioned toward her profile.

"Any dream that makes your beautiful face shine like
that." He studied the painting and then Josie.

When she glanced toward the stairs, he quickly moved them over to the handprint painting. "I had my assumptions on this one, and over the last month and a half it's been confirmed."

Brows pinched, she kept her eyes trained on the picture. "What's been confirmed?"

"Although our hands are different sizes, you have to admit we make a perfect pair." August reached over and aligned their palms. "Each project we've worked on together is proof. Our styles vary, but put them together and look . . ." With his free hand, August gestured to the three pop art paintings. "We create masterpieces."

"Perfect pair?" Josie took a guess at the translation of the words written at the bottom of the canvas.

"*Oui. Paire parfaite.*"

Josie nodded and took a step over to the last painting, holding her questions until he was done.

August brushed his fingers over the three words added to the bottom. "*Rêve, Audace, Brillance.*"

Josie shook her head, not quite understanding the translation.

"*Dream, Bold,* and *Shine.* It's the three words I envisioned for this piece. This painting is busy and chaotic, but with reason . . . with purpose. It reflects our lives. One I want us to work on together as a team."

Josie wasn't sure if he meant a personal relationship or a professional one, but she was too much of a coward to ask. Better to wait and let him explain when he was ready. At the moment, she didn't think she needed any more to worry about.

"I have one more piece to show you." August led her to an art easel in the corner and pulled the cover off to reveal a collage of surprising beauty.

Josie gasped. "How'd you get these?" She pointed to the various pages displaying her elaborate designs. Designs she thought were hidden among stacks of books in Dalma's living room.

"Funny story." August chuckled and ran his fingers through his hair, brushing the thick locks away from his eyes. "Dalma has been giving me books over the last few weeks every time I'm at her house. I kept sticking them in the truck and had no idea I was driving around stunning artwork. I discovered the hidden treasure the same day we danced in the rain."

Josie's face warmed as her eyes remained fastened to the collage of book pages. "But . . . how'd you know I did this?"

August turned and stood blocking most of the collage so she had to look at him. "Give me some credit, Jo. I can spot your artwork, but one page in particular confirmed it." Wearing an impish smirk, he reached behind the easel and came back with a single page. The familiar *A* fashioned from the Eiffel Tower caught her eye first. "I love the design you made with my name."

Josie attempted to snatch it from his hand, but he yanked it out of reach. "I can't believe that rascally woman gave you my books," she growled and tried again to grab the paper without success, trying not to panic. Some of the books actually held more than just her designs, and she made a mental note to swing by Dalma's and try finding them before August got his hands on those too.

August wrapped his arm around Josie's waist and firmly planted her at his side. "Your heart is on display all over those pages. Jo, you're doing the world an injustice by not sharing this." He waved the page toward the collage.

"Life hasn't given me the opportunity to share it," she whispered, turning her eyes to the wood floor.

"Looks to me like you're finally getting an opportunity. What do you think?" His eyes brightened.

With so much on her plate, did she want to go there right now? *No.* Too tired to go anywhere near it, she said instead, "I think I'm ready to eat."

August took it as a joke, his head inclining as he let out a rumble of laughter. "Then I guess I should feed you." He halted her retreat when she turned away from the paintings. "Whoa. Before I do, I'd like to steal this memory." He turned Josie so she was facing the paintings.

"Okay. Tell me how we're going to steal this one." She wrapped her arm around the crook of his and waited to be wooed a little more. The man even had wooing down to an art form, even though she didn't think he realized it.

"When I look at these paintings, I'll remember when I began drawing them as a surprise for you and the moment I realized I was willing to do whatever it took to have you in my life." He pointed to the canvases. "You see, your soul is painted in the same colors as mine, so I knew this was all it would take to convince you."

"Then I'll remember it the same." She smiled, thinking the ruggedly handsome artist had a poetic side to him as well. "August, my life is a hot mess right now, but I want to thank you for allowing me to be a part of yours."

"The pleasure is all mine, ma'am." August placed a gentle kiss on her forehead before leading Josie to the dining table. He pulled a chair out for her to have a seat.

As she settled in the chair, she watched him tug on oven mittens. From the savory smell of garlic and oregano perfuming the air, she just knew he had prepared lasagna. Instead, he pulled a pizza box from the oven. Now she had to laugh. "I thought you were actually cooking me something."

"I've kept it warmed to perfection." He placed giant slices on two plates and sat them on the table before moving over to the fridge and reemerging with two glass bottles of soda. "Confession: if it's not going into a deep fryer or on a grill, I'm useless."

Josie snickered. "Thank goodness."

"Why?" August asked while grabbing a handful of napkins.

"I was beginning to worry there wasn't one thing you weren't good at." She took the napkin he offered.

August joined her at the table. "Hope this doesn't ruin my superhero status."

Josie eyed him. "Superhero?"

He gave her a coy smile. "I heard y'all that day on the beach."

Heat circled her neck and climbed over her cheeks, but she decided to play it off. "I won't tell Opal about your lack of cooking skills so she can keep thinking of you as her superhero." They both laughed.

After saying grace, they dug in.

A few bites in, August wiped his mouth and said, "Seriously though, I got caught up at the camp with some supply deliveries. I had good intentions of coming up with something a little more elegant than this for you . . . but you know how it is."

"Truly, I do." Josie reached for her cola as she let out a sluggish yawn.

"Busy lunch shift?" August asked.

"Yes. The season is gearing up, so I have to adjust the work schedule and put in more food orders from our suppliers. It's a bit daunting." She shook her head. "Enough about that. Are y'all set to open the camp on time? Is everything a go?"

"Seems close to it. We hired a few more camp counselors and a recreation director today. We only have one more instructor position to fill and the staff lineup will be complete."

"That's good. What position is left?" She knew what position but played ignorant and plucked a banana pepper off the slice of pizza and popped it into her mouth.

"Art instructor." August wiped his mouth with a napkin and grew serious. "That position has been set aside for you, but Carter says time is running out. Are you still considering it?"

Her stomach did a flip. "I don't know . . . Honestly, between helping you and my diner duties, I don't think I can make it work."

August nodded his head in the direction of the paintings hanging on the wall behind her. "You know you want to shine. That position will allow you to."

She chose not to look at them and stared down at the half-eaten pizza. "It's not that simple. I don't think I can, and I figured you would have found someone else by now."

"What happened to that girl eating sand to show off that she *can*? You didn't let anyone or anything get in the way back then."

Josie considered talking it out with August to see if they could find a way to make it happen, but she ended up choosing silence and another bite of pizza instead, knowing it was ultimately her problem and not his.

She was worn thin and her dad was looking equally haggard lately. She was worried about him. All the man did was work, work, work, and for some reason he'd started taking on her job, too.

Something had to give before someone broke. She

couldn't stand the thought of losing another parent, so the *give* part was clear to her.

The tension seemed to build around the silence until August broke it. "If the diner wasn't an issue, you'd be saying yes to my offer to work at the camp, wouldn't you?"

"Sure." Josie shrugged a shoulder and placed her napkin on her empty plate.

August looked at her thoughtfully for a while and then gave his head one quick nod as if to confirm something she was too tired to ask about. "Okay . . . it's time for you to head home, young lady, and get some rest that I've been responsible for stealing from you." August stood and Josie did the same.

"I'm returning your money for those paintings."

"No, you're not."

"Yes, I am. You're not paying me for your own art. That's silly."

"It's the best money I've ever spent, so don't rob me of that." His grin showed just how proud he was to tease her with her own words from several weeks ago. August moved over to the brass pole. "You wanna?"

When Josie's eye fixed way down to the cement floor below, her stomach did a somersault. "Nah. I'm good with the stairs. Don't feel like plunging to my demise."

"Suit yourself." Without hesitation, August wrapped himself around the pole and whirled to the floor before Josie could blink.

Shuddering, she took the stairs and met him by the door, where he walked her to the truck.

After helping her climb in, August leaned in and brushed a tender kiss to her lips. "We still have a little time before the camp opens, so just think about it. And in the meantime, I promise to leave you alone."

Josie didn't like the idea of him leaving her alone but

kept the comment to herself. She gave him one final kiss before closing the door.

• • •

Josie veered down Miss Dalma's avenue just as she did most nights, wanting to check on the little lady before heading home. The porch light was on and made it easy to see her sitting on the porch.

"What are you doing out so late, dear?" Dalma asked as soon as Josie made it up the stairs.

It was barely nine, but Josie didn't point that out. She sat beside Dalma in the glider swing, closed her eyes, and said on a yawn, "I had dinner with August."

"That fellow has overcome so much in his young life. Don't be another difficult part of his story."

Josie's eyes snapped open and glared down at the little woman beside her. "Where in the world did that comment come from? It was dinner. Nothing difficult about it."

"Humph." Dalma scoffed as she smoothed the lapels of her robe, the porch light glinting off the oversize sapphire ring on her pinkie. How her bony finger could support such a giant gem was beyond baffling. "Did you know he came to me for help the summer before he began high school?"

"No, ma'am. What kind of help?"

"Good. You shouldn't have known about it. It was a secret, but now I'm going to share it with you because it shows just how much August has had to fight for the life he's dreamed of, and when I'm done telling you, you better promise to never tell a soul and to not make him fight for you." Dalma gave Josie such a scolding look even the swing paused to take notice.

Josie only nodded, feeling right shameful over being called difficult.

"August was already pretty far behind with his education, so he came into the library one day and asked me to help him learn to read better before starting high school. The poor thing was basically illiterate. Couldn't hardly read a lick." Dalma pushed her foot against the porch planks to start the swing back into motion. "It was a struggle for him, and we had to start with some pretty basic books, but once I introduced him to the Magic Tree House series, he really got into it and his reading improved. Our August liked the adventure those books took him on." Dalma smiled warmly.

Josie listened to the roar of the ocean off in the distance as they silently rocked in the swing, impressed yet heartbroken for everything August bravely overcame. "I had no idea."

"As you shouldn't." Dalma patted Josie's knee, the ring clinking around and making the gesture have more of an impact. "That young man is tenacious to a fault, so don't be a scaredy-cat when he invites you to be part of his adventure."

"And you're cunning to a fault." Josie waggled a finger at her as Dalma gave her an innocuous look. "Don't even play innocent with me. You've been giving August my books."

Dalma clucked her tongue and waved. "Oh, that. Someone had to share your artwork, since you're too chicken to do it yourself."

"I am not chicken. I just have more important things on my plate besides drawing."

"It's more than just drawing and we both know it. God gave you that gift to share, so shame on you for being disobedient."

Josie cleared her throat. "I thought I was sharing the gift of compassion with the world . . . Doesn't that matter?"

"Oh, my sweet Josie, it does matter and you have a heart of gold. Truly, you do. The world would be almost perfect if it were filled with Josies." Dalma patted Josie's knee again.

"Almost?" Josie teased.

"Yes, almost. A perfect Josie would be showing off how great and mighty her Savior is by sharing the talented gift he created in her."

They grew quiet again until a fish breached the water in the inlet and disrupted it.

Josie sighed. "I'm going to work on it, okay?"

"Good enough for me." Dalma smiled.

Josie wrapped her arm around Dalma, cherishing the lucid moment with her. They were becoming fewer and farther between. "Please agree to move in with me. I promise to be a good roommate."

"That idea ain't even an option, dear." Dalma huffed.

"Why not?"

Dalma pointed over to the window behind the glider swing and clucked her tongue. "Because the Knitting Club had a vote about a roommate. Those ole heifers moved Vanessa Sánchez in here without my permission."

Josie looked over and saw Miss Vanessa sitting by the window watching them. She was a member of the Knitting Club who had lost her husband last year to colon cancer. At only sixty-eight, she was considered the baby of the group. Josie offered her a small wave, feeling grateful for the Knitting Club's meddling for once and relieved that Dalma would no longer be living alone. "I like Miss Vanessa."

Dalma clucked her tongue again. "She's all right as long as she doesn't get wound up and start mouthing off at me in Spanish. I told her I didn't understand a word she was blathering, but she keeps doing it just to get a rise out of me."

Josie laughed and followed it with a yawn. "I'm going to call it a night." She hugged Dalma close once more before dropping her arm and standing. "You know I love you, Miss Dalma."

"Yes, and you know I love you more than my teeth, dear."

Josie waved her silly comment off and started descending the porch steps, even though she knew it was the truth, considering Dalma had never misplaced her. She felt a weight lift from her shoulders knowing someone was watching over Dalma around the clock. But then the weight of August's offer took its place and made a restful night's sleep impossible.

22

Tug-of-war had never been August's favorite game. The tedious back-and-forth always grew old on him fast. He wanted results and didn't like the constant pull and give the game demanded—one where if he allowed just the slightest bit of slack, he chanced losing all that he'd worked so hard for. He wasn't sure if it was Josie's intention to make him participate in that private game of tug-of-war, but he found himself once again with the rope growing slippery in his hands.

At the moment, he stared down another challenge and was determined to be victorious in that matter. He narrowed his eyes and gave his opposition all the attitude he could muster in the particular situation facing him. And that was no easy feat.

"You listen up and listen up now . . . You're gonna take this like a man," August said slowly while his opponent narrowed his own eyes in a similar manner, looking as if he was ready to do battle with the problem at hand. August wrapped the line taut around his finger and gave it a slight tug, causing Zachary to reach out and grab his wrist.

"No, not wet. I not wetty." The little guy's words came out in a lisp due to the fishing line wrapped around his loose front tooth.

They were hunkered down in the corner of Derek and

Nan's office at Sunset Seafood House, where August was trying to solve yet another problem. The one where the little guy was walking around with his first loose tooth barely holding on to the gum and no one else was brave enough to do anything about it. Never August's style, he cornered his youngest brother as soon as Zachary arrived from his day at school.

"Dude, you're making a big deal out of nothing. What part scares you?"

Zachary continued to grip August's wrist, a petition not to yank the line. "It's gonna huwt."

"Nah, man. You just need to chill." Before the *ill* was out of his mouth, August flicked his wrist and the tension of the fishing line gave, producing a tiny pearl-size tooth on the end of it. Before August could celebrate, Zachary's hand lashed out and connected to the unsuspecting man's face.

Both brothers sat on their knees in shock with rounded eyes, the older one holding his cheek while the younger one cupped his mouth.

"You slapped me!" August finally bellowed out.

"You pulled my toof!" Zachary lisped as his little face grew pink.

"Yeah, and did it hurt?" August hitched an eyebrow way up, giving the expression as much attitude as he could while rubbing at the throb in his cheek.

Zachary stilled and gave the question some thought. "No . . ."

"That's what I thought." August gave him a smug look and stood. "Come on."

"August, you mad at me?"

August looked back and saw the little guy's eyes were growing watery. "Nope. Lesson learned."

"What lesson?"

August lunged for his brother and slung him over

his shoulder and did a quick spin until he had Zachary giggling. "Next time I'll hog-tie you first." He playfully popped him on the backside. "Seriously, I know you didn't mean to hit me. Just a knee-jerk reaction."

"It wasn't my knee, though. It was my hand."

Bellowing in laughter, August placed the boy on his feet and opened the office door to lead them out. "It's just an expression."

They shuffled into the kitchen, both looking a little worse for wear, on a search for iced tea.

"Why is your cheek all red?" Nan asked. She sat the clipboard down and walked over to where August was pouring two glasses of tea.

"Just a slight misunderstanding." He shrugged and handed his little brother a glass before taking a long swig from his own.

"And that would be?" Nan's attention was zeroed in on August's sore cheek.

"Zachary thought smacking me was part of the tooth-pulling ritual."

August's cheek seemed to be instantly forgotten as Nan knelt in front of her little boy. "Y'all pulled it?"

Zachary grinned wide, showing the new space between his teeth.

Nan clapped her hands. "Aww! Ain't he so cute?" She glanced over her shoulder where August was swiping a few fried shrimp from the basket one of the cooks just placed on the prep table. It was the way of the kitchen. If a plate or basket was placed on the prep table and not the order-up counter, it was considered a treat for the taking. "I knew you were on a mission when you showed up here earlier. Where's my baby's tooth?"

"On your desk."

Nan headed that way with August following. He

watched her get teary-eyed over the tiny tooth, wishing he had a sketch pad with him to capture the sentimental moment. He picked up a surfboard that he and Zachary had knocked over during their tooth-pulling scuffle and leaned it against the wall. Once he was satisfied the board wouldn't fall over again, August released it and took a seat. "Your message earlier said you had something to talk to me about?"

Nan sat behind her desk. "Yes. Jasper Slater came by here last week and we had an interesting conversation. I wanted to get your opinion on it."

August's smile faltered. "Why's that?"

"Well, it's something we've not wanted to see happen, but as it is, the time has come."

Two hours later, August felt an odd mixture of relief and apprehension. Relieved because Nan and Jasper had actually come together to work on something, but apprehensive about how Josie was going to take it. His gut told him it wasn't going to be so simple. Nothing so far had been with the beautiful blonde.

He sat on the deck at Driftwood Diner and watched through the window as Josie led a meeting with the staff, probably about the upcoming Memorial Day weekend. He knew from past years at his own family's restaurant that they would need to have a game plan laid out to get through the hustle and bustle of the holiday. He longed to go inside and steal her away from the stress of it, but he stayed hunkered down in the Adirondack chair and tried to be content with only watching her from afar. It's what he'd promised after all—to give her space—but the promise was testing his patience.

"You just gonna sit out here and stare at my girl?" Jasper asked as he shuffled up the steps and plopped down in a chair beside him.

"I promised to leave her alone for a while." August brushed some sand off the arm of his chair, trying to focus on something besides what he couldn't have.

"Why would you go and promise something dumb like that?" Jasper kicked the side of August's leg with his bare foot.

August moved his leg out of reach. "She was getting a little twitchy on me again."

"It's my fault." Jasper released a pensive sigh and slumped in his chair. "I knew she used to be interested in art, but I thought she was like most teenagers with a fleeting hobby and she'd lose interest in it . . . I didn't realize just how much my daughter gave up for me until you showed me those pictures of her painting that bus." He paused and shook his head. "But that's Jo-Jo for ya. Always putting everyone else before herself. She's even doing it with you now too. Adding you to the list and sending herself further down it . . . I've been trying to make things easier and lightening her load around here, but she's too dang loyal and I think I gotta fire her."

"From what Nan told me earlier, that's the plan."

"Yeah." Jasper looked at him from the corner of his eye.

"Sir, no offense, but I think you're going about this the wrong way. You need to have a talk with Josie instead of leaving her in the dark. She's a grown woman."

"She'll just convince me she's fine and can handle it and then she'll brush off your offer and . . . it's the best answer I could come up with to solve all our problems."

The two men sat on the deck and rehashed the entire conversation August had earlier with Nan. They both seemed to have everyone's best interest in mind, but he felt a little incredulous over their plan. He hoped Josie would still be on talking terms with them once she found out.

Jasper stood. "Come on with me to the docks."

"What's at the docks? You're not planning on feeding me to the fishes, are ya?" August tried for a mobster impersonation, sending Jasper's eyes to roll.

"We ain't got time for your goofiness. Now get the lead out."

August followed the older guy down the steps and over to his pickup truck. "You didn't answer me."

They settled into the truck that smelled like an unappealing mixture of fishing bait and peppermints. "The fishing boats are coming in. I want to beat your momma to the draw."

"Ah, man. You're trying to get me in trouble with both women in my life." Before August could climb out, Jasper took off, causing the pickup truck to backfire in protest.

"Nan always beats me. That stingy woman takes the best-looking shrimp and fish every time, but *not* this time. A buddy of mine gave me the heads-up that one of the boats is making its way up the waterway. That seafood is mine this time."

"You know it's dirty of you to pit me against my own momma." August crossed his arms, thinking he'd thumb a ride back as soon as they made it to the docks. "I'm beginning to think you really don't like me."

Jasper's only response was a loud cackle.

August settled in. The tongue-lashing he was sure to receive from Nan as soon as she got wind of him aiding and abetting her competitor had better be worth it in the end. He knew it would be if he ended up with Josie by his side, but boy, was he going to get it over that seafood swiping. "You know I'll probably end up being banned from my family's restaurant because of this."

"Yeah. So? Ain't like you don't know of another good

one to eat at." Jasper parked the rusted truck, slid on a hat and shades, and started booking it to the dock.

"You don't have another hat and a pair of shades, do ya?" August called out while plundering around inside the cab.

Jasper barked out in laughter but didn't slow. "Come on! The boat's here!"

Letting out a defeated sigh, August turned and noticed a familiar SUV pulling up. His stomach did a flip as a shot of adrenaline overtook him. "Ah, shoot! Jasper, hurry up! She's here! She's here!" His deep voice rumbled out in warning, sending a flock of seagulls scurrying off the dock.

August sprinted down the dock, actually passing the portly man to get to the goods first. If August was going to help the guy, they were going to do it at lightning speed. He managed to swipe the seafood and dodge his mom from snatching it away from him, but he didn't walk away unscathed.

Drenched in sweat and smelling strongly of ripening seafood from where some was spilled down the front of his shirt, August slumped in the old truck and took in a few jagged breaths as Jasper made their getaway.

"You managed that pretty good, boy." Jasper let out one of those hee-hee laughs.

"I can't believe I just got into a scrap with my own momma over seafood." August frowned and focused his annoyance out the window as they passed by rows of colorful beach houses. His hand moved over the tender spot on his neck, remembering how Nan got her claws in him at one point of the scuffle.

"Ah, you're just a young whippersnapper. It's your own fault if you let a woman get ahold of you like that." Jasper pointed to August's stinging neck.

"I'm never going to live this one down," August mumbled to himself, knowing he'd just secured his place as Jasper's accomplice while getting on Nan's bad side, neither of which he was comfortable with.

23

The diner was abuzz with a bountiful mix of patrons and tourists, and if it was any indication for the season ahead, it was going to be one of their busiest to date. With three order slips in hand, Josie wove between the packed tables, promising more tea and hush puppies as she went. She practically ran into her dad in the kitchen.

"Oops." She laughed, pretending to dance a jig around him. "Didn't see you there."

"I ain't got time to deal with you being distracted," Jasper said, taking the order slips out of her hand. "Take the rest of the day off."

"That makes absolutely no sense." Josie huffed, thinking *he* was the one acting distracted. "We're slammed." She pointed out the kitchen door but Jasper pointed to the time clock.

A mood crawled up Josie's back and began pinching her neck. She rolled her head this way and then that way, but nothing would alleviate it. Not even taking the time to clock out, she untied her apron and stormed out the side door. She left the truck in its spot behind the diner and took off on her bike.

After riding around aimlessly for a while, Josie decided to go check on Theo's mother. There were things they needed to discuss now that Deandrea had finally agreed to let Theo stay at the camp and work there for the summer.

Carter and Dominica gave him the title of campgrounds manager, and Josie couldn't recall a time she'd seen the young man beam so brightly. Theo needed purpose and some guidance from some good people, and she was relieved he was finally getting the opportunity for both.

"Knock, knock!" Josie called out as she let herself in, knowing Carter was giving Theo a tour of the camp at the moment. She found Deandrea balled up on the couch, staring at the blank screen of the TV.

Deandrea blinked a few times before looking at Josie. "Did Jasper kick you out of the diner again?"

Josie sat on the opposite end of the couch as Deandrea sat up. "Yes. I don't know what's wrong with that man lately, but I've about had my fill of it." She chanced asking, "Did Doc Nelson and his wife come by yet?"

"Yesterday." Deandrea focused on her nails, her bottom lip quivering. "Y'all think I'm crazy?"

Josie reached for her hand. "Not at all. You're going through a rough patch, is all, and this facility will help you overcome it and get healthy again."

"Doc mentioned chronic depression. That doesn't sound like a rough patch." Deandrea wiped under her nose and sniffed. "I'm so embarrassed."

"There's no reason for that." Josie plowed on before Deandrea could rebuke her. "After my mother died, I was put on antidepressants and went to counseling for a while. Sometimes I still have milder bouts of depression. Should I be embarrassed by that?"

Deandrea shook her head but said nothing.

"Then neither should you."

"I just . . ." With her shoulders slouched, Deandrea looked close to giving underneath the weight of her burdens.

"You check yourself in, and if it doesn't suit you, you are free to check yourself out. You owe it to yourself to get some help, and you owe it to Theo. That young man adores you so much that he's willing to rob me at gunpoint!" Josie joked. Deandrea cracked a small smile.

After discussing the details and Josie reassuring her friend that Theo would have the best summer of his life, Deandrea agreed to give it a chance.

Josie phoned Doc to let him know. "Doc and his wife are on the way to pick you up," she told Deandrea as she hung up the phone. "They'll take you by the camp so you can see for yourself how great it is and say goodbye to Theo. Okay?"

Deandrea nodded and gave Josie a hug. "Thank you for being our angel all these years."

Josie embraced her tightly. "We both know I'm no angel, but I do care deeply for you and Theo and have always been honored to be your friend."

Josie helped Deandrea pack and then stayed until she was picked up before taking the long way back to the diner, choosing to bike along the seashore instead of the road. She rounded the bend of the beach just before reaching the diner and immediately spotted the big black truck parked beside it.

"What's going on?" she mumbled while slowing the bike and hopping off to walk it the rest of the way. She came to a screeching halt as the screen door swung open with August walking out with his arm draped over the shoulder of a beautiful woman.

"See, I told you there was nothing to worry about. Problem solved." He gave the woman a quick squeeze before releasing her to open the driver's door of a van and helping her inside.

The woman said something to make August's handsome face light up, but the sudden roar of a crashing wave drowned it out.

As a knot formed in her throat, Josie hurried inside the diner at a clipped pace and found her dad walking out of the office. "Just what are y'all up to?" Her scold came out sharp enough to startle him and send his hand to clutch his chest.

"You can't scare an old geezer like that!" Jasper sucked in a stuttered breath.

Josie placed her hands on her hips. "And you don't need to be messing behind my back!" She jabbed a finger toward the back door. "Who was that with August?"

"I ain't got time for this." He reached around to lock the office door, but Josie wedged herself in the way.

"Then make time." The irritated mood from earlier had escalated into a full-blown hissy fit with foot stamping and finger jabbing to drive the point home.

Huffing, he muttered, "That was our new manager."

"What?"

"Her name is Marta. I just hired her." He gave Josie a don't-mess-with-me look.

Squaring her shoulders, she gave the look right back to him, resembling the Slater she was. "That's my job!"

"Not anymore. I've trapped you around here long enough."

"But—"

"I got somewhere to be." Jasper gave up on locking the door and hurried through the dining area. "We'll talk about this later. Be sure to lock up!"

"Dad!" Her protest did nothing to slow his escape; if anything, it put a shot of vigor into his stride. Giving up, Josie let him get away for the time being while she headed into the office to figure out what was going on.

Sitting on top of the desk was a résumé. Josie settled into the chair and skimmed it. Marta Holmes. Forty-three years old. Listed as her last employer was Sunset Seafood House, where she'd been the night manager for the past thirteen years.

"Why on earth would August help such a devoted employee jump ship to come work at Driftwood Diner?" Josie shook her head and pushed the paper to the side. She sat there, arms crossed, and stewed on it until she heard the screen door creak open.

Springing up from the chair, she rushed out front and found August walking toward her, a warm expression on his face.

"You have a lot of nerve," she snapped and side-stepped him when he leaned forward for a hug.

"Something wrong?"

"Seriously?" She let out a huff. "I should have seen it, but I've been too blinded by you in these last two months."

"Seen what?" He stuffed his hands into his jean pockets and lifted an eyebrow.

She flicked her hand between them. "What this was really all about. The painting and the wooing . . . all of it just to secure Marta a job!"

The neutral calm of his features began to sharpen with irritation as he tossed his palms up in surrender and let out a growl. "I told Jasper he needed to tell you first. This was your dad and my mom's idea. Not mine."

"Why didn't you tell me?"

"Because I encouraged your dad to. Seriously, Jo, you and Jasper suck at communicating. I don't think he went about it the right way, but I'm honestly glad he finally did something with your best interest in mind."

She batted a sweaty lock of hair off her forehead. "How would you feel if you were in my position?"

"Relieved!"

"Since Daddy won't talk to me . . ." A whine slipped into her tone without permission, so Josie paused to clear it away on a hasty cough. "So you need to explain what's going on."

"Marta is a single mom. Her daughter starts school next year, so she needed to switch to a day shift. One Nan couldn't offer her, considering they already have a stand-up day manager. Jasper got wind of it and talked to Nan about Marta working here. It's a win-win."

They stood staring at each other with all the hurt they were feeling reflecting between them.

August pushed off the counter, seeming ready to leave. "Your dream isn't inside this place. I've watched you over the last two months while you're here, and not once have you shone while doing it . . ."

"I've done what I've had to do. Dad needs me here. And Miss Dalma . . . Theo and Deandrea—"

August shook his head. "No one asked you to take all that on!" A huff escaped in a haggard grunt as he raked his fingers through his hair, tugging at the ends before dropping his hand. "I think you're being a martyr when it's not really called for. You're setting your dreams aside to make sure your dad and everyone else in this town is taken care of." He took a step forward and leaned close to her ear. "News flash, Miss Slater: Jasper is doing just fine. Everyone else will survive too."

"Why is it so bad to want the best for others?" She tossed her hands in the air.

"You're all about helping someone out but won't allow anyone to do the same for you. How messed up is that, Jo?" He looked so defeated that Josie reached for him, but he took a step away before her hand made contact with his arm.

"August . . ."

"I've done all I can do . . . I guess it still wasn't enough."
He released a humorless laugh. "Mercy, Jo! I've always
prided myself on being a patient man. You've shown me
just how wrong I am. Not sure if your intentions were to
make a game out of breaking August, but you've finally
won." Shoulders slouched, he turned around and exited
the diner as quietly as he'd entered, but the message he
was conveying was rather loud.

Later that night her phone lit up with an incoming
message from August. It contained two images. The first
picture was of a sketch he'd drawn of her leaning against
the counter at the diner. She looked longingly out the
window. The second picture was a sketch of her looking
up at the building with the fairies flying overhead. He
was absolutely right. Josie shone when her hand held a
paintbrush but was nothing more than shadows when
she held an order pad.

Placing the phone on the nightstand without replying
because there was no need to, Josie burrowed under her
quilt and allowed the frustration to wash over her. She
quietly begged the ocean melody to tug her under, but
sleep wouldn't show up. As she lay there tossing and turning, something else showed up instead. Or she should say
someone. Her eyes were focused on the ribbons of moonlight that were filtering through the open window when
a leg popped through. She jumped up and was ready to
whack whoever it was with the ever-ready baseball bat,
but she left it by the nightstand when several coils of red
sprang into view.

"Opal Gilbert Cole, what are you doing?" she
whisper-yelled and tossed a pillow, nailing her friend
upside the head.

"The moon is alive tonight. We need to have a chat

with it." Opal grunted, trying to leverage her other leg through the window.

"I'm half-tempted to push you back out and then call your husband to come get hold of you." Josie grabbed her arm and pulled her inside instead. "Does Linc even know you're here?"

"Of course he knows I'm here. He's the one who drove me over on the golf cart, silly."

"Me, silly? You're the one sneaking in my window and yammering on about the moon being alive." Josie placed her hands on her hips while Opal beamed at her.

"But it is alive." Opal pointed outside. "See!"

Josie leaned around her friend and regarded the giant glowing ball in the sky. It did seem like it was dancing with all of the stars gathered around it. "You're such a hippie."

"And that's perfectly all right. Come on!" Opal beckoned Josie to follow her to the window.

"This is my place, *silly*. We're allowed to use the door." Josie pulled on a pair of yoga pants but decided not to change out of her long nightshirt. Surely at that late hour they wouldn't have to worry about bumping into anyone. Well, besides the giant on a golf cart somewhere . . .

"Nah. It's more adventurous this way." Giddiness wove through the quirky woman's voice as she scooted over the window ledge and hopped down to the sand below but miscalculated her landing and tumbled sideways.

"Girl, you're going to end up breaking your collarbone again." Josie recalled an incident in grade school where Opal's flip-flop got tangled up in the monkey bars as she tried hanging upside down. After a few wiggles this way and that, the sandal released before she was ready, sending the girl crashing to the ground and earning a broken collarbone. Unfazed by the injury, she kept the pain to herself until arriving home later that afternoon.

"I think perhaps I've broken something," she had admitted to her mom over a bowl of ice cream. Sure enough, a trip to the emergency room proved her correct.

Josie watched now as Opal picked her petite self up, brushed off the sand from her backside, and rotated both shoulders. "All's good. Come on!"

With Josie's height advantage all she had to do was step over the window ledge and her foot met the sand. They didn't slow until they were at the end of the pier. Opal was uncharacteristically quiet on the walk over, not making a peep. That unnerved Josie a bit, making her wonder what this Sand Queens meeting was really about.

Once they were settled on a bench, Josie commented, "I miss Sophia the most on nights like this." She peered up at the moon taking a prominent spot in the dark sky. "It's not quite right without her here."

Opal sighed. "I know, but if my heart is nudging me right, I think she'll be back soon."

"She's scheduled to be here for Memorial Day weekend," Josie reminded.

"No, not like that . . . I have a feeling she'll be moving home again."

Josie let the psychic jab die on her tongue before delivering it. They'd already had several concerned conversations about Sophia recently, worrying about what she wasn't telling them. "I just hope she and Collin are okay." She inhaled a lungful of briny air and searched for the Big Dipper.

"Lincoln and I have added several prayers to our treasure chest for them. I guess that's all we can do for the time being."

"I suppose you're right." They lapsed into a silence for a while, but Josie had a feeling the meeting was only beginning when she noticed Opal was fidgeting.

"Your daddy came in this afternoon to pick up that table I restored for him," Opal mentioned nonchalantly, making Josie cringe. "Says he's working on firing you."

And there it is . . .

"Please don't." Josie groaned, scrubbing her hands down her face.

"I think it's time you let him fire you."

Josie dropped her hands and gave Opal a sidelong glance. "Are you even listening to yourself right now?"

Opal nodded slowly. "Yes."

"You know my life is in those four walls. It's my duty."

"No, it's been your trap. Your dad finally understands he needs to set you free. Let him."

Josie stewed on that until she finally admitted, "I'm scared."

Opal wrapped her small arm around Josie. "Scared can be fun and exciting if you allow it to be."

Josie snorted. "Says the girl who falls into open windows in the middle of the night because she thinks the moon is coming to life."

"Nah. I'm just the girl who falls into open windows in the middle of the night because my dear friend is on the verge of coming to life. I want to be here to see her through it."

Josie's smile wobbled as a sting hit her eyes and nose. "I really am scared, though."

"I know." Opal patted her arm and gave Josie just enough strength to fall for a spell.

24

A live band was set up on a nearby deck and was holding a breezy rhythm with the ocean waves as bikes whirled by on the congested beach. Laughter and conversation filled the air, along with footballs and Frisbees. With the menagerie of events, the jovial sounds of celebration, and the savory scents of nearby grills cooking in abundance, Sunset Cove was beginning to wear its summer wardrobe rather well.

"The Sand Queens always win. Ain't any use in trying," Tucker grumbled while lugging the supplies needed to the beach for the Memorial Day Festival.

"You have me as a partner this year. Have a little faith, punk." August popped him playfully on the backside with the long-handled sand shovel. He emitted a playfulness he wasn't feeling but had no intentions of ruining his brothers' fun with a sour mood.

"But they always have the best sand castles," Zachary said as he waded through the sand.

August dropped the shovel and container filled with other tools in the designated area for the sand castle contest, mindful of not getting anywhere near Josie, and started unloading stuff. "Yeah, but I've created us a pretty cool design. Be positive." He had to stifle the eye roll at his own words. Seemed he'd been giving that pep talk to almost everyone lately, but he was beginning to feel like he was in need of one.

"So start lugging buckets of water up here?" Tucker asked, grabbing the largest pail.

"Yeah, man. And I'll start packing the sand." August yanked his T-shirt over his head, applied a good coating of sunblock to himself and his little brother, and then knelt in the sand. "All right, little dude, let's get to working on making this pile of sand into a masterpiece."

"I ain't little," Zachary lisped out, having even more of a hard time sounding out words with the other front tooth gone as of yesterday. He'd called August up after school and asked his big brother to bring his fishing line, saying he was gonna take it like a man this time and promised to keep his hands to himself. He held true to both declarations and walked away with one less tooth.

"Okay, *big* guy, get to work." August smirked at him before setting in to the side of the sand mountain.

It didn't take long for a tall blonde in a bright-teal bikini to draw August's attention from the moat he was digging. He watched Josie scrape away slices of wet sand from her castle. She wore a frayed pair of jean shorts with an array of tools sticking out of the pockets. His sunglasses had him at an advantage with being able to freely watch with Josie unaware of it. Or so that's what he thought until she began glancing over at him, maybe sensing his eyes on her.

"Dude, you gonna ogle Josie the entire time or are you gonna actually help out?" Tucker tossed a shovelful of sand against August's arm.

August flicked the sand off, sending it back in Tucker's direction, but decided not to lob any comment. He picked up his trowel and went to work until the wet sand was transformed into a detailed castle surrounded by a moat with a gnarly crocodile lurching around it with his teeth bared in warning.

"Not bad, but I don't think we've outdone the Sand Queens." Tucker pointed over to the women's creation. Their castle sparkled in the sun from sea glass and shells adorning the walls in a mosaic design, helping it stand out in the sea of beige creations.

"Ah, man. Theirs is more pretty." Zachary scrunched his little nose and pouted his lips.

"No worries. We're about to brighten this baby up." August knelt by his giant duffel bag and pulled out a plastic canister with a spray nozzle attached to it by a thin hose. "We got this." With a wide grin, he pumped the device on top of the canister a few times before bathing the crocodile in neon green. Several onlookers gasped.

Before he made it to the long tail that wrapped around the side of the castle, they had a good-size audience.

"Th-that's against th-the rules." The stuttering mess came from behind him.

"Hello, Jo," he greeted without turning around to face her. "I read over those rules and this falls within the guidelines."

"How so?" Sophia asked as she and Opal joined the group gathering around.

"This is simply nontoxic food coloring mixed with cornstarch. The rules state that nontoxic materials can be used." August hitched a thumb in the direction of the Sand Queens' castle. "You used nontoxic materials, too."

"Real bricks are nontoxic, but you don't see us building with them. Sea glass and shells are found on the beach," Sophia, always the hard sell of the group, pointed out.

August dropped the nozzle and hitched his hands onto his hips. "You didn't find that sea glass and those pristine shells on this Carolina coast, and we both know it."

"I-I found some of them," Josie stuttered out.

August briefly cut his eyes at her, wondering why the

stuttering was suddenly prominent again. It didn't take long before the realization hit him that she was no longer comfortable around him. That rubbed him the wrong way more so than the sand trapped in his swim trunks.

"You queens are just jealous you didn't think of it first," he fired in Sophia's direction, sounding as childish as he felt, but continued on by moving his attention to Josie. "Go on back over there to your monotone world, Jo, and leave me be to paint mine up with life."

Her face grew a bright shade of pink as she sucked in a shocked breath, letting him know his condescending attitude and sharp words had effectively done their damage.

Too bad it only served to make him feel worse.

August turned his back to her, picked up the container of neon blue, and began painting the moat.

Josie stood there for a while, seemingly chewing on something she wanted to say. In the end, she stayed true to character and chickened out.

Once she returned to her sand castle, Tucker reached over and punched August in the upper arm, sending a line of blue to streak across Zachary's back. The little guy squealed and the oldest guy growled.

"What was that for?" August glared at Tucker.

"Dude, could you have been any harsher?"

"She asked for it." August brushed by his brother, bodychecking him in the passing, and continued to color their creation. "Zachary, sorry about that. Grab up the coral-colored bottle and I'll let you paint the castle walls."

Zachary rummaged around the duffel bag. "What's cowal?"

"Pink."

It took a good part of the sunny morning to finish up their creation, but once done, the boys stood back and admired it.

"We've got this in the bag," August said with confidence.

"That cornstarch paint is pretty cool, man." Tucker offered his fist and August bumped it.

The guys set up foldout chairs and settled in to wait for their turn with the judges. As the day wore on, the sun heated the beach up. August couldn't keep from watching Josie, and he noticed the sun was reddening the tops of her shoulders.

He dug around in a drawstring bag until finding the sunblock. "Tucker, take this tube of sunblock over there to Josie. Her shoulders are starting to burn."

"Take it over there yourself," Tucker mumbled in a drowsy tone.

"I asked you to."

"No, you didn't. You ordered me to. You're the one concerned over her skin, so you handle it."

Before the two older brothers could continue bickering, little Zachary plucked the tube from August's hand. "I like Miss Josie. Her says you shouldn't talk ugly to people like you were doing to her. And her says you should always help a friend when they need you." Done with his reprimand, Zachary walked over to the Sand Queens as they were putting the final touches on their creation.

"We just got *told* by a kindergartner." Tucker snorted. The women were out of earshot, but Josie's giggle somehow skipped over on one of the breezes as Zachary said something to her. "And now look. He's going to school us on how to court a girl." Both brothers sat up in their chairs, a bit miffed, as their baby brother began helping rub sunblock on the blonde beauty's shoulders. He even stayed a while and chatted up the three women before making his way back over to his brothers.

"What all were y'all talking about over there?" August questioned before Zachary even took his seat.

"Nothing much." The little boy shrugged with a grin planted on his face.

"Fibber." August reached out and poked him playfully in the side.

They sat a little longer as the panel of judges wove closer and Zachary grew antsy. He stopped squirming in his chair suddenly. "August, I hear the ice cream cart."

August inclined his head and listened for a few beats. Sure enough, the tinkling of the bell on the cart reached them. He fished out some money and handed it to Tucker. "Y'all grab us an ice cream and also get some for the Sand Queens."

Tucker looked over to the women and then to August with a dubious look on his face. "Why?"

"Because it's hot out and they look like they could use a treat," August answered while digging his toes deeper into the sand.

Tucker chuckled and shook his head. "Dude, you're the kindest jerk I've ever met."

"Whatever. Go on before the line gets too long."

His brothers walked over to the cart and then took the treats to the Sand Queens. Instead of just dropping the ice creams off, they sat down and enjoyed their treats with the women.

"I guess that's what I deserve," August muttered to himself, knowing he wouldn't be getting an ice cream himself.

"If it isn't the famous August Bradford," a high-pitched voice called out from behind him.

Cringing, he sank down in his chair, but it was too late. All at once, he was surrounded by an entirely different group of women than the Sand Queens. More like *Drama*

Queens! "Nothing famous here," he mumbled, putting as much detachment into the three words as possible.

One of the women he remembered as the head cheerleader from high school swatted him on his shoulder. "You're just being too modest."

"My work may have made a name out there, but I'm not famous. Sorry, sweetheart." August meant the endearment as a jab, but when she batted her fake eyelashes at him, he knew he failed.

Another former classmate boldly ran her fingers through his hair. "You look so different without the piercings and blue hair. Seriously, August, you've matured into one good-looking man."

Who do these brazen chicks think they are? He really didn't want an answer to the question. Just wanted them to go away. "I'm the same guy I was with the piercings and colored hair. You know, the one everyone called the *freak.*" He leaned away until her hand dropped from his hair. He stretched out his arms to give them a good view of the well-placed tattoos. Three in all, the paintbrush, a reference to his favorite Bible verse, Psalm 20:4, and the French word for family, *famille.* Each was a symbol of what mattered most to him. "And I still have my tattoos. Really not different at all."

The cheerleader popped him again, and it was all he could do to keep his anger in check while trying to brush her advances and his agitation off, but it was like trying to get rid of a nagging sand gnat, near about impossible.

"Do you plan on traveling anytime soon? I would just love to travel some." She looked at him with an expression filled with hope, and it was all he could do not to snort in disdain.

"Nah. I'm done with that part of my life. It's time to settle down," August answered with a measure of aloofness.

The aggravating group of women giggled like he said something cute. He didn't, and he was close to abandoning the sand castle to make a run for it.

As they kept yapping on and on about nothing of importance to him, August studied the group of plastic women. They were the same snooty clique who used to make fun of him and considered him nothing more than trash. Now they stood before him in some sort of hero-worship stance all because they thought he'd turned into a somebody. He'd been somebody way back then, bright hair and all, and he had no patience for shallow individuals who looked no further than outer appearances.

August pulled out a casual tone he wasn't feeling to address them. "Look, ladies, we know I wasn't your cup of tea back in school, and to be quite honest with you, you're most definitely not mine. So how about y'all go cluck somewhere else."

All four gasped and then transformed it into sucking their teeth, and he could barely refrain from raising his hands and shooing them away. A large shadow overtook him and seemed to be the final push the women needed to stomp away.

"That was impressively rude," Lincoln said in a lazy drawl.

August looked over his shoulder and noticed a giant brace covering most of Lincoln's left leg. He sent his eyes way up and rolled them. "They asked for it." He waved to one of the empty chairs. "Have a seat."

"Nah. Better not take my chances of being unable to get back up."

August hadn't taken into consideration how low the chairs were, so he stood and moved to stand beside Lincoln. "Leg giving you a fit today?"

"Yeah. Overdid it in PT, but no worries." Lincoln shrugged. "What I am worried about is you not knowing how to woo a woman."

"I ain't got any desire to woo any woman like those I just chased off." August crossed his arms and huffed. His patience for all women was at an all-time low at the moment.

"I'm not talking about them. I'm talking about that shy blonde over there." Lincoln ticked his chin in Josie's direction.

August rolled his neck and grunted. "Man, if you have a magic wooing potion that'll work on that stubborn woman, by all means, hand it over."

Lincoln let out a bark of laughter and clamped him on the shoulder. "I got nothin'."

"Thanks for the help." August was beginning to think nothing and no one was on his side when it came to Josie Slater.

"Let's go fishing in the morning. That'll cure 'bout anything that ails ya."

"I'll have to take a rain check."

"Don't be all pouty," Lincoln goaded.

"I'm not. I have a flight to catch tomorrow."

Lincoln took a hobbled step and turned until he was blocking August's view of Josie. "You better be coming back."

Frustration was coursing through August like hot lava, so the only reply he gave was a haughty jerk of his shoulders. When he kept his lips firmly pressed together, Lincoln imparted some stern words about keeping promises and then he limped away. Not long after that, his two brothers finally decided to rejoin him.

"Thanks a lot, you punks."

"For what?" Tucker asked as he plopped into his chair.

"For leaving me to defend myself and for not even having enough decency to at least bring me an ice cream."

"I told you we forgot something," Tucker remarked to Zachary.

By then the ice cream cart was long gone and so was August's appetite, anyway.

After it was all said and done, the boys ended up taking first place in the sand castle contest, but August felt far from a winner.

25

The three Sand Queens sat upon their thrones, aka lounge chairs, as the festivities continued on around them in the late afternoon. Some grills were cooling while others were just being lit. One band wrapped up their performance as another set up shop on a deck a few down from them. That was the beach life—one gathering morphed into another and seemed the party never completely concluded.

"I can't believe we lost . . . We've never lost!" Sophia scoffed at the ill-fitting notion while adjusting her sun hat.

"August Bradford is being talked about as the next big thing in the art industry, honey. Are you seriously shocked?" Opal gave her friend a wry look as she poked Sophia's leg with her teal toes that glittered just as sweetly as their sand castle had earlier.

"I suppose you're right." Sophia huffed and resettled in her chair. "Thank goodness Momma took Collin home with her. I needed this time-out."

"How are things going?" Opal asked Sophia. When she received no answer, she prompted, "Come on, Sophia. Let's talk about it."

"There's really nothing to say." Sophia sniffed, saying more in that gesture than not. "I don't know the man I married. . . . Do y'all think fame and fortune changed Ty that much? Or do you think it just revealed who he really was all along?"

"Are you referring to his overinflated ego?" Josie asked, never having had much use for Ty Prescott from day one. He'd always been too polished and too perfect in the beginning, like he was hiding something.

"I wish ego was the only problem." Sophia sniffed again.

Opal exchanged a worried look with Josie before saying, "Sophia, there's something you're not telling us."

Sophia sat straighter as her expression hardened, and before she even opened her mouth, Josie knew she was shutting the conversation down. "Nothing. I'm just in a sour mood." She flicked her wrist as if that could shoo away her troubles. "Opal, you have any snacks in that giant bag?"

"Go ahead and brush it off all you want. Just know we're here for you when you're ready to talk about it." Opal reached into her bag and began passing out saltwater taffy, adding something sweet to help chase the bitter away, as she liked to say.

Josie noticed Sophia's frown was as severe as her own, so there wasn't much hope in chasing the bitter away today.

"This is the biggest sham on the Grand Strand. People think it's made from ocean water." Sophia unwrapped the wax paper from her candy and gave it a good sniff before popping it into her mouth.

"It's all about nostalgia. It doesn't matter if this stuff was made up with only a pinch of salt and a little water. Stop being such a grump about everything." Opal shook her head and chewed on her own piece. When Josie made no move to eat hers, Opal swiped it back and nearly growled. "And what's wrong with you, Josie?"

Josie lifted a shoulder and huffed. "Y'all ever feel like a loser?"

Opal interjected a quick "Never."

At the same time, Sophia supplied, "All the time."

Opal scoffed. "Both of you need to straighten up. God didn't make us to live down in the mouth." Opal turned her attention to Josie. "Clearly August presented you with a challenge and you couldn't hang."

Josie snorted. "Thanks for that vote of confidence there."

"You're the one moping about it instead of proving to him you're not a coward. From what I've gathered, he and your daddy only did what they did to give you the freedom to live out your dreams." Opal stood up and gathered her bag.

"Where are you going?" Josie mumbled.

"It's a holiday weekend that should be spent paying respect to the men and women who sacrificed their lives for our freedom. A freedom you two want to sit here and take for granted." Opal began stomping away, light-auburn curls bouncing every which way.

"Where are you going?" Sophia hollered.

"Going to go make out with my husband as a thank-you for my freedom. Ya know, the war hero who almost died while rescuing others in a bombing. Linc had to go home to rest from overdoing it earlier, but he insisted I stay and spend time with my friends. Yet all you two have done is grouch and whine about ridiculous nonsense!" Before Opal disappeared past the sand dunes, she yelled over her shoulder, "I have had my fill of the both of you!"

"Guess we deserved that," Sophia muttered.

"Yep . . ." Josie pushed out a long breath. "Sophia, I'm truly sorry for what you're going through. All I know to tell you is just give it some time to see if it works out. If it doesn't, you know Opal and I will be here for you."

"I know. Thanks . . ." Sophia reached over and patted Josie's hands. "What do you plan on doing?"

Josie shrugged. "Stop being a fraidy-cat, I guess."

"I think it's time you had a heart-to-heart with your daddy. Clear the air between the two of you. That's what your mom would have wanted."

At the mention of her mom, a sting hit her nose and rose to her eyes. Sniffing it away, she stood. "You stay awhile and relax. I'm going to go see about hemming Daddy up in a corner and getting this mess straightened out."

"Good for you." Sophia squeezed Josie's hand as she passed by. "Jolene would be so proud of you."

Josie bent down and hugged her friend, saying a silent prayer that God would be able to fix whatever was broken. Sophia was too dynamic and too much of a go-getter to wear the ill-fitting look of defeat. "Remember I'm looking up to you . . . always looking up." She gave Sophia a squeeze before letting go and heading in the direction of getting things straightened out in her own life—starting with her dad.

It wasn't hard to find her dad considering it was Memorial Day weekend. He had his grill set up on the diner's deck and was grilling burgers, bratwursts, and hot dogs for any veteran who came by. Locals would wander up on the deck and swipe food too, but Jasper never minded.

Josie took a seat in one of the Adirondack chairs and watched him chat up several locals.

"Jo-Jo, you want a burger or bratwurst?" Jasper asked as he served up a burger for an elderly man.

"Bratwurst, please." She decided to allow him to reach out with an edible olive branch. It would give her time to gather her words and calm her nerves. She was never one to have a confrontation with her dad, and the idea of doing it then didn't feel right but needed.

She accepted the plate he passed to her and ate slowly and quietly until the deck only held the two of them. "Dad, can we talk now?"

Jasper sighed. "Jo-Jo, I'm sorry."

"For what?" She dropped the half-eaten sausage onto the paper plate and set it aside.

"After your mom . . ." He cleared his throat and concentrated on flipping the burgers for a moment. "After she passed, I was just so lost. You're all I had and I clung to you." He shook his head. "I should have never held you here. Should have forced you to go on to college, but . . ."

"Dad, we both did what we had to do then. It was for the best." Josie knew deep down it was the right choice.

"Yeah, but it's been six years and I've been too chicken to let you go." His eyes reddened as a waft of smoke rose from the grill. Blinking several times, he moved the patties away from the direct flame.

"And I've been too chicken to let you." Josie stood and moved over to help him plate the burgers. "Seems I'm a lot like my daddy."

They gave each other a wobbly smile before Josie slid her attention over and regarded the weathered diner. Even though Mother Nature had stomped up the beach a time or two over the years and pitched quite a hissy fit on occasion, Driftwood Diner always held its ground. The place fit her daddy to a T and she wanted to be more like him in that aspect as well.

"August told me about offering you an opportunity to work with the camp. I think it's something you shouldn't pass up. Jo-Jo, I honestly forgot how talented of an artist you are until I saw those pictures of the bus you helped him paint. Sweetheart, you're really good." His eyes rounded as he nodded his head, looking right impressed and downright cute in Josie's opinion.

She leaned into his side and placed her head on his shoulder. "I love you, Daddy."

"Love you too, baby girl."

"What am I going to do?" she mused out loud, thinking about how peeved August was with her earlier. Clearly he'd reached his patience limit with her wishy-washy attitude.

"You're going to help me settle Marta in and then you're going to show that boy you're worthy of that position at the camp."

"Yes, sir." It sounded easy enough, but Josie knew she had some work ahead of her. She lifted her head and turned to leave.

"Jo-Jo."

She glanced over her shoulder. "Yes, sir?"

"We both know August is a fine feller. Don't take our mess out on him. He just wants to see you happy."

"Why you reckon he cares so much?" She gripped the railing.

Jasper scoffed. "'Cause that boy loves you. You love him too, don't ya?"

Josie bobbed her head and moved down the stairs. She decided it was also time to show August just how much he meant to her. That was, if she hadn't already ruined things with him.

●   ●   ●

It took three days to find enough courage to go see August. Josie put her pride to the side and drove out to the firehouse on a sunny afternoon. As she parked in her usual spot, an eerie feeling of arriving to where she belonged washed over her. She shrugged it off and headed over to the dark-haired guy pushing a noisy lawn mower along the side yard. Although he was tall with a head full of black hair, the guy was on the lanky side and that hair was a bit too shaggy to be the one she was seeking.

Tucker waved before shutting the mower off and heading in her direction. "Hey, Josie. What's up?"

"Hey. I came to see August." She looked around, hoping he would appear.

"Oh, well, he's in New York until next week." Tucker wiped his brow with the hem of his soggy T-shirt.

"New York?"

"Yeah. He brought some more paintings up there and some fancy people wanted to talk to him about commissioning a few pieces." Tucker gestured over to where the rocking chairs were slowly rocking in the humid breeze, reminding Josie of that day dancing in the rain. He grabbed up a bottle of water and gestured toward it to see if Josie wanted one as well, but she shook her head.

"Do you really think your brother will stay around here?" She waved a hand around, thinking the country fields and small woods were too small to contain such an extraordinary soul as August Bradford.

Tucker took a long pull from his bottle of water and plopped down in one of the rocking chairs. "Oh yeah. He's here to stay."

Josie took a seat beside him and gathered a long, satisfying inhale, loving the sweet smell of freshly mowed grass. "How can you be so sure?"

"Because he promised me," Tucker answered in a matter-of-fact tone.

Josie glanced at the teenage boy, thinking he might have been a bit naive. "But sometimes life presents unexpected challenges or opportunities that you can't control. What if someone makes him an offer he can't refuse?"

"Then you don't know August very well." They rocked in silence for a spell until Tucker looked over at Josie and asked, "Can I share something with you?"

"Sure."

"I know I was pretty young when . . . *it* happened and we had to move in with our grandpa, but I remember things. We were left alone most of the time and his house was right beside a bar. Things would get rowdy sometimes. I was only like four, so it scared me. August promised me each time things got crazy in the middle of the night that we would be okay."

An ache settled in Josie's chest from just thinking about what those boys had to go through. "I'm glad you had August."

"Me too. He also promised me he'd find us a new family. One that would want us." Tucker's voice grew raspy on the last part. Clearing his throat, he grabbed up the bottle of water and drained it. "Everybody thinks the Bradfords just found out about us and took us in, but what no one knows is August went fishing for them." Tucker's lips hitched into a crooked smile, looking uncannily like his older brother.

"How'd he go fishing for parents?"

"Nan was holding job interviews one of those days we went looking for food. August swiped one of the applications, filled it out, and requested an interview with both her and Derek." Tucker chuckled, but Josie could hardly breathe. She'd never had to go looking for food, but here the young man sitting beside her mentioned it so casually like it was totally normal.

Josie tried to do a quick calculation of his age at the

time. "He was what, eleven or twelve? She couldn't give him a job." She watched as the breeze picked up and sent a blade of grass that was nestled in Tucker's dark locks flying off.

"He wasn't seeking a job. Derek has told me this part 'cause I was too young to remember. But anyway, August sat in their office as they reviewed his application. The line where you are to put the position you're applying for, August wrote *son*. Scribbled my name beside it, too."

"Oh, Tucker—" A sheen of tears blurred her view of his face, but Josie still noticed there wasn't a lick of self-pity in his features. Only pride for his older brother.

"Derek said August looked him square in the eyes and told him it was ridiculous for them to own a six-bedroom house for only two people. Said we would gladly take two of those rooms off their hands. And in return he would keep their house clean and the yard work done. He promised the Bradfords that day he would do whatever it took to secure us the positions as their sons."

They grew quiet again, Josie unable to say anything and Tucker being enough of a gentleman not to draw any attention to her crying. Her entire body hurt from what he'd just shared. She couldn't fathom a twelve-year-old boy being brave enough to go out looking for a proper family for him and his brother and then promising to do anything he had to in order to secure a healthier life for them.

Tucker cleared his throat after a while. "So when you asked me how I can be so sure about him not leaving, this is why. August never makes a promise unless he knows he can keep it. He promised me he's here to stay, and I take the guy at his word."

Josie wiped her damp cheeks and nodded.

"And that mess of him acting like a mouthy fool on the beach the other day . . . that ain't like him. You just had him riled up. He didn't mean it." The teenager's dark-blue eyes lit up with humor.

"He sounded like he meant it." Josie offered a watery laugh.

"For some reason, August came home on a mission for you. I've never seen him so crazy about a chick. You're special to him, for sure. . . . Can I ask you a favor?"

She wished she could give the young man the world on a silver platter for all of the life storms he'd already had to live through. "Anything."

Tucker scanned the yard before settling his focus on Josie. "When my brother gets back, will you go fishing for him?"

"*With* him?"

Tucker shook his head. "No. *For* him. Let my brother know how important he is to you." He reached out and nudged her knee. "I know you care about him just as much as he does you, and y'all already wasted enough time. August taught me one line of French. Told me if I didn't learn any more, at least I had to know this phrase."

"What's that?"

"*La vie est trop courte.*" The words rolled off his tongue, showing he'd given it much practice.

"Translation?"

"Life is too short."

"Ah, I should have guessed. That sounds like your brother." Josie snickered but quickly grew serious as she reached out her hand and grasped Tucker's forearm briefly. "Thank you for sharing about how you became a part of the Bradford family with me. I'll hold that close to my heart forever."

"Good, good. Now we need to figure out what bait we want to use." Tucker rubbed his palms together and helped Josie strategize the most important fishing trip of her life.

Later on, as Josie headed back to her truck, Tucker called out, "I almost forgot to give you this!" He came jogging over with a canvas wrapped in brown paper and handed it to her.

"What's this for?"

"I don't know. August asked if I would make sure you got this. It was on my list for tomorrow, but since you're here and all." Tucker shrugged. "Okay, let me know if I can help with the fishing trip."

"Just what we already went over will be great."

Tucker tipped his head, much in the same fashion his older brother was known for, and made his way to the abandoned mower and fired it up.

Josie took a moment to watch the young man, thinking August had done a stand-up job in raising him. Once Tucker pushed the mower on a track behind the firehouse, she climbed into the truck and headed out.

Curiosity followed her all the way home, but she refrained until making it to the small table on her deck. With trembling fingers, she carefully tore the brown paper away to reveal a sentimental memory from her youth.

An antique birdcage sitting on a wooden table took up most of the canvas with clues tucked into the details to hint at the complexity of it. She traced the paintbrush serving as the hinge on the open door of the cage and the paint pallet that made up the bottom of the cage. The pale-yellow bird with a crown on top of its head clung to its perch even though the door was wide-open. A key sat on top of a mound of sand just outside the cage.

As Josie grasped the canvas a little closer, her hand landed on a piece of paper on the back. Flipping it over, she hiccuped on a sob at what she found.

You've always held your freedom. I simply wanted
to help you unlock the door. Step out of the cage, Jo.
~August

"I'm trying," she whispered to the note as a waterfall of tears set a path down her cheeks. It was time to grow up and stand up for what she wanted.

26

"This is like *Where the Wild Things Are*, neon edition," August muttered as he watched kids run around squealing and laughing while heavy bass music piped out from the camp sound system. The night was painted up in vivid disarray on the recreation field in the midst of a neon color party, but August wasn't feeling it.

"Why'd you come back from your trip so cranky?" Carter asked as he sidled up to August, where he was squirting more glow-in-the-dark color onto the tops of several sets of drums. As soon as he stepped away, a couple of kids came at the drums and attacked them. With each pounding from the drumsticks, splashes of neon dotted them along with August and Carter.

"I ain't," August grouched. He moved over to a long clothesline they set up and refastened a few crooked camp flags. They were set up for campers to paint with the neon paints, but most of them had yanked the flags down and were wearing them as capes while they chased one another with Super Soakers filled with glowing paint.

"This is killer!" Tucker yelled out as he ran by with his own flag cape billowing behind him.

"Yeah, but those black lights are a pain in the backside." August pointed up to the portable poles that held the lights even though Tucker had already disappeared among the sea of glowing figures.

"No, you're being a pain in the backside with this

attitude. Seriously, did they try wooing you to move to New York or did something else happen while you were there?"

"They're always trying to woo me to move up there." August adjusted a pole that was starting to lean again. "We need to figure out a better game plan before the next neon night."

"You're not considering leaving us, are you?" Carter crossed his arms over his glowing chest.

"Nah, man. I promised Tucker I'm here to stay."

"You don't sound so sure about that."

August waved a hand, brushing Carter's concerns away. "I just have a lot on my mind. No worries." He moved back to the drums and dumped more paint on top of them.

"She'll come around," Carter yelled over the loud music. "Just be patient."

August huffed. "I used to think I was the most patient guy in the world."

Carter chuckled. "Seems Josie Slater went and stole that from you."

August agreed 100 percent, thinking that one last ace up his sleeve had ended up as another fail from where he stood. If sending her the painting he'd kept hidden all those years hadn't done him any good, then to continue the chase would only prove that he was a glutton for punishment.

Mad with Josie and mad with himself, August left the glowing festivities and skulked off into the dark to head home. Too keyed up to sleep but too distracted to paint, he went straight up to the loft to at least straighten it up a little. After washing the few dishes in the sink and tossing out some trash, he moved to the small living room to find another mindless task. The only thing to catch his attention was the stack of books Dalma had given him.

Plopping on the couch, August decided to go through

them page by page just to feel near Josie. Tracing the
scrolling loops of blue on the title page, he missed her to
the point of pain. He continued the self-torture until the
epilogue and was about to close the book when he felt the
need to flip just one more page. It was a blank extra page
in the back with no colorful drawings, but what it did
hold had August blinking several times and then rubbing
his eyes to make sure it wasn't his imagination. When her
delicate handwriting remained, he gave in to temptation
and read her words.

*Blessed with a happy childhood where my parents
took pride in loving each other and loving me even
more. They realized the potential in my doodling
even before I did. Cultivating it through art classes,
camps, trips upstate to galleries until my little
glimpse of a dream became my passion.*

*Age seventeen, I was on the cusp of adventure,
prepared for my life to merge with my dreams.
And what a life I'd lived so far, untouched by
the bitterness that struck so many other lives. I'd
counted myself one of the lucky ones who coasted
through childhood unscathed. Accepted to an art
program, I would be heading toward my vision
of happiness with a certain enigmatic man by my
side. His vision so in tune with my own. He'd been
in the periphery of my life from as far back as I
could remember, but I was finally ready to share
the spark I'd kept hidden in my heart with hopes
of it igniting the idea of us. Together, side by side,
claiming a life of vivid color and wonder.*

*Then the spark faded in one momentous storm.
One that came out of nowhere and destroyed my
bubble of happiness. I had no idea how delicate*

that bubble was until it was destroyed. In the wake
of losing the bright, colorful life of my mother, only
shadows remained. Creeping in to underscore any
color. It consumed me for a while, and when I
somehow managed to reemerge from a dark bout of
depression, smudges of it never washed completely
off. It took months, years, even seconds sharp as
shards of glass, before I woke up and realized he
had continued painting his life with adventure
and dreams without me.

August read the note three times before placing the
book on the coffee table. Elbows braced on his knees, he
stared at it while coming to terms with the message it
relayed. He'd learned early in life how to keep his emotions in check for Tucker's sake, so he'd never been one to
shed tears, but something in her raw honesty had his eyes
and nose stinging.

Sniffing, August swiped the book and headed out.
The clock in the truck read three in the morning, declaring it too early for a confrontation, but he drove over to
the beach house anyway. He made himself at home on the
back deck and waited for the first rays of day to show up.

Just shy of two hours later and before the sun was up,
the door creaked open. "Ain't this a fine surprise." Dalma
wrapped the fluffy robe tighter around her tiny frame
before taking a seat beside August on the daybed swing.

He flipped the book to the page and showed it to her.
"You knew what you were giving me."

"Yes."

August closed the book and set it between them. "I
didn't realize she battled depression."

"Don't beat yourself up, dear. She hid it well from
most everybody."

"But not you," August pointed out.

"Because I pay attention. Something these new generations don't know how to do." Dalma shook her head. "But back to our girl. Josie's made this whole thing with you more difficult than she should, but you deserved to know why. It's her story to share with you, but I was beginning to worry she wouldn't ever get around to it in my lifetime. Call me selfish, but I wanted to witness your HEA."

"HEA?"

"Happily ever after," Dalma said slowly while giving him a *duh* look.

"Well, ain't nothing happy at the moment."

"Young man, your life made you grow a thick skin from the very beginning in order to survive it. Josie's didn't. She lived a pretty sheltered life behind that counter at the diner. Losing her mother flipped the light off inside her for a good long while. She got some help to turn it back on, but when it comes to you . . . well, you represent the world she thought would be hers. Can't blame her for being scared you'll vanish again."

August scrubbed his palms down his face, the sleepless night catching up with him. "I'm not going anywhere. I've told her that over and over and *over*."

"Josie didn't think her mother was going anywhere either."

"Dang it. When you put it like that . . ." He raked his fingers through his hair while casting his eyes to the dark water slowly rolling out with the tide, which was exactly what Josie had been waiting for him to do. "I don't know what to do."

"You do absolutely nothing. It's that young lady's turn. Make her come to you."

August looked at Dalma out of the corner of his eye.

"That sounds too much like playing games. I'm not about that."

Dalma snickered. "Games can be fun. I just love when the hero or heroine in a romance novel makes some big gesture to show the other how much they love them."

August didn't have anything against big gestures, so he asked, "How about in exchange for more books, I buy you breakfast?"

By the time they'd loaded up the books, the cab of his truck resembled a mobile version of the little lady's living room.

●   ●   ●

The week-ending festivities at Palmetto Fine Arts Camp were geared up with everyone in a celebratory mood. The second week of camp went off without a hitch just like the opening week. It was almost perfect.

"The special-effects makeup booth is a big hit," one of the camp counselors said to August in passing.

August looked over to where a makeup artist was applying a scar to one of the camper's foreheads. He nodded his head and tried to take it all in as music began pumping through the speakers. Vendors lined the circle in front of the fine arts buildings. The coloring-book facades were slowly coming to life after two groups of campers had contributed, with color from his paint session as the backdrop.

The entire scene emanated the vibe of a big party and the kids running around seemed to thrive in it. A twinge hit his stomach with knowing someone else who would thrive in that environment, too, if she'd just get over herself.

Several colleges had booths, offering kids information about their fine arts programs and scholarship opportunities. Various artists and musicians also had exhibits and demonstrations set up. They were all hands-on and the campers were eager to participate. August spent the day exploring the booths with several art students and even tried out composing music through pieces of fruit that were wired to a computer program.

He and Carter didn't want to just offer kids a week of exploring their gifts. They also wanted to direct them to paths leading to a future. He knew Josie would love that aspect of the camp if she were there to witness it. She should have been there to help make decisions for the art department and leading the sessions he had always envisioned her teaching.

Someone tapped him on the shoulder, so he turned to find Theo looking up at him expectantly from underneath the brim of his navy sun visor. "Yeah, man?"

"Carter said for you to get your tail over to the amphitheater. The performance is about to start."

"That was my plan," August retorted and kept walking in that direction with Theo following beside him. "What? You my escort?"

"Carter said to make sure you got there." Theo shrugged, fiddling with the walkie-talkie he proudly carried at all times. They explained that his assistance could be needed at any time and for him to never be caught without it, but it was more to keep a close eye on him as they'd promised his mother and Josie. "I'm just making sure."

And sometimes Carter would give Theo a task such as the one he had at the moment to keep him busy, so August decided to just let the guy do his job without giving him any more lip. By the time he made it to the amphitheater, the place was packed, so he had to take a seat near the back.

Large fans were set up around the perimeter, adding a muted hum to the atmosphere while pushing the humidity and mosquitoes away the best they could. August sat behind one and as it made a rotation, the words from Freda, their events emcee, onstage kept being washed out.

"Our first performance is . . ." The fan moved over again and whispered into August's ear. He watched on as Freda moved off the stage and a punk band set up. He'd caught a few jam sessions of theirs during the week. The boys liked to serenade the camp most evenings after supper, too. He stretched his legs out in front of him and draped an arm along the empty chair beside him, knowing he would enjoy this last hoorah from them.

After they rocked out a few cover songs, a familiar blonde began lugging easels onto the stage. August suddenly sat up, nearly knocking over the fan, as a blushing Josie Slater hurried offstage. She was back in a flash, carrying two blank canvases as Dalma followed her with a cart full of paint supplies. Dalma placed the cart beside the easels and turned to give the audience two thumbs up before shuffling offstage.

Once they had everything arranged, Freda introduced, "Our next performance is a little unusual, but I'm sure you will all enjoy a paint-off!" The emcee's ecstatic voice beckoned the audience to join in with whistles and loud applause. "Now, I would like to introduce our first artist, Miss Josie Slater." Freda gestured toward her, making Josie fidget while her hand clung to a paintbrush for dear life. Freda walked over and handed Josie the microphone.

After taking several long inhales, Josie held the microphone to her lips. "Good evening." She paused to clear the hoarseness from her voice. "I, umm . . . I'm here tonight to challenge the great August Bradford to a paint-off." The crowd erupted at the mention of his name.

Freda retrieved the mic and spoke rather loudly, "August Bradford, get your handsome self up here!"

August eased to his feet and moved toward the stage. Josie had a gravitational pull set up just for him, and he couldn't get to her fast enough. He climbed the steps and came to a stop beside Josie.

"Now for the rules of this paint-off. Artists have five minutes to create something. If Josie wins, August has to offer her the art assistant position again *and* go on a date with her." Catcalls rang out, interrupting Freda. She was good-natured about it and grinned until they quieted down. "And if August wins, Josie has agreed to eat a mouthful of sand."

August reined in the laughter threatening to bubble out, covering it with a cough. He spoke out of the corner of his mouth, "What are you doing?"

"Fishing," Josie answered with a good bit of poise, and it took every ounce of his willpower not to toss her over his shoulder and run away with her.

Tamping that idea down, August grabbed a paint-brush. "So we just go at it?"

"Whoa! Not so fast. We need some inspirational music." Josie nodded to the band behind them and the boys launched into a cover of "Wipe Out."

August let out a rumble of laughter. "You planning on wiping out this time, Miss Slater?"

"Not a chance, Mr. Bradford." There was a determined gleam in her blue eyes, and it was all he could do not to toss the paintbrush and wrap her in his arms instead.

Freda held a stopwatch up and yelled, "Go!"

Both artists scrambled to take their places behind the canvases and slipped into the seriousness of the challenge. August smirked while adding strokes of translucent watercolor to the canvas, knowing his sidekick had put a lot of thought into the challenge. Even the detail of what song she had the band play emphasized it.

The five minutes flew by with August languidly working on his piece while he watched Josie paint with fervor out of the corner of his eye. The woman shone so bright he couldn't look away.

"And . . . that's time! Put your paintbrushes down!" Freda shouted as the band closed the song.

"Ladies first." August tipped his head in Josie's direction.

She swiped a wisp of hair from her cheek, leaving a streak of red paint behind, and August was certain he'd never seen her look more beautiful. Josie turned her canvas to the audience to show off the quick depiction of the renovated firehouse. The bay doors were up with their rocking chairs set up at the opening. She signed the piece *La vie est trop courte pour vivre sans toi. Life is too short to live without you.*

"Now that is quite impressive, young lady," Freda complimented with the audience joining in by clapping and whistling. "How on earth are we to decide a winner?"

"Won't be difficult," August yelled out over the noise.

"Says who?" Josie glared at him. "You've not even shown us your artwork yet."

His lips curved up on one side. He liked her spunk and also the fact she'd not stuttered once. "Like I said . . ." August revealed his painting to the crowd, causing them to break out into a raucous round of applause. The background was a modest smearing of delicate watercolors with two simple words written in bold black paint in the center of the canvas. *You Win.*

Josie scrutinized the canvas in confusion until understanding lit her face. "You're going to make it that easy on me?"

"I'm not a complicated man." August placed the

canvas on the easel and took a step closer to her. "Are you going to allow me to make it that easy?"

"Well, that's not really my style." She wrinkled her nose and picked up the small jar of wet sand, swiping a small dollop onto her palm.

August reached over and grabbed the jar and did the same. "We need to get something straight right now. We're a team. We're going to do this and everything else *together*. No running from the scary parts."

Josie nodded her head. Both artists braced themselves and slurped down the mushy sand with the kids in the audience chanting their names.

"Josie! Josie! August! August!"

Even as he struggled to get the grit down his throat, August savored the moment. Once he choked the sand down, he leaned over and whispered, "Each time you walk along the shore and your toes sink into the sand, you'll remember the day you made me fall even more in love with you."

Josie choked a bit on her sand, until finally getting it down. She wrapped her arms around his neck and said close to his ear, "And you'll remember I went fishing for you—used sand and paint as my bait—because you are worth it . . . I love you."

"Well now, that's my kind of fishing." August leaned down and brushed a gritty kiss to her smiling lips.

●   ●   ●

Later that night, once they were finally able to escape the camp, August took Josie to the firehouse to share his grand gesture with her. As soon as they stepped inside and he flipped on all the lights, she released a loud gasp.

"Oh, August . . ." Josie walked to the middle of the

floor and stared up at the giant shimmering sun. He'd constructed a wire-and-mesh form and then glued page after page of her designs to cover the sun.

"I hope you don't mind that I added to your artwork." August sidled up behind her and wrapped his arms around her waist. "I filled in the voided areas you didn't color in with gold metallic paint and then sealed the entire piece with an iridescent clear coat."

"I love it," she whispered, leaning against his chest. "I love you."

"And I love you." August smoothed her hair and placed a kiss against her temple. "Josie Slater, you are my sun. My rainbow of color. Without you, I've had shadows and smudges, too."

Josie turned in his arms as tears cascaded down her cheeks. "You found my note."

"Yes. I wish I'd understood sooner." He used his thumbs to wipe the tears away, but they continued to trail down her face. Needing to experience those tears, he pressed his lips to the damp warmth of her skin. "I only want to be your sunshine. Your rainbow of color. Baby, I can't promise the shadows won't show up every now and then, but I can promise we'll get through them together." After caressing several more tears with his lips, he angled away just enough to take her in. "Whaddaya say, Jo?"

Blue eyes glittering with more tears, pink cheeks the perfect shade of passion, brilliant-white teeth showcased by smiling ruby lips, Josie's beautiful face gave him all the answer he needed. When she finally breathed a delicate yes against his lips, August sensed the shift. One whispered word collected all the drifting dreams and created the vibrant world meant for the two artists to share together.

EPILOGUE

The Sand Queens stood inside the art studio at the camp, stealing peeks at the guests getting settled in their seats around the courtyard. It was a breathtaking spring day with the subtle breeze swaying the palmetto trees above the guests to offer just enough shade and comfort from the early afternoon sun.

"All right, Jo-Jo. Time to get this show on the road. I'm going to go sit with Dalma." Jasper gave Josie a hug and scooted outside.

"Are you absolutely sure you want to do this?" Opal, of all people, asked as she handed Josie the white bouquet.

"Absolutely. August insisted I walk the aisle to a remix of 'She's a Rainbow,' so this is what he gets." Josie giggled at the absurdity of it all, right proud of herself for being brave enough to do what she was about to do. "I can't wait to see August's reaction."

"You definitely get points for boldness, my friend." Opal directed Josie to bend at the knees so she could better reach her hair.

"That man would marry you regardless of this or any other stunt," Sophia commented, a small yet sincere smile on her face.

Josie took the opportunity to study Sophia closely as Opal fussed with placing a few white roses throughout Josie's thick braid. The physical signs of last month's nightmare had finally healed, which was why Josie and August decided to push the wedding back a month, but from the vacancy in Sophia's teal eyes, she had a long way to go before the emotional wounds would heal. Josie still wanted to hunt down that awful excuse for a man and put a whooping on him for what he did to Sophia. She felt remotely better from knowing August and Lincoln had taken care of matters already.

"I think August and I are going to postpone the honeymoon to Italy until the fall."

Josie's comment snapped Sophia out of her careful facade. Sucking her teeth, she wagged a finger at Josie. "No ma'am, you are not! Your behind will be on that plane this evening with your husband. It's time for Josie *Bradford* to go on an adventure."

"I agree." Opal moved around Josie and locked her arm with Sophia's. Both petite women wore identical pale-blue dresses and determined looks.

"We'll be right here when you get back in two weeks and expect at least one postcard while you're gone." Sophia wagged her finger one last time before moving over to the table to gather her bouquet and satchel.

"Linc and I'll be keeping a close eye on her and Collin. Promise," Opal whispered as she gave Josie a hug.

Josie knew Sophia would be safe while she was gone. Lincoln Cole had already put the fear of God in Ty Prescott, so it was highly unlikely that idiot would show up anytime soon. It was baffling that they'd all missed the signs, and Josie continued to carry a good bit of guilt for not pressing Sophia to open up when her friend refused to share the extent of what she was enduring last year.

"Stop worrying. You know she'll have a hissy fit if you don't go." Opal stepped back, gave Josie one last once-over before grabbing her own bouquet and satchel. "Now come on. Let's go make a mess of your perfectly white wedding day. We've waited long enough."

"We sure have." Josie grinned, trying not to get teary-eyed.

Settling into a relationship with August had been the easiest thing she'd ever done. Their days were filled with painting and stealing more memories together. Between surfing, teaching Sunday school side by side, and spending time with their family, the two had gathered quite an impressive collection.

Of course, August had big plans to add even more and shared them with her one night back in September, after the first summer session of Palmetto Fine Arts Camp was in the books. August finally talked Josie into sliding down the fireman's pole that night. She recalled screaming like a lunatic but surviving the descent, only to nearly pass out at the sight of August waiting for her on one knee with a diamond ring placed on the palm of his paint-stained hand. Josie held her own paint-stained hand out and allowed him to slip the ring on her finger, knowing he would lead her on an adventure filled with every color of life under the sun.

Grinning at the memory, she was ready to go show August Bradford just how colorful they were going to make their wedding day. As "She's a Rainbow" began filtering through the outdoor speakers, she followed her friends out into the sunshine. Her eyes landed on August where he stood with their pastor, Lincoln and Carter by his side in matching gray tailored suits.

Josie waited until her two friends were in place up front before taking her first step down the aisle, and as

instructed, the guests lifted small pouches of colored powder and launched a flume of rainbows at her. Through the
colorful cloud, she watched August tip his handsome face
skyward and bellow out in laughter as his buddies and the
Sand Queens doused him in color as well.

By the time she reached her groom, they were both
living examples of the Rolling Stones song. August
wrapped Josie in his arms and led her in a dance. As the
song concluded, he dipped her and laid one memorable
kiss on her smiling lips, mixing their rainbows, until the
pastor cleared his throat.

"Do you two mind knocking it off until at least after
exchanging your vows?" It was hard to take him serious
with most of his head dusted in blue powder.

"We can try. Just need to steal a moment with my
bride first." August righted Josie but kept her gathered in
his arms, sending laughter and whistles moving through
the group. His silvery-blue eyes glittered with unshed tears
as he skimmed his knuckles along her cheek. "Every time I
hear that song, I'll remember the moment my wife made
herself my rainbow and painted my dreams to come true."

"She ain't your wife yet. The vows. Sometime today
would be great," the pastor tried again, this time laughing
with everyone joining in.

August finally agreed and moved them to stand up
front like a proper bride and groom should. Josie kept her
gaze on the charismatic man she was about to have the
privilege to call husband, knowing she'd remember the
moment just as he described. Truly, it was a magnificent
one to steal.

Turn the page

for a preview of

book three in the

Carolina Coast series,

Sea Glass Castle

Available in stores and online summer 2020

JOIN THE CONVERSATION AT crazy4fiction.com

TYNDALE
FICTION

www.tyndalefiction.com

CP1301

1

"I'm so tickled the Sand Queens are back together!" Opal scooted around the table on her back deck and grabbed a glass of lemonade. The summer day was warm and sunny, with a breeze carrying laughter from beachgoers and squawking from seagulls.

"Me too," Josie agreed as she tucked a wayward wave of white-blonde hair behind her ear. "Two months is too long to go between meetings. I'm glad I talked August into giving me the afternoon off from the camp."

"Your husband knows how important we are to you, so of course he'd give you some time off," Opal said in that reassuring tone, the one that was trying to relay a hidden meaning.

Sophia caught the meaning but chose to ignore it. Yes, it was she who had stood up the other two, but tough. That was life. And for the past several months—closer to a few *years*—life had served her a platter brimming with unfairness.

"Sophia, aren't you glad to be spending time with us today?" Josie asked in that small voice that never really suited her.

Sophia looked at Josie's long, paint-stained fingers where they rested on her forearm. "Nothing against the two of you, but I'd rather spend my Monday alone. . . . I have a lot on my mind." Yes, the warmth of the sun and the softness of the breeze felt good on her skin, but that was neither here nor there.

"Oh, I bet. Are you considering signing Collin up for the preschool program at the church this fall? I heard Momma talking with you about it after Sunday school yesterday." Opal took a sip of her drink and gave Sophia an innocent look that was really her meddling expression.

Sophia let go of a long sigh and decided not to call her out on it. Instead, she gave the excuse, "He has to be potty-trained before they will accept him."

"That's easy enough." Opal shrugged. "YouTube some tutorials and go get him one of those tiny toilets."

"I'd rather he decide when he's ready. So far there's no interest." Sophia tucked her left thumb underneath her ring finger and couldn't contain the cringe at finding it bare. It was a habit she had formed right after Ty slid the flashy engagement ring onto her finger. Touching the back of the ring had always offered comfort and a reminder of his promises. She was still struggling to grasp that the wedding ring—and the promises—no longer belonged to her.

"I'm sure you want to help Collin along. The preschool would be a great opportunity for him to interact with children his age. And it would allow you to get a job." Josie smiled but seemed uncertain. She wasn't nearly as good at meddling as Opal.

Sophia narrowed her eyes at both women, wondering what their game was. "I have alimony and child support and a nice severance package. I don't need a job."

Ty's PR team had been quick to get most of his dirt swept under the rug, and his lawyers even quicker to finalize the divorce. Sophia had only been required to sign nondisclosures about the abuse allegations that prevented her from ever speaking about it publicly, and that was fine by her. She agreed after they added a clause that Ty had to undergo anger management counseling and could have only supervised visits with Collin.

"That's hogwash. Never has your strong backbone stood for someone else taking care of you and—"

Before Opal could carry on her rant, Josie piped in. "But a job would be a great reason to get out of the house and be around adults. Plus, you're too talented not to be out there doing something with yourself."

Sophia had recently endured not only the demise of her marriage, but also the demise of her career. When Southeastern Public Relations had to choose between a replaceable consultant and their star athlete, the decision to let Sophia go was more than easy.

"Really? Southeastern seemed to think I'm nothing more than a grunt worker who somehow deserved to be beaten up by her famous husband for catching him in bed with another woman." Sophia growled and slammed her glass down, sending a fountain of pale-yellow liquid sloshing onto the table. That didn't release enough of her pent-up anger, so she added stomping her feet against the sandy deck and another growl.

Sophia's intuition had always been spot-on. She was an ace at using that skill for the betterment of others and keeping her firm's clients out of hot water. Herself, not so much. It didn't do her a darn bit of good when it came to the bronze-haired Adonis with his lustrous skin tone and that aw-shucks smile. Ty Prescott's stunning facade had fooled her right along with the masses. Months had passed since Ty had completely removed his mask while taking a part of her soul with it, yet she was still dealing with the wreckage. She was so mad at herself for allowing it to happen in the first place. The worst part was that she'd failed not only herself but also her son.

"Then why are you allowing their opinion such power if you don't believe it to be true?" Opal asked, knowing exactly what button to push. "You sure have been acting like you believe it."

For months, Sophia had allowed circumstances to dictate her self-worth. The only days she had any hope of turning things around were the days she could make her baby smile, and that wasn't nearly as often as it needed to be. A saying her grandmother shared once flickered through her thoughts as she pounded her fists against the arms of her Adirondack chair. *"Never underestimate the power of a good ole hissy fit."*

The haze of despondency cleared momentarily as Sophia had herself one glorified conniption. "I'm not a nobody! I have just as much talent as that giant schmuck running around a dumb field with a ball! I want to slap that smirk off his lips! I want to show him he didn't break me!"

Opal nodded exuberantly. "This is good!"

"What?" Sophia snapped back, hot tears cascading down her flushed face. She caught Josie echoing the question in a much more subdued whisper.

"You're alive!" Opal fist-pumped and jumped up and down. "She's alive! Hallelujah!" She turned back to Sophia and shook her by the shoulders. "For a hot minute I thought you'd turned into a robot." Opal giggled, followed by Josie snickering, and that had Sophia snorting. And from there it escalated to an outlandish round of laughter.

And that was Opal for you. Always twisting and turning a touchy situation until she could figure out how to defuse the tension. It was one of the reasons Sophia loved her so much—and also the reason she wanted to pinch Opal's little button nose half the time.

"Y'all, I'm sorry . . . I'm just having a hard time getting my act together." Sophia shook her head. "I never thought I'd let a man manipulate me or lay a hand on me out of anger."

Josie moved over and knelt in front of Sophia's chair. "I sure wish you had confided in us about what was really going on."

"I was embarrassed. Still am." Sophia watched Opal join Josie in front of the chair, their wall of support causing a heaviness to press against her chest. Clearing her throat, she whispered, "It didn't happen that many times, but it was enough to leave a lasting effect. Made me doubt my strength and character. I hate being weak."

"One time is way too many times." Opal squeezed Sophia's knee. "But who says you're weak?"

The question had Sophia coming up short, so she only responded with a half-hearted shrug.

"You are the owner of your self-esteem. Don't let circumstance dictate it. Show Ty and everyone else you're still that crazy-smart, fiercely driven woman who lets no one and nothing get the best of her."

Josie bobbed her head in agreement. "Opal's right. You've achieved everything you've ever set your mind to. You are the former reigning Miss Sunset Cove, you were the captain of the cheerleading squad, valedictorian of your graduating class, you formed Beach Preserve Coalition for your senior project when the rest of us only took the time to write a research paper—"

"Oh! I love that charity." Opal's face lit with admiration, mirroring Josie's. "Girl, you got the entire town *and* my daddy, the senator, on board with keeping our beach a litter-free, healthy environment."

They were doing what the Sand Queens did best. Lifting one another up when life tried beating them down by redirecting the focus to all of the good and positives.

Sophia's tears of anger transformed into tears of appreciation as she leaned forward and hugged both wonderful friends God had blessed her with for as long as she could remember. Even though she was a year ahead of them in age and school grade, their bond had always been ironclad.

After the three women hugged it out and resettled in their own chairs, Sophia finally asked, "What was all that talk about a mystery neighbor?"

"There's no mys—"

"I think a vampire moved in last night." Opal was quick to cut Josie off, but Sophia dismissed it when she processed what the silly woman had just spouted off.

"A vampire?" She wiped the last of the tears from her cheeks and rolled her eyes at Opal's absurd words.

"Yes. Possibly two of them." Opal leaned toward Sophia and Josie in a conspiring fashion and glanced around. She nodded her head to the cookie-cutter, saltbox-style beach house to the right of Opal's. Instead of the orange-sherbet paint job, it was whitewashed with dusty-blue shutters. "A moving truck showed up late last night. I saw two men slinking around in the dark and they kept at it until sunrise. Then all went eerily quiet over there."

Sophia pulled her sunglasses down the bridge of her nose and looked for any sign of life. A nice set of outdoor furniture had been placed on the back deck and a beach bike was propped against the side of the house, but nothing looked amiss. She slid the shades back into place and was about to look away when the curtain at the kitchen window fluttered, revealing a hint of a shadowed figure. Sitting up taller and angling her head to the side, she whispered, "Someone's in the kitchen." She heard Opal gasp and Josie snort.

All three leaned over the railing, like that would actually get them close enough to see more clearly. Sophia knew they looked like a bunch of nosy rubberneckers, but she kept leaning until a loud boom ricocheted from the neighboring house. Three sets of feet cleared the deck as squealing burst from each of the women.

"What was that?" Sophia whisper-yelled, ducking down behind the deck railing and clutching her pounding chest.

"See!" Opal crouched beside her. "I told you something's not right with him."

"How do you even know it's a *him*?" Sophia narrowed her eyes and glanced over to find Josie settling back into her chair, obviously the only sane one out of the bunch. She stood and followed suit.

"I already told you. It's two guys and I saw them hauling in things last night. One of which was a long box." Opal stretched her arms as wide as they would go while her eyes bugged out. "I'm pretty sure it may have been a coffin."

Josie snorted again. "Get up from there, silly, and knock it off."

Opal stood and dusted the sand off her brightly colored shorts. "I'm serious. That house has been sitting there vacant since Mrs. Clark vanished last year—" Her eyes rounded again. "Oooh! The neighbor did it!"

"With the candlestick in the dining room!" Josie interjected with a thick coating of sarcasm.

"I have the weirdest friends," Sophia muttered,

propping her cheek on the palm of her hand and slouching against the side of the chair.

Josie disregarded the jab and said to Opal, "You know Mrs. Clark went to live with her sister in Florida."

"So they say . . ." Opal's words trailed off as she jabbed a finger toward the house. "She could have been holed up in the basement all this time."

"Your husband oversaw the renovations to the house just last month. To be sure, Linc would have noticed an old lady tied up somewhere." Josie rolled her eyes and picked up a cookie from the plate. She gave it a cautious sniff. "You didn't bake these, did you, Opal?"

"You know Linc doesn't let me near the oven. Momma made them." Opal drummed her fingertips against the table while eyeing next door. Suddenly she jolted in such a spastic manner that it caught Sophia's waning attention. "The curtain moved again!"

Sophia blinked slowly at her friend before moving her sights over to next door. All she could see were shadows moving past the windows. They appeared to be drifting about in no particular direction. Much the same way she was doing as of late.

"I think we need to go over there and check things out."

"We're doing no such thing," Josie ordered while swiping two more cookies and handing one to Sophia. "Seriously, Opal, that's enough. You keep on and I'm calling Linc to come get ahold of you."

Sophia sniffed the cookie out of habit since it came from Opal, finding only the delicious aromas of vanilla and chocolate chips. She took a bite and chewed absently, realizing her sluggish attention was missing something. From Opal's outlandish behavior over the new neighbor and Josie's snorting responses to it all, clearly she wasn't catching on to whatever was happening. But she didn't care enough to try figuring it out.

● ● ●

The smell of fresh paint mixed with a lemony scent the cleaning crew had left in their wake had been welcoming the prior evening. But after pulling an all-nighter and sorting through moving boxes until the sun showed up, Weston Sawyer was over it. Squinting his tired eyes at his watch and finding it past noon, the only scent he wanted assailing his senses was coffee. Stat.

"Looks like the neighborhood watch is already on to you," Seth mumbled as he peered out the kitchen window of Wes's new home.

Wes rummaged through the third box marked *kitchen*, hoping to unearth the coffeemaker. If his search came up empty once more, he was heading out the door to find some form of caffeine. "Why's that?"

"There are three women sitting on the deck next door watching us. Been there for a while now."

"Aha!" Wes held up the coffeemaker's carafe as if it were a grand prize. At the moment, it certainly was, to him. He yanked the machine part out next and walked it over to the counter to put it to work. He glanced out the window as he filled the pot with water and spotted his audience. A blonde sat chowing down on cookies while another woman in a giant sun hat looked to be melting into her chair from slumping down so much. He couldn't help but chuckle at the wild one with her hands flailing around. "The redhead is my new neighbor, Opal Cole. Her husband remodeled the house and the doctor's office for me." Wes surveyed the space and was quite impressed with the clean lines of the kitchen. The white marble countertops with the subtle veining weren't like anything he'd ever had in a home. Taking in the espresso wood floors and the crisp gray walls, he concluded nothing was, for that matter. *Lincoln Cole nailed it.*

"Oh." Seth kept looking out the window. "She dropped those cookies off earlier, right?"

"Yes. She promised she didn't bake them. Whatever that means." Wes scooped the ground coffee into the filter and inhaled deeply of the robust scent. "They'll go good with some coffee. I hope between the sugar and the caffeine, we can muster enough energy to set up a few rooms before I have to take you to the airport." He glanced at his brother out of the corner of his eye. It was like looking in the mirror, but his brother's image reflected an untarnished spirit that Wes's never would. "Sure wish you could stay longer than just one day."

Seth turned away from the window and grabbed up another box. "I drove that stinking moving van all the way here and helped you unload it for a better part of the night. I call my brotherly duties done." Seth's teasing smirk vanished as he stumbled and dropped the box, sending an explosive clanging ringing out.

"Man, if you messed up my pots . . ." Wes moved over to work the tape off the lid so he could inspect them.

Seth let out an obnoxious snort. "You're so peculiar over everything, old man. They're just pots and pans."

"There's nothing wrong with wanting to take care of my belongings." Wes's words choked off as soon as he realized what he'd said. He'd failed at taking care of what belonged to him when it had mattered the most. Without inspecting the contents of the box, he straightened and walked back to the coffeemaker. His eyes fixed on the ribbon of rich-brown liquid filling the pot as he gripped the back of his neck with both hands.

"I hope you give this fresh start a real chance, Wes." Seth moved behind him and clamped him on the shoulder. "You know it's time. You deserve to be happy again."

Finalizing the sale of the house that held too many broken dreams and walking away from the successful practice he'd helped to build from the ground up in Alabama was supposed to be the ending of a long, difficult chapter.

Signing the paperwork to purchase the beach house and small medical practice in Sunset Cove was supposed to be the beginning of a new, calmer chapter.

Thus far, Wes found himself trapped in the tragic-twist part of the story. He wasn't sure he'd ever figure out how to give a new chapter any real hope.

Seth squeezed his shoulder. "You hear me, man?"

Wes dropped his hands away from his neck and worked on filling two mugs with coffee. "I already had happiness once." He lifted one of the mugs and breathed in the scent before taking a sip, as the what-ifs began a worn-out mantra. "I'm not here looking for that. I just want some peace and quiet."

Seth reached over and took the other mug. "It's been well over three years—"

"Yet it feels like just yesterday." Shaking his head, Wes moved over to the spacious breakfast nook surrounded by bay windows and plopped down in a chair that faced the ocean. The table set, with a custom-built bench seat along the back and chairs on the other three sides, was stark white and chunky. Clean-cut, yet comfortable. It was new, just like the rest of the furniture pieces. His old furniture, along with the rest of the material belongings from his last chapter, was left behind in storage.

Too bad he couldn't do the same thing with his memories.

DISCUSSION QUESTIONS

1. *Driftwood Dreams* is not only the book's title, but also the name of Josie's beach house. How does the book's name relate to the main characters, Josie and August? For instance, how is Josie like driftwood? What are Josie's and August's approaches to fulfilling their dreams?

2. Dreams and achieving life goals are a common theme throughout *Driftwood Dreams*—August grasping his dreams and going after them with abandon, Josie allowing her dreams to die along with her mother. What obstacles do they have to overcome in order to allow their dreams freedom?

3. Other characters in the book deal with dreams in different ways too: Carter and Dominica, Lincoln and Opal, Sophia and Ty. Each couple has to revise the dreams they had for their lives. Discuss the revisions and roadblocks presented to each of them.

4. The author enjoys infusing comic relief into her stories. Does any particular scene from this book come to mind?

5. Even though the sun can be brightly shining, a darker struggle can be hidden just below the surface. What effect does Josie's private struggle with depression have on her "passive" personality? How does her struggle with depression help open her eyes to others around her?

6. At first glance, August is a free-spirited artist who is known to be easygoing. What are some instances that come to mind where he lets that slip away enough to reveal another side of him?

7. August finally gets Josie on board to paint a vivid life with him. The two artists have a few romantic, artistic scenes. Which ones stand out to you?

8. The next book in the series is *Sea Glass Castle*. It centers around Sophia Prescott and her attempt to rebuild a life for herself and her son in the aftermath of a turbulent marriage that ends in divorce. Dr. Weston Sawyer moves to Sunset Cove to take over Doc Nelson's pediatric practice. His life is in shambles as well. From what you've learned about Sophia in the first two books, where do you see her story heading? What do you look forward to discovering in the next book?

DRIFTWOOD DINER BISCUITS & GRAVY

(T. I.'s simpler version)

Ingredients:

8 Pillsbury Grands! Southern Homestyle frozen
   biscuits
4 strips bacon, chopped
1 lb. extra-large shrimp, peeled and chopped
¼ cup flour
2 ½ cups whole milk
1 teaspoon Old Bay seasoning
Salt and pepper to taste
2 tablespoons chopped chives

Bake biscuits according to package directions. In a large skillet, cook bacon, then add shrimp once the bacon has browned and sauté together. Sprinkle with flour. Gradually add milk and bring to boil, stirring frequently. Reduce heat to medium and let simmer until thickened. Add Old Bay seasoning, salt, and pepper, and sprinkle with chopped chives. Pour gravy over split biscuits and enjoy.

A NOTE FROM
THE AUTHOR

I am a lot like Josie Slater in many ways—just not the tall, skinny part. I have had dreams from an early age, and just as Josie did, I allowed life circumstances to stand in the way of achieving them. Through her journey and also my own, I hope you will see that dreams are attainable as long as you're brave enough to go after them. The journey wasn't easy. It took a lot of work and dedication to pursue my passion for writing, but I eventually stepped out in faith and stopped allowing excuses to hold me back. Now, I don't advise you to wait until reaching close to age forty as I did, but even if you're forty or beyond, I say go for it!

I'm thankful for each "Opal," "Sophia," and "August" in my life who have encouraged me to go after my dreams. I bet you have those special people in your life as well. Listen to them and allow them to be a part of your journey. And don't forget to be a part of the cheering squad for others.

I like to write lighthearted books that address deeper topics. I chose to highlight depression in this story because I want readers to be aware of its relevance. Depression is something I've struggled with over the years. At one point in my teens, I attended counseling, and in my young-adult years I used antidepressants for a while to help combat depression and anxiety attacks.

If you're struggling, be brave and ask for help. No one is immune from bouts of depression, small- or large-scale. And I also want to encourage you to be a Miss Dalma and take a closer look at those around you. You never know what someone is struggling with internally. We need to be more aware and compassionate. I'm thankful for those who were looking close enough at me to realize I needed help and then encouraged me to get it.

I pray the same will be true for anyone struggling through their own life storms.

DRIFTWOOD DREAMS
PLAYLIST

"One of Us"
by New Politics

"Rhythm & Blues"
by the Head and the Heart

"Oh, Carolina"
by NEEDTOBREATHE

"Suit and Jacket"
by Judah & the Lion

"It's Not Over Yet"
by For King & Country

"Limitless"
by Colton Dixon

"I Want to Live"
by Skillet

"Fearless"
by Jasmine Murray

"She's a Rainbow"
by the Rolling Stones

ACKNOWLEDGMENTS

My Lowe family and Bethlehem church family, you have poured out your support throughout this journey. Wouldn't take anything in exchange for you or the journey.

I couldn't, in good conscience, share the recipe for this book without the tasting approval of Zachary and the Rosenau family. Thank you for taste testing my concoctions. My little buddy gave me a "yum" and thumbs-up for the shrimp gravy, so I feel good about sharing it with my readers!

Trina Cooke, I appreciate the help you've given me along the way with this series. From helping me name Opal's store, Bless This Mess, to allowing me to use your grandma's name for one of my favorite characters, Miss Dalma. I hope I did you proud.

A special thank-you to Tyndale House Publishers and Browne & Miller Literary Associates for this opportunity.

God has allowed my dream of writing and sharing stories to come true. He has also blessed me with such lovely reading friends. Thank you.

ABOUT THE AUTHOR

Tonya "T. I." Lowe is a native of coastal South Carolina. She attended Coastal Carolina University and the University of Tennessee at Chattanooga, where she majored in psychology but excelled in creative writing. Go figure. Writing was always a dream, and she finally took a leap of faith in 2014 and independently published her first novel, *Lulu's Café*, which quickly became a bestseller. Now the author of ten published novels with hundreds of thousands of copies sold, she knows she's just getting started and has many more stories to tell. A wife and mother who's active in her church community, she resides near Myrtle Beach, South Carolina, with her family.

Don't miss book one in
the Carolina Coast series

Available in stores and online now

JOIN THE CONVERSATION AT crazy4fiction.com

TYNDALE FICTION

www.tyndalefiction.com

CP1532

Settle in for a cup of coffee and
some Southern hospitality in

OVER 100,000 SOLD

Lulu's Café
a novel
T. I. LOWE

Available in stores and online now

JOIN THE CONVERSATION AT

crazy4
fiction
.com

TYNDALE
FICTION

www.tyndalefiction.com

TYNDALE HOUSE PUBLISHERS IS CRAZY4FICTION!

Fiction that entertains and inspires

Get to know us! Become a member of the Crazy4Fiction community. Whether you read our blog, like us on Facebook, follow us on Twitter, or receive our e-newsletter, you're sure to get the latest news on the best in Christian fiction. You might even win something along the way!

JOIN IN THE FUN TODAY.

 www.crazy4fiction.com

 Crazy4Fiction

 @Crazy4Fiction

FOR MORE GREAT TYNDALE DIGITAL PROMOTIONS, GO TO TYNDALE.COM/EBOOKS

CP0021